how to be bad

E. LOCKHART

We Were Liars
The Disreputable History of Frankie Landau-Banks
The Ruby Oliver series
Fly on the Wall
Dramarama

SARAH MLYNOWSKI

Ten Things We Did (and Probably Shouldn't Have)
Gimme a Call
Don't Even Think About It
The Magic in Manhattan series

FOR YOUNGER READERS:
The Whatever After series

LAUREN MYRACLE

The Internet Girls series
Shine
Bliss
The Infinite Moment of Us
Peace, Love, and Baby Ducks
Rhymes with Witches

FOR YOUNGER READERS:
The Winnie Years series
The Flower Power series
The Life of Ty series

e. lockhart
lauren myracle
sarah mlynowski

how
to be
bad

HOT
KEY
BOOKS

First published in Great Britain in 2015 by Hot Key Books
Northburgh House, 10 Northburgh Street, London EC1V 0AT

Originally published in the United States of America in 2008
by Harper Teen, an imprint of HarperCollins Publishers,
1350 Avenue of the Americas, New York, NY 10019

A CIP catalogue record for this book is available from the British Library.

ISBN: 978-1-4714-0484-9

1

Here's to good friends. Be kind,
be brave, and eat lots of mangos.

FRIDAY, AUGUST 20

1

JESSE

AT THE END of July, back when I was still fun, I bought Vicks two tufts of fake armpit hair from Jokes-A-Plenty. They were like Band-Aids with fur. She cackled and wore them all day, calling herself She-Woman of Fantastical Florida, and she kept them on for her date that night with her boyfriend, Brady McKane. She wore a camisole.

She told me the next morning that Brady nearly spit rocks when he saw her, although she was probably just making the story good. Brady adores that girl and wouldn't care if it was fake nose hair she was sporting. Heck, he'd adore her even if it wasn't fake.

I'm thinking about that as I pull into the parking lot of the Waffle House, where me and Vicks work. The armpit hair, not how much Brady adores Vicks. 'Cause I remember that jokey girl I used to be, and I remember how easy it was with me and Vicks, making each other laugh and being best buds. Now there's something off between us, and I can't stand it.

Part of it's me, I don't deny it. Ever since Mama first found the lump, I haven't been myself. That was seventeen days ago, which is a long time to stomp around all pissy and full of secrets.

But Vicks has also gotten herself into a big ol' funk, which I pin on the fact that Brady left town almost two weeks ago. Still, can't she look past her own troubles and see that I'm hurting too? Besides, it's not like he left the country. He's in Miami, not Timbuktu.

I want Vicks back. I *need* her back, especially now.

I cut the engine of Mama's sherbet green Opel and gear up to go into the restaurant, even though Friday's my day off and by all rights I should be lounging on the sofa and watching one of those birth stories on Lifetime, where the baby almost dies but at the last second is saved, and everyone is full of tears and happiness and second chances. Life is good, and look at those eensy perfect toes and fingers. What a blessing. Praise the Lord.

It's just that these days, there hasn't been much in my life to praise.

"Oh, babe, I must'a pissed God off something serious," Mama said to me last week when she got the official news from the oncologist. She laughed, but her eyes were holes of worry ringed with jet-black liner.

And I'm obviously filled with worm rot, because what I shot back was, "Yeah, I guess you did."

This came the day after the wet T-shirt contest, mind. My mama, my *mama*, in a wet T-shirt contest! With truckers spraying her boobs with ice water! And R.D. standing there all proud, I'm sure. Grinning and nudging his buddies and saying, "That's my woman. Ain't she something?" No doubt serving Icee Gator Aid from his frozen drink cart, which he thinks gives the truck stop a touch of class.

Well, I am here to say that there is nothing classy about the goings-on at that truck stop.

Mama claims she knew what that fancy clinic doctor would be telling her, and that the contest at R.D.'s Truck-o-Rama was her chance to give "the girls" a final whirl. Plus, it won her a hundred bucks. Doesn't that mean she'd taken something sour and created something sweet?

Um, *no*. What it means is that R.D.'s a perv, Mama's a sinner, and those horny truckers are pervs and sinners for going along with it.

I wish I could erase the entire last week: Mama, the lab reports, and most definitely R. D. Biggs, who yesterday left me a twenty-dollar tip for no reason at all, other

5

than I'm Mama's daughter and apparently he wants to share the love.

I used to like R.D., or at least I liked him more than some of Mama's other boyfriends. I liked his belly laugh, and I liked that he'd play Pictionary with me and Mama on our weekly game night. But I no longer want him around, his worried eyes following me as I deliver eggs, toast, hash browns, grits. And waffles, of course. The Awful Waffle, that's what me and Vicks call this place. Though the waffles are actually delicious.

"Listen, Jesse," he said, after he'd practically licked his plate clean. He leaned in, his expression all fatherly, and I could tell in a flash I did *not* want to hear what was coming. "Your mama's experiencing some hard times."

"No. Uh-uh." I got real close and lowered my voice to a furious whisper, 'cause no way did I want anyone hearing our business. "You do not come talk to me about hard times, not after . . . what you made her do!"

"Jesse, what the . . . ?" He splayed his greasy fingers on the counter. "Are you talking 'bout the other night? I didn't make her do nothing. She's a grown woman—ain't she allowed to make her own choices?"

I stalked away 'cause he's not worth my time anyhow. But when I got home, I informed Mama I didn't want that fool in my trailer no more.

"*Your* trailer?" she said.

"Why'd you have to tell him, anyway?" I said.

"Tell him what?"

I glared. She knew. Stupid R.D., coming in and blabbing about her medical woes.

She sighed. "Baby . . . when you're hurting, you lean on your friends."

"You call him a friend? Making you act all nasty in front of his trucker buddies?"

"I wasn't . . . he didn't—" She broke off. "Listen, Jesse, maybe he's not the friend you'd pick for me, but he's still a friend. More than a friend. And you know what? I'll take them any way I can get them."

"You'll take *anything* any way you can get it," I said under my breath.

"'Scuse me?" She put down her dishrag. I walked out of the trailer's dinky kitchen and into the equally dinky living area, which smelled like dogs. She followed me and grabbed my arm.

"You think it helps my situation knowing how you're taking this?" she said. "Knowing my daughter thinks I'm a . . ."

"Whore?"

She sucked in her breath.

I couldn't believe I'd said that—though I didn't take it back.

"God, Jesse," she finally said. "R.D. was *right there*. No way was he going to let anyone disrespect me. If he can stand by me, why can't you?"

"You shouldn't take the Lord's name in vain," I said.

She stared at me like she didn't know who I was, this daughter who would act so hateful.

"I can't fix this," she finally said. "*You* can't fix this. We just gotta hope for the best, that's all we can do."

"And pray," I said.

She barked out a laugh. A laugh!

"Fine," she said, "you pray for me. That'd be nice. Know what'd be even nicer?"

I stood there, feeling trembly.

"If you'd live your own damn life instead of passing judgment on mine. I mean, I *swear*, Jesse. You're so set on following God's rules that you've turned into a goddamn Goody Two-shoes."

"Mama—"

"No. You act like you're so special, like you're racking up points in heaven by being so *good* and looking down on the rest of us, but all the while, you're missing out here on Earth."

I looked away. She grabbed my head and turned me back.

"I mean it, Jesse." She kept ahold of her voice, but just barely. "You better live this life of yours while you can—*real* living, the kind where you get a little dirt on your halo—'cause, babe, not one of us knows how long we got."

Fine, Mama, I said in my brain. Not then, but later,

once the heat of it had turned to a hard, fierce, teary ache. *If that's what you want, then fine.*

The midmorning sun toasts my skin through the windshield. I spot Vicks inside the restaurant, and I can just bet she's sweating up a storm. *Four eggs, over easy. Waffle on two. Three hash browns, scattered, smothered, chunked, and diced.* She's the only fry cook who's a girl, and the only cook under the age of twenty. She's seventeen like me, but I just wait tables. Anybody can wait tables.

From my primo parking space, I can also see the new girl, Mel. Mel's been hostessing here for just two months, meaning she's got less rank than anyone. But she doesn't act like it. Not that she's out and out rude, but she watches everyone with her big blue eyes, and I can see the thoughts running through her head about how redneck we all are. How redneck *I* am, because I don't wear four-hundred-dollar jeans.

For real, four hundred dollars! I noticed them right off. See, our uniforms consist of black pants and a gray-and-white-striped shirt. The shirts we get from Waffle House, along with the butt-ugly bow ties. The pants, however, are our own. Most people buy a pair at Kmart or Mervyns and don't think another thing about it, 'cause they're going to be filthy by the end of the shift anyway.

My pants are bad. I admit it. They snap shut too high

on my waist, and they've got these dorky pockets that fluff out and make me look fat, which I'm not. Put me in a pair of cutoffs and a tank top, that's the real me.

MeeMaw—that's my grandma—likes me better in church clothes, but I'm not wearing skirts and dress-up shoes on my days off. I can be close to the Lord in shorts just as well as in a skirt, I figure.

Anyway, last week Mel showed up in a new pair of black jeans, and I told her they were cute. I was trying to be nice, since Vicks had gotten on me for being so snarky.

"Thanks," Mel said. She seemed surprised I was talking to her.

"Where'd you get them? I have the hardest time finding good jeans in this town."

"Um . . . ," she said. She tugged a strand of her hair and drew it to her mouth, like maybe she didn't want to go sharing her jeans secrets.

"Well, what brand are they?"

She twisted around, searching for a label. "Um . . . Chloé?"

Chloé? That was a brand of jeans?

That afternoon I took the bus to the public library and used the Internet to look up Chloé jeans. No stores in Niceville stocked them, but I could order them from some place called Bergdorf Goodman for the low low price of three hundred and ninety dollars, plus shipping. I felt like an idiot, knowing that's why Mel didn't tell me.

The next day I asked Mel why she was even working here. It just slipped out, and Vicks shot me a look like, *Cripes, Jesse. Be a little cattier?*

But c'mon. We'd all seen Mel climb out of her dad's silver Mercedes, and the diamond studs she wears glitter in a way my cubic zirconias never do. Plus I'd heard Abe, our manager, making conversation with her about the African safari she'd gone on before she started working here. Mel had fidgeted, but she confessed that yes, she'd seen actual lions and zebras and giraffes doing their thing in the wild.

Me? There's no call for any trip to Africa. Mama's got a zillion and a half boarder dogs stinking up our trailer on any given day. That's *my* wildlife adventure.

Anyway, that's when I finally asked Mel what I'd been wanting to know since the day she started: Why was someone like her working at the Awful Waffle?

Her answer: "Um . . . because no one I know would ever eat here?"

Vicks thinks she didn't mean it the way it sounded, but those were her exact words.

I climb out of Mama's Opel, and the door squeaks when I shut it. Mama's going to be madder than tar that I took it without asking, but tough.

I tug at my shorts and smooth down my tank. I push my fingers through my hair, combing out the tangles. One thing I've got on Mel—not that I'm counting—is my corn silk, ultra-blond hair.

Mel's longish brown hair is cute enough, but she keeps it in a ponytail 24/7, so it's not like she gets any mileage out of it. Same with her face. Cute enough—maybe even pretty—but a touch of eyeliner and a swipe of lip gloss would go a long way. As for her body . . . well, fine. She's hot. Sure she folds her shoulders in like no one ever told her to stand up straight, but she's like a size two and has one of those athletic bodies that's probably from years of private tennis lessons. Goody for her.

Vicks is so much cooler looking. She might not see it that way, but she is. She's got this awesome shaggy haircut that she did herself, and she dyed it jet-black with a couple streaks of white. The black came first, and then she got sick of it and was like, "Think I'll bleach it out." The streaks frame her face and make her dark eyes stand out. Plus, unlike Mel, she isn't afraid of a little eyeliner.

The bell on the door jingles as I step into the restaurant. The smell of waffles and bacon hits me hard, and suddenly those stupid tears are back.

"Hey there, Jesse!" Abe calls, glancing up from the cash register. "Just can't stay away, can you?"

"That's right," I say. I blink and paste on my smile. "I need my toast burnt like only you can do it."

"Uh-uh," he says. He steps out from behind the counter and makes as if to swat me, and I sidestep the blow.

12

I call out "hey" to Dotty, who's got two All-Star Specials balanced on her arms, and say, *"Hola, amigo,"* to T-Bone.

"You looking for Vicks?" T-Bone says from the griddle.

"Yeah, she was just here. Where'd that girl get to?"

"She's on break, but it isn't on the schedule," Abe complains. "Tell her to quit ruining her lungs and get back here, will you?"

I head for the back exit, then stop and turn. "Hey, Abe. Can I have tomorrow off? Sunday, too?"

"You gotta be kidding," he says. "Tell me you're kidding."

"It's just . . . I need a break, that's all." My heart starts pounding. What if he says no?

"Aw, Abe, take a chill pill," Dotty calls. "I can cover for her. I was supposed to have the kids this weekend, but Carl Junior's taking them to Disney World. Did he *ask* if he could take them to Disney World? No, he did not. Did he stop and think for one second that maybe *I* was taking them to Disney World? No, he did not."

Disney World! I think, which is a sign of how twitchy my brain is. I've always wanted to go to Disney World, especially Epcot, which stands for "Experimental Prototype Community of Tomorrow." I've seen the brochures, and the whole thing's done up like a miniature world, with itty bitty countries snuggled up side by side:

13

France and Germany and China and all those amazing places. There's even an Eiffel Tower stretching clear to the sky.

Miami, I remind myself. *Miami's the thing to focus on, not Epcot and the Eiffel Tower. Geez, girl, get your head out of the clouds!*

Out loud, I say, "Thanks, Dotty."

"You bet." She deposits a side of bacon in front of a woman in a pink T-shirt. "I've told Abe a dozen times—ain't I, Abe?—that you've been working yourself too hard these past few weeks. I been worrying about you, darlin'."

She wipes her hands on her apron and heads my way, and I sense I'm in for a hug. Which would undo me.

"Well, don't," I say sharply. Right away I feel bad, 'cause she knows about Mama's health problems, and she knows *I* know she knows. She and Mama play bingo together, and of course they get to talking. It's just that no one else at the Awful Waffle knows: not Abe, not T-Bone, not even Vicks.

Mama doesn't understand why I haven't told Vicks. I don't know why, either. Not in a way I can explain.

"I'm fine," I say to Dotty. I don't like the way she's looking at me, so I let my gaze slip off sideways. "Really. So, uh . . . see you kids on the flip side, 'kay?"

I find Vicks in the back parking lot, leaning against the concrete wall with a cigarette between her fingers.

Beside her is Mel. I suck in my tummy, because that's how Mel makes me feel.

"Jesse!" Vicks says. She pushes off the wall and slaps my palm. "What's up, toots? Thought you didn't work today." Her smile is big, like she's genuinely glad to see me, and it makes me wonder if I've imagined all the weirdness between us lately.

"Hey, Jesse," Mel says. She's got some kind of accent that I haven't figured out yet. Up north or something, somewhere snooty.

"Hey," I say back. I angle my body to shut out Mel, though not enough that anyone could call me on it. "Listen, Vicks. I've got an idea."

"Oh, yeah?"

"An *awesome* idea," I say, thinking about Vicks and Brady and how she'll jump at the chance to go see him for sure. Brady left early for the University of Miami because of football workouts, though by now he's probably started classes and everything. He's a freshman, and he's playing for the Miami Hurricanes. Pretty cool. Heck, Miami in general sounds pretty cool.

Niceville, on the other hand, hosts the "world famous" Boggy Bayou Mullet Festival. Now there's a whomping good time. You can eat fried fish while cheering on your top picks for Baby Miss Mullet, Junior Miss Mullet, and Miss Teen Mullet, which I was in the running for once, but I couldn't figure out a talent, so too bad for me.

Vicks flicks me. "So are we going to hear this awe-some idea?"

"Oh. Right. Well . . . how's Brady?"

She looks at me funny, like I'm changing the subject. But I'm not. I'm just warming up to it. "He's busy," she says. "Practice starts every morning at six, then they run them again in the afternoon."

"It's not good," Mel says, all sympathetic, like she's got the inside scoop. "I can't believe he's only sent her one pathetic text message since he left."

What? This is news to me, and I don't like it. I especially don't like that Mel's the one reporting it.

"That true?" I ask Vicks.

"'The U rules, wish you were here. Heart ya!'" Vicks says. She looks uncomfortable, like she knows she done wrong by me. When you're best friends with someone— even when things aren't quite right—you give *her* the inside scoop. Not some new hostess girl.

"He sent it at two A.M.," Mel goes on. "When he knew Vicks would be asleep."

"Whatever," says Vicks. "I'm not going to be some whiner-baby girlfriend, all freaked out because he doesn't check in every morning and every night." Her tone is ballsy—classic Vicks—but her brow furrows as she draws on her cigarette. And her foot, which is pressed against the concrete wall, is tap-tap-tapping away.

"But . . . how can he not call you?" I say. "You've been

going out for almost a year."

She sighs. "Tell that to him."

I'm floored. Whenever me and Vicks and Brady went out for wings this summer, or when the three of us went to the movies, Brady would hold Vicks's hand and give her little kisses and not care a whit that I was looking on. "You are just gone over this girl, aren't you?" I said once. Brady just smiled.

"No, listen, *you* tell him," I say to Vicks. 'Cause this is my great idea: to drive to Miami so Vicks can see Brady. "Let's go down and see that bum in person. The U is only six hours away."

Vicks snorts. "Six? Try nine."

"You *know* he loves you, Vicks. We'll kick his behind for not treating you like he should!"

"How would we get there?" Vicks says. "Take the bus? That's classy. I'd hop off the Greyhound, all grubby and smelly, and be like, *'Dude, it's me, your stylin' girlfriend. Wanna take me with you to Freshman Composition?'*"

"I've got my mom's car," I tell her. "I've got it for the whole weekend."

She snorts again. She's no stranger to the Opel.

"Don't be rude," I say. I'm trying too hard, and it's making me sweat. "Think about it: you and me and the open road. We can do whatever we want, whenever we want to do it. And I got the radio working again, so we'll have music."

"I need to find a good radio station around here," Mel puts in, as if we're all three having a conversation. "All I can find is country, so I pretty much just listen to my iPod. Hey, does your mom's car have a built-in iPod?"

I glare at her.

"No iPod in the Opel," Vicks says. "I regret to inform."

"Is there a CD player?" Mel asks, and I glare harder. Plus my cheeks heat up.

"No, o innocent one, the Opel is a minimalist outfit," Vicks informs her. "No power windows, no AC, no cup holders, no CD player, and definitely no built-in iPod."

Now I glare at Vicks.

"And the windshield wipers are kaput," she adds.

"They are not kaput!" I protest. "They get a little sticky sometimes, that's all. Anyhow, who needs wipers? We're in Florida! The sunshine state!"

"Yeah, right."

"'The sunshine state,'" Mel says. "I like that." She blinks and smiles, and it's like she's trying to smooth things over or something. Which is so not her place, it's not even funny.

She gazes at me with her too-blue eyes and says, "That's so cool that your mum's giving you the car for the entire weekend."

"*Mum?*" I say. Who says "*mum*"? I turn to Vicks.

"So . . . you up for it?"

Vicks stares into space.

Mel fidgets. Out of nowhere, she goes, "Um . . . I am."

I'm speechless. Did anyone ask her to go with us to Miami? Did anyone ask her to go sticking her nose where it isn't needed and sure as heck isn't wanted? I mean, really. Where does she get off?

With my body I shut her out for real.

"C'mon, Vicks. A little bit of fun before school starts? We can swing by—" I almost say *Disney World*, but I don't, 'cause I don't want Mel knowing I've never been, or even just guessing. Mel's traveled to Africa, and I've never crossed the state to Disney World? That's sadder than a hound dog who's lost her pups.

"We can swing by that museum place you told me about," I improvise. "See the giant lizard."

Vicks crushes her cigarette and flicks the butt on the ground. "It's not a lizard. It's a gator. Old Joe."

"Fine, see Old Joe," I say. "We'll make a road trip out of it, go to any of those tourist sites we want!" Vicks adores that crap. She's got a whole book of roadside attractions involving mermaids and albino squirrels and monkeys wearing Beatles wigs.

Vicks checks her watch. "I've got to go back in."

"But . . . what about my idea?"

She sighs. "Who would I get to take my shifts?"

"T-Bone. You know he needs the extra cash."

"Yeah, and speaking of—how would we fund this adventure? I bet you've got, what, all of fifteen dollars?"

"Thirty!" I reply indignantly.

"And I've got maybe ten dollars, tops, since I blew my entire last paycheck on booze and Lucky Strikes."

"You did not."

"But I did buy Brady a laundry hamper for his dorm room, the kind that stands up on its own. The rest I socked away in my college fund." She shrugs. "Sorry, Jesse. We can't go anywhere on forty dollars."

"We can if we want," I say. There's a wobbling in my chest. I drive my fingernails into my palms.

Mel clears her throat. "Um . . . I've got money. I can pay."

I turn and gape.

"Fuel, snacks . . . whatever." She gives an awkward hitch of her shoulders. "I could get us a room at a hotel."

I throw up my hands, because she is insane. *Why?!*

"I want to see Old Joe?" When Vicks and I stare, she juts out her chin. "What? I *do*."

This isn't the way it's supposed to play out. Mel's ruining everything. Except the truth is, Vicks isn't helping much, either. And when I think on that, my insides twist tighter. After all, she's the one who's been on me for being a wet blanket—so why's she being like this?

Can't she see how much fun we'd have, dang it?

Then I realize how to make it happen. It's a gift from God, which proves it's true, I guess, that He works in mysterious ways. Mysterious, annoying, Chloé-clad ways, but who am I to go against His will?

"Fine," I say to Mel, knowing there is nothing Vicks hates worse than not being Tough Girl Numero Uno. "We'll go to Miami. It'll be awesome."

Mel looks slightly alarmed that I've accepted her offer.

I turn to Vicks, trying to stay cocky. "So what do you say? You in?"

2

VICKS

JESSE KNOWS ME way too well. I do want to see that gator. I read all about it in this guidebook called *Fantastical Florida*. Back when my brother Penn and I had to share a room, we used to read to each other out loud, whispering because we were supposed to be asleep. That book is full of weird stuff. A building shaped like an orange. A bat tower built by a guy named Perky that no bats ever lived in. World's smallest police station. A twenty-two-foot statue of Jesus Christ built entirely underwater. Xanadu, home of the future, which looks like it's made of marshmallows.

Penn and I used to try to get my dad to take us to some of these places on vacation, but he always made us go visit Grandma Shelly in Aventura. No stops, except for gas—a straight drive down.

According to *Fantastical Florida*, Old Joe Alligator is three hundred years old. He used to sunbathe in the town square and even swam with kids in the fountain. Never hurt a flea. Then some stupid poacher shot him, so now he's stuffed and displayed in a glass case in a Florida history museum only a couple hours from Niceville.

Maybe we can hit Coral Castle, too, on this trip. Years ago, Ed Leedskalnin, this hundred-pound weakling from Latvia, got dumped on his wedding night by his sixteen-year-old fiancée Agnes Scuffs. Then he spent twenty years carving a memorial to her out of coral, working only in the middle of the night. He moved blocks of coral that weighed thousands of pounds, and no one knows how he did it.

Now it's a palace to unrequited love.

Ed Leedskalnin. What a wimp.

If Brady never calls me, if he never ever calls me again and just goes around humping cheerleaders at the U like we never were each other's first time and it never meant all the things we said it meant—to be actually doing it like we might be together forever—and he acts like we never built that matchstick house for our six-month anniversary, or made our own potato chips in his mom's deep fryer, or stayed up all night talking, or like we never used to see each other every day and tell each other everything and text each other nearly every minute we were apart . . . If Brady just disappears on me the way that sixteen-year-old Latvian girl did to the hundred-pound weakling, no way am I building him a coral castle.

I'm not the kind of girl to take shit from a guy. You don't grow up with five older brothers and not know how to fend for yourself when it comes to the opposite sex.

Anyone building coral castles has got to be an only child.

Me, I'd just—I'd do something else, for sure.

Make him come back.

Force him to remember. How he noticed me sprinkling vinegar on my school pizza, to give it some kick. How he noticed me again when I dyed my hair black. How he hadn't known I'd noticed him, too, until I slammed his locker shut that day with barely enough time for him to get his hand out safely, then went running down the hall. How all of a sudden I wasn't Penn Simonoff's little sister, I was something else. How he asked me to come watch a football game of his. He played outside linebacker for the Travers Manatees.

"No thanks, dude," I had told him.

"You don't like football?" Brady asked, wrinkling his forehead.

"I love it," I answered, glad to surprise him. "But I like touch games on Sunday afternoons, or watching it on the national level. Super Bowl Sunday? I'm your girl."

"Really?" he said, raising his eyebrows. He was flirtatious.

I went on. "The problem is, I spent way too many years watching my brother Tully's high school games, and let's just say it was a losing streak for the Manatees. Before Coach Martinez took over. Can we catch a movie instead?"

Brady laughed. It was the first time I'd seen that huge smile break across his face just for me, and the first time that bouncing laugh had shaken up the room because of something I did.

I made up my mind just then that I wanted to make him smile, over and over, every day.

"Yeah, we can catch a movie," Brady said, but then even before we set a time or figured out what to see, he leaned in and kissed me on the neck, like he was aiming for my cheek but kind of went astray, and he giggled while he was doing it, but it felt good, and I could tell he liked me the way I liked him.

This was something real. Not just a date, not just a crush, not just a fling.

So, yes, I will be taking Jesse up on her offer. I want to

go down to Miami, and when I get there, I want to make Brady remember what it seems like he's forgotten in ten days of summer practice and half a week of classes.

Because I know he hasn't forgotten at all.

What I *don't* want to do is ask why he hasn't called. That's certain death. Steve, Joe Jr., Tully, Jay, and Penn taught me that. They had so many girls my head spun as they banged the screen doors going in and out, but if there was one thing that made my brothers cool off fast, it was the way some flowery girl would whine, "Why didn't you *call* me?"

Because there's no answer to a question like that. "He didn't call you because he didn't want to call you," I'd say, if they asked me when I answered the phone. "I think you should take that as a message."

"Well, tell him I called," the little Rose would say, "and ask him why he didn't call when he said he would."

"You got it," I'd say, and write it down in large letters and stick it on the Frigidaire. "Your girlfriend's nagging at you again. Call the droopy little flower and get her off my back."

And Steve, Joe Jr., Tully, Jay, or Penn—whoever it was—would never bring that girl through our screen door again. Not because of what I wrote. They didn't care if I hated their girlfriends or wanted to be just like them. Why they didn't call was, guys don't like to be pegged on bad behavior. They like you to overlook it, or coax them round to something better from the side, not with the head-on relationship jabber.

And the girlfriend, poor flowery girlfriend, would probably go and build a little coral castle of her own, writing in her diary or sobbing on the phone with some other Roses, or sending cutesy photographs or heart-shaped notes to our mailbox that my brothers would open and then forget about, leaving them lying on the kitchen counter for anyone to see.

Guys respond to action. They respond to a body sitting next to them on the old couch while they flip through the channels. They respond to a girl who understands football, a girl who keeps her mouth shut and doesn't yammer on like it's important what she bought at Target that afternoon. A girl who eats when they take her out to dinner.

Jesse's waiting for me to answer, to say yes or no to her crazy plan. She's starting to look worried, and I feel like a wench.

I know she's sad I didn't tell her right off about what's been going on with Brady since he left for the U. Instead I kept quiet about it for days and days—and then told little Mel.

I don't know why, really.

My friends from Travers—to them, Brady and I are the perfect couple. Me and Brady, walking down the

27

halls with our hands in each other's pockets. Going to the Halloween dance as Superman and Lois Lane. Kissing during assembly. Me sitting at the seniors table surrounded by a crew of Brady's friends, me wearing Brady's old Mr. Bubble T-shirt. Me and Brady, all the time.

I don't want to deal with their reactions. Their sympathy. It's a lot easier to tell a girl your boyfriend hasn't called you back when the whole way she thinks of you doesn't hang on your being the girlfriend of a senior starter on the district champion football team.

Jesse—I could have told her. Should have told her. We've been close ever since we started at the Waffle last year. She goes to public, but not to Travers, which makes it a lot easier to be real friends. Because Jesse doesn't think about "VicksandBrady" like the girls from Travers do. To Jesse, I'm the person willing to wait while she goes through giant bins of discount makeup at Eckerd. I'll sit through her boring Christian network TV shows and let her pick all the cashews out of the nut mix. I'm the one who'll help her think up questions for the funny surveys she posts on the wall of the staff room, asking people to write in their favorite word, their least favorite sound, their most beloved song. I buy her a toasted almond ice cream bar when I bike down to the 7-Eleven on my break, because I know that's her favorite, and I'll even go out to Applebee's with her slightly bat-shit mom and say stuff like "Oh, Ms. Fix, what happened to the

unhappy pit bull you were telling us about last time?"—
and then listen to the answer, because her mom will
seriously talk about dogs for an hour and a half at a go.

To Jesse, I'm not one half of "VicksandBrady." I'm just
me. Her best friend.

Mel and I aren't really friends, but somehow everything about the Brady situation came pouring out of me
when she stepped outside to—I don't know what she
was doing, really. Watching me have a cigarette break.

I feel sorry I didn't tell Jesse first. There isn't a truer
friend than Jesse when my parents are driving me crazy
or I'm freaking about a test or if I just need a little retail
therapy—but I haven't been honest with her about me
and Brady.

She's really Christian, Jesse is. The one time like five
months ago when I hinted that Brady and I were maybe
going to do it—*sex* it—and asked her to come to Planned
Parenthood with me, she got all uptight about how sex
before marriage is a sin, and how Planned Parenthood
just supports that kind of sinning. Then it was as if she
decided she'd said too much, because all of a sudden she
clammed up.

Like she couldn't even talk about it, it was so bad.

I wonder if her spaz had to do with her mom not
being married. And obviously, doing it, since Ms. Fix
ended up with Jesse. Or maybe it's got more to do with
Jesse's dad, whose name I don't even know, and how he

29

split before Jesse was even out of diapers.

Brady would never pull a trick like that, but also—I'm never giving him any reason to. Hello? We have Planned Parenthood now. Anyone can go, and you barely have to pay.

Jesse must figure that by now I'm not a virgin, but since she made it clear she didn't want to hear about it, I'm not telling her.

Lately—since right before Brady left, actually—she's made remarks. Like God is taking up more room in her brain than usual, so Christian stuff pops out. Like she wants to help me be saved.

It is really, really not fun to be around.

Still, here she is, standing in the lot behind the Waffle, waiting for me to say something. And she's got to be hurt I told Mel instead of her about Brady not calling, but she's not showing it except maybe in her eyes. There's a crazy-strong yearning coming off her, how she's jingling her keys and stalking this grease pit on her day off. Just to get *me* to let *her* give me a ride.

I gotta love her. Plus, I want to see Brady so bad it's making my eye twitch. And then she pulls this thing of pretending she wants to go with Mel, which I know she doesn't at *all*; she's just trying to make me say yes—and I can't tease her anymore.

"What the hell," I say. "Let's do it."

* * *

Jesse wants to leave from the Waffle the minute our shifts are over, but I don't want to show up at Brady's dorm covered with grease and smelling like sausage patties and eggs. So we decide that Jesse'll swing by my house at three thirty, and then we'll go get Mel, who writes down her Fort Walton address on a napkin and takes my cell number. I think she wants a way to get in touch with me—in case Jesse tries to stand her up.

I fry up about a zillion more eggs, and then bike home to find a note from my parents. They've gone to Babies "Я" Us to buy stuff for Steve's kid that's not born yet. I know they won't mind if I go to Miami so long as I tell them where I am and take my cell. Even if they do think it's a bad idea to go out with Brady long distance, which they do, they don't have the time or the energy to make a fuss about it. By the time you get to kid number six, your rules are pretty lax.

Mom and Dad are electricians. They run their own business, Simonoff Electrics, though Mom took a lot of time off to have us. My eldest brother, Steve, is a chip off the block, now an apprentice electrician down in Broward. Joe Jr.'s in the navy, Tully's a senior at Florida State in Tallahassee. Jay's on summer break from community college, living with his girlfriend and hauling boxes at Wal-Mart for a couple months. And Penn, my favorite of all my brothers, graduated with Brady and moved in with a couple friends for the summer, living in a junky apartment across from the mall. He's been working a prep station at P.F. Chang's, which is like a giant step up from the Waffle in terms of restaurants, and come September, he's going to culinary school three towns over.

Anyway, he moved out in June. Which means, it's just me and the folks.

It sucks to be the one left behind. Next June I'll be the one graduating, but still.

I call Penn while I pack. "Hey, it's me."

"Vicks."

"This house is silent like a morgue. I'm going to Miami to see my long-lost boyfriend."

"Didn't Brady just leave?"

"No, it's been two weeks."

"Like I said, he just left. Can't you live without him?"

"Shut up," I say, and mean it.

Penn can tell, so he changes the topic. "How you getting down there?"

"Jesse's driving me."

"Jesse, the one you brought to Fourth of July?" he asks, all innocence.

"Uh-huh. The one who always gives you free Coke when you come in the Waffle."

He chuckles. "Oh, yeah. Jesse."

"So, what are you doing?" I ask him.

"I'm in Publix," Penn answers. "I just got off the lunch shift."

"So did I. I'm totally sweaty and greasy."

"Me too!" he cries. "You wanna hear about the state of my T-shirt?"

"I'll pass."

"Disgusting is the state of my T-shirt. I'm in the detergent aisle right now, looking for a box of—oh, there it is. You think Tide is better, or All?"

"Which has a prettier box?" I ask.

"I don't want a pretty box. I want a dude box."

"Uh-huh," I deadpan. "You want a dude box of laundry detergent."

"Yes, I do."

"Good luck with that."

"Okay," he announces. "I made my decision."

"Whadja get?"

"I'm not telling you. Mocking my dude detergent."

"When are you coming over to the house?"

"Not till next weekend."

"Come sooner. Come for dinner Monday."

"Won't you still be in Miami, following Brady around?"

"Shut up! And no, I have to work Monday morning. So you gonna come over?

"Nah, I got stuff to do."

"Come on, Penn. It's so boring here. There's no one around if you don't come."

"Vicks, I gotta go. I'm at the checkout."

"Fine," I say. "But don't leave me alone in this house for too long or I'm gonna die of boredom. You won't have a little sister to boss around when I'm dead, now will you?"

"Guilt me later," he says. "I gotta run." And he clicks off.

Does Penn really think that two weeks is "just left"? Does Brady? Because two weeks is a very long time in the Vicks department.

I head to the pantry, which is overflowing. There are, like, eight sacks of potatoes in here. My parents think every meal should include a potato and they're still buying food at Wal-Mart like they've got five boys to feed, instead of one girl who's working all summer at a restaurant. I snag a pack of Fig Newtons and some chocolate snack cakes.

Next, I open the fridge. Rummage past potato salad, leftover baked potatoes, and a Tupperware filled with a disgusting invention of my mother's called Potatoes à la King. Hey, mangos. My favorite. I grab them.

Jesse honks the Opel outside, I write a note to the proprietors of Simonoff Electrics—and I'm out.

3

MEL

"HEY, NIK?" I ask, over the noise of the blow-dryer. "You almost done?"

No answer.

I knock on the door to our shared washroom. Again. "Hello?"

"I'm doing my hair!"

"Nikki, I *really* need to use the shower! Can you dry your hair in your room? Please?"

"I need the mirror! Use Blake's shower!"

"Rosita's cleaning it!"

"Mummy's?"

"She's in the bath." I close my eyes and take a deep breath. "Come on, Nikki, please?"

"I'm almost done! Stop being annoying."

I sink onto the carpet. She's been in there for forty-five minutes.

Something soft hits me on the nose. I look up to see Blake bounding up the stairs in his climbing gear: weird shoes, climbing harness, gym shorts, T-shirt. Another harness is resting beside me on the carpet, where it landed after bouncing off my face.

"Can you belay me?" he asks. He and my dad built a climbing wall on the back of the house.

I shake my head. "Sorry, Blakester. I have plans."

"What are you doing?"

"Going to Miami."

He stretches back his arm until it pops. "With who?"

I try to sound nonchalant. "Friends from work."

"Really?"

"Shocking, I know," I say, and then force a laugh. My phone hasn't exactly been ringing off the hook since we moved here in January. Even Corey Perkins never called. Not that I expected him to.

Tara from bio called a few times, but that was to ask about assignments, not plans. Of course I told her I was really busy with family stuff so she wouldn't think I was pathetic. She must have known anyway, because she got her friend to invite me to her house party. I felt so awkward, worrying if everyone was wondering why the new girl was there, so I kept drinking wine coolers until I forgot about how uncomfortable I was, and until Corey's tongue was in my mouth. I don't know what I was thinking. I mean, he's cute in a messy, stoner-boy kind of way, but I barely even know him. Now I'm the new girl who gets drunk and hooks up with random guys at parties.

Awesome.

Not that we *hooked up*, hooked up. I've never done *it*, though I'm not saving myself or anything. Back in Montreal I might have done it with Alex Bonderman, if things had turned out differently. After five years of carpooling and my family basically adopting him since his parents were always in Paris or Hong Kong, after five years of me being secretly in love with him, he finally kissed me at eleven thirty on a Wednesday night when we were popping Halloween candy and studying for a math exam. His breath smelled like Reese's Peanut Butter Cups. We spent the next few weeks making out whenever we found a second alone. In the stairwell at school. On our walk home from school. In my basement.

Until he stopped coming over.

I dropped by his house to see what was up and found my so-called best friend, Laurie Gerlach, in his room, her beige C-cup bra tangled on the wheels of his computer chair. They felt terrible, they said. But they *liked* each other.

That was the week before Laurie's sweet sixteen party. Which I went to, even though I shouldn't have. I drank wine coolers in the club's bathroom with some random people in my grade. It made watching Laurie and Alex's slow dances to John Mayer a little more bearable.

I should have known Alex didn't really feel that way about me. I mean, come on, he belonged with someone like Laurie. Glossy hair and all that.

And I should have known not to trust a friendship based on the two of us sporting identical sheepskin winter coats. Back in grade seven, Laurie had rushed up to me and screamed, "Omigod—look! We're twins!" And there we were. Instant BFFs.

I bet Laurie and Alex have done *it* by now.

I don't speak to either of them anymore. I rarely speak to anyone from Montreal. We're still friends on MySpace but everyone always seems so busy.

I bet Vicks has done *it* too. A girl like Vicks doesn't date a guy for a year and not do it. I doubt Jesse has. Judging from the gold cross that dangles from her neck, I'd say she's probably one of those chastity-belt-till-I'm-married girls. She could use a massage. Vicks is the opposite. All relaxed and "No problem, dude."

Nothing shakes her. If my boyfriend didn't call me for two weeks, I would be under my covers whimpering.

Vicks is not afraid of anything. Not boys. Not what people think.

"Oh, come on, you can come belay me for five minutes," Blake says now.

"I can't. I'm leaving in five minutes." To go away with friends. *Friends.* Almost. I smile. I can't help it. Vicks opened up to me today, telling me about Brady and everything. Sure, Jesse doesn't seem to love me, but she invited me along, didn't she?

Fine, I invited myself along. And basically offered to pay for the trip if they'd take me.

Oh, God. I can't believe I did that. Tried to buy friends.

"Hey, Nikki!" Blake yells, banging on the door. "Come belay me!"

She hollers back, "No way, pipsqueak!"

Nikki hates the climbing wall on the back of our house. As does our mother. Mum worries daily that Blake is going to bust his head open, but Dad's an adventure junkie like Blake—the two of them got scuba certified in Aruba two years ago. There wasn't much Nikki or Mum could do since it was three against two. I voted for the wall, even though I'm too uncoordinated to use it. It makes Blake happy, so what the hell?

Most things around here happen by popular demand.

Grilled salmon or wheat-crust pizza for dinner, Hono-lulu or Mexico for winter break, BMW X3 or the convertible as the new kids' car. Blake wanted the truck; Nikki was obsessed with the convertible. I didn't really care. But like with the climbing wall, I was the swing vote. I had a vision of myself on the highway, the top down, windswept hair . . . and then I had a vision of the car flipping over and my head being cracked open. I chose the X3.

I'm often the swing vote. The swing sibling. That's what I called myself to Dr. Kaplan, the psychologist my parents sent the three of us to, to help us adjust to starting a new high school in January. Blake as a freshman, me as a sophomore, and Nikki as a senior. Kaplan laughed when I called myself that. She didn't really get it, though. She said that the swing vote is the power seat. I tried to explain that being told to choose between Nikki's choice *A* and Blake's choice *B* makes me power*less*, because I don't have a choice *C*. She asked me if being the middle child made me feel insecure or like I didn't belong, and I thought, *Well, yeah, Nikki's the pretty, 4.0, popular one, Blake's the rebel baby, and I'm just . . . the other one. The tiebreaker.* But then Nikki started talking about how she felt *she* didn't belong in Florida and then she was off and running. Everything is always about Nikki.

Blake rolled his eyes at me, and then we both almost cracked up. I gave him a "don't start" look, because Nikki would have gone mental if we laughed. She hates when we gang up on her. Blake got the message and kept a straight face.

Blake's the only one who understands why I wanted to work at the Waffle House. Nikki and Mum couldn't grasp why I'd be a hostess, why I didn't want to work at Dad's office, like Nikki, where I could choose my own hours. Or—judging from the fact that Nikki is doing her hair in the middle of the afternoon—lack of hours. But at Dad's, everyone would know that I was Mr. Fine's daughter. People would be nice to my face because I was their boss's kid, but then whisper about how I was just some spoiled rich girl behind my back. No, thanks. I'd rather hostess at the Waffle House. Sure, occasionally having to bus tables is not good for one's spa manicure, but I like that no one even notices me. The customers barely know I'm there. I tried to explain that to Jesse when she asked me about why I was there, but I don't think it came out right.

I hope Abe gets my note about missing my shift tomorrow. I apologized about the short notice, of course.

I can't believe I invited myself along. But when Jesse mentioned the trip, all I could think about was that I wanted to go with them. Vicks is so strong and cool and Jesse is so sure of herself all the time. Plus they're both so different from everyone I knew back home, and from everyone at Rawling Prep. Vicks would never stop by Brady's to find Jesse's bra tangled on the wheels of his computer chair. And not just because Jesse's all Christian conservative. They're loyal. They trust each other.

I want that. With them.

I lied about wanting to see that alligator.

On the safari we went on in June, we had to sit in an open Jeep, watching four cheetahs rip a gazelle apart limb by limb. Blake and Dad thought seeing a kill was the highlight of the trip. We had driven around for four hours searching for one.

I mentioned that to Vicks once, when I was trying to think of something interesting to talk to her about. She arched an eyebrow. "That's some wacked shit," she said.

Tell me about it. Blood. And skin. And internal organs everywhere. I had to cover my eyes with my hands.

Last week I dreamed about that drive. Except I was the gazelle.

Nikki finally opens the door.

"How does it look?" she asks, fluffing her hair and blocking the entrance.

"Perfect, but I need to get in there."

"Look how straight I got it. Do you believe? In this

heat? You have to try my antifrizz gel. It's amazing. I'm obsessed."

"Will do. Can I get in now? Please?"

She sweeps past me. "Don't be too long, I need to do my eyes."

Postshower, I yank the sliding doors open, climb out of the Jacuzzi tub, and wrap a hot, fluffy, lemon-scented towel around my body. Rosita must have just done a wash. Then I hurry to my room to find Nikki riffling through my closet.

"I'm borrowing your Alice + Olivia sundress, 'kay?"

"Sure. But didn't Mummy get you one too?"

"Yeah, but yours is nicer. The stripes on mine make me look fat."

"They do not." Nikki is being ridiculous, because she weighs only five pounds more than her ideal weight, max. She has big boobs, a mane of gorgeous shiny blond hair, and has always been considered one of the best-looking girls in her grade. Boys love her. Honestly, they fight over her. Even though she was the new girl in school, she had five invitations to senior prom.

Nonetheless, Nikki is always on a diet. As is Mum. Since the two of them are currently obsessed with the South Beach diet, we keep having weird things like

cauliflower purée that's pretending to be mashed potato.

Nikki pulls my dress off its hanger and examines
the tag. "Ugh. It's a size two. You're such a rexi."

I hug my towel. I hate when she calls me that. If
I eat the cauliflower or whatever South Beach thing
they're eating, I'm anorexic; if I sneak out with Blake
and Dad for McDonald's, I'm a traitor. "Nikki, I have
to get ready. I'm going out with friends."

"You have friends?" Her phone line rings and she
runs off to get it. Nikki is very busy with her Florida
friends, her Montreal friends, and her future college
friends.

I open my drawer to get dressed. My white cotton
underwear are all folded to look like little envelopes,
courtesy of Rosita. I pull on a pair of black shorts and
a tissue-soft white T-shirt that Mum must have just
bought me because I've never seen it before. Then I
yank a red carry-on bag out of my closet and start tossing stuff inside. Jeans, shorts, a few shirts. Running
shoes. In case I have to take off in a hurry. Ha-ha. I'm
sure it'll be fine. Fun even.

I hear a car pull up outside and separate my blinds
to see the world's oldest two-door station wagon in
our circular driveway. With the engine still running,
Jesse is in the driver's seat staring up at the house
while Vicks is checking out the X3. I open the win-

dow and yell down, "Sorry, I'll be three secs!" I grab two towels from the linen closet—one for showering and one in case we go to the beach—and then run to the toiletries closet and pick out a travel toothbrush and some hotel-size bottles of conditioner, shampoo, and body wash. I stuff them in my bag and knock on Mum's bathroom door. "I'm off!"

"Where are you going again?" she asks through the door and over the sound of the elevator music she's playing in there.

"To Miami. With friends from work."

"From the Waffle Shop?"

"Waffle House, Mum, Waffle House. I keep telling you that." It's like she has a mind block.

"When will you be back?"

"Sunday night."

"Who's driving?"

"Jesse."

"Is she a good driver?"

"Yes. Mum, I gotta go."

"Do you have enough money?"

"About a hundred. A hundred and fifty, maybe?"

"Take my AmEx card from the credenza," she says. "Just sign my name. Have fun! Be good!"

She would never give Blake or Nikki her credit card. She'd worry he'd charge a Jet Ski and she'd buy a diamond tennis bracelet or whatever. But she trusts me.

45

"Thanks!" Maybe I should buy a Jet Ski. Or a diamond tennis bracelet. Right. Maybe I should take my iPod. And my pillow. Yes, I definitely should. I run back to my room, toss in my iPod, and then unsuccessfully try to cram my pillow into my bag. I resort to carrying it under my arm. "Bye, Blake! Rosita! Nikki!"

I hear Blake and Rosita wish me good-bye.

I knock on my sister's door. "Nikki? I'm—"

"I'm on the phone!"

"Okay, I'm—"

"Mel, I'm on the phone!"

Whatever. "Have a good weekend. I'm leaving."

"Wait. You're not taking the car, are you? I need it."

Oh, now she's paying attention.

I never take the car. Nikki's convinced it'll get stolen out of the Waffle House parking lot, so my dad drops me off for the morning shifts and whoever's around picks me up. Today I just called a cab. Honestly, I don't even like driving. I just got my license a few months ago and sitting in the driver's seat is just too scary. "I'm not taking the car," I say, and then hurry down the stairs. At the sound of two loud honks I slip into my flip-flops, heave my bag over my shoulder, and firmly close the front door, leaving my family and the over-air-conditioned house behind.

I skip down the concrete steps, waving to the girls.

Instead of waving back, they both stare at me like I'm some sort of alien. Jesse's left hand is draped out the window, and she's tapping her long, soft pink nails, decaled with tiny silver angels, against the side of the door. Nikki would never let me get away with decals, but I kind of like them.

"Finally," Jesse says through the rolled-down window.

"Sorry you had to wait," I say, the wet heat enveloping me like bathwater as I walk around the car to the trunk. "Would you mind popping it?"

"I just did," Jesse says, sounding annoyed.

I try to lift it, but it doesn't want to go up.

"What is wrong with her?" I hear Jesse grumble, and my back tenses.

"Don't be like that; you know it gets stuck," Vicks says, and then adds, "I'll do it."

Vicks comes around to help. Even crouched over, she towers over me. The tallest building on the skyline, someone you can't help but pay attention to. Someone who won't be ignored.

"Rockin' Beamer," she says, fiddling with the trunk while still checking out the car. "Your dad's?"

"My sister's," I say. "And mine. And my brother's eventually, but he's only fifteen so he can't drive yet."

"Lucky." She heaves the trunk open, tosses in my bag, and then slams it closed.

"Thanks," I say. I struggle to figure out how to push forward her seat, but then Vicks does it for me, and I climb into the back.

Jesse shifts the car into reverse.

"Mel, someone's looking for you," Vicks says, pointing to the porch.

Nikki is staring at the car, confused. She must have assumed the honks were for her. She beckons me back inside.

Now she wants to talk to me? Now that I'm leaving?

"Just go," I say, looking down and pretending I don't see her. And just like that, we're on our way.

4

JESSE

"AT LAST!" I put the pedal to the metal, and my mood soars. The windows are down and the late-afternoon air rushes in and I yell, *"Whoo-hoo!"*, not caring if Mel thinks I'm a hick. Mel with her fancy house and fancy cars—that girl has more money than anyone I've ever met. Not that I want to trade places. As the Bible says, "It is easier for a camel to go through the eye of a needle than for a rich man to enter the kingdom of God." Her sister even looked like a camel, all prissy at the door, like she wanted to spit or nip or whatever it is camels do when they're cranky.

I laugh out loud, and Vicks says, "What?"

I shake my head. I still don't have the slightest clue why Mel wants to go to Miami with us, and my hopes of a last-minute back-out have just been dashed. To her credit, she did climb right into the backseat like she knows that's where she belongs. Vicks is up front with me, where she belongs, so I've decided to think of Mel as, like, a mosquito. If she gets too annoying, *smack*.

"This is great, huh?" I say. "Don't you think, Vicks? Aren't you glad I kicked your fanny into gear?"

Vicks doesn't respond. She's fiddling with the radio, which, okay, fine, maybe isn't working quite up to par like I said it was. Her forehead is getting that frown that makes her look like a bear.

"Dude," she says. The only station she can hit is Klassic 103.9, home of the golden oldies. "These Boots Are Made for Walkin'" blares from the speakers, and I shake my booty to the beat.

"'These boots are made for walkin'!'" I sing. "'And that's just what they'll do!'"

"Oh, vomit," Vicks says.

"'One of these days these boots are gonna walk all over—'"

Vicks twists the knob.

"Hey!" I protest. I try to find it again, but all I get is static, static, and more static.

"Noooo," Vicks complains. "I thought you said we'd

have music! *Can't* have a road trip without music!"

Then Mel's hand is snaking up to the cigarette lighter, fiddling with some cord, and out of nowhere, "Drive" by Incubus fills the car. It's coming from the Opel's speakers, and yet I know it isn't the radio because Niceville's alternative rock station is way down on the register, and I've got the red doohickey up in the hundreds.

"Leave it," Mel calls as my hand goes to the knob. "You have to keep it on the same station for it to work."

"Duh," I say. I understand about reception; I just don't know what miracle station we've somehow landed on. I turn the knob, and Incubus is no more. Vicks shoves my hand away and re-tunes. Incubus returns, and Vicks's forehead smoothes.

"It's iTrip," Mel explains. She holds up her iPod, thrusting it between the front seats. It looks like a normal iPod, only it's connected to a black cord she stuck in the cigarette lighter.

"See?" she says. "Now we can listen to whatever we want."

She's far too pleased with herself, and Vicks is far too appreciative.

"Mel, you rule," she's saying.

Whatever. I'm irked that Mel picked "Drive" because Vicks loves indie rock. Her brother Penn got her into it.

"I would have pegged you as more of a pop-star girl," I say.

"Oh, I like pop too," Mel says. "But isn't this the perfect song for a road trip? I think I heard it in a movie, or maybe on *American Idol*."

I glance at Vicks to make sure she's catching this. Vicks isn't an *American Idol* fan, which normally I would rip all over her about, 'cause *American Idol* is, like, the American dream. I love *American Idol*. But in this particular instance, I'm happy to let Mel take the fall.

Only Vicks doesn't take the bait. She throws it right back at me, saying, *"'These boots are made for walkin''?!"*

"Please," I say. "I was singing ironically."

"Uh-huh." She holds her hands palms up, pretending to be a scale. *"American Idol . . .* golden oldies." Her hands go up and down to show that the two are awfully close in the corn category.

I slug her shoulder. "Irony!"

"I don't get it," Mel says. "What are you guys talking about?"

Vicks and I laugh.

"Sorry?" Mel asks.

"Nothing," I say, turning up the volume.

At the next intersection, as I ease into the left-turn lane, Vicks scans the road signs and says, "No, dude, turn right."

I shake my head. "I-10's north of here."

"Yeah, but we don't want I-10."

"Are you wigging? To get to Miami, we take . . ." I

trickle off, watching as she leans down, fishes in her back-pack, and comes up with her battered copy of *Fantastical Florida*. Ah. Her guidebook.

She flips to a dog-eared page and scans the print. "Ha," she says triumphantly. "Not even three hours away."

"Old Joe?" I say.

Mel leans forward. "Um, when you said giant gator . . . could you maybe explain exactly what you meant?"

Vicks picks up on something in Mel's voice—I hear it too—and turns toward her. "You're not wimping out on us, are you? This early in the game?"

"What? No!"

"I thought you wanted to see Old Joe."

"I do!"

Vicks cocks her eyebrows.

"I *do*!" says Mel.

Uh-huh, I think, my spirits rising. *Sure you do.*

"Okay, seriously, I'm not wimping out," she says. "I just kind of need to know if he's in a cage, that's all." She swallows. "He's in a cage, right? With bars? It's not one of those natural habitat places where there's just a ditch or something?"

"Now, come on, who wants to be locked up in a cage?" I say. "Anyway, I thought you've been on a safari." I stretch it out all hoity-toity. "What's one wild and free gator compared to a whole passel of wild and free lions?"

In the rearview mirror, I see Mel blanch. Old Joe is

stuffed—he hasn't been wild and free for a long time—but Vicks doesn't correct me. I love how we're teasing Miss Scaredy-cat together.

The light turns green. I flip my blinker and switch out of the left lane.

"Now what?" I ask Vicks.

"Your next turn's on White Point Road," she tells me. She twists around. "But don't worry, Mel. We're not off to see Old Joe."

"We're not?" I say. "Then what were we just talking about?"

"We'll get to Old Joe eventually," Vicks clarifies. She holds up one finger as if lecturing a roomful of eager students. "First, the world's smallest police station."

"Aw, girl!" I say. "You crack me up."

She grins. "I do? Why?"

"The world's smallest police station?!"

"It'll be awesome. Miniature desks, miniature squad cars . . . maybe even itty-bitty policemen! What's not to love about that?"

"Uh-huh," I say. "I know what you're up to. You're stalling, that's what."

"What are you talking about? You said we could go see that stuff! 'Anything you want,' you said."

"Hey, sure, happy to oblige. I'm just saying: Mel's scared of Old Joe, and you're scared of sweet ol' Brady. That's why you're sticking in so many detours." I mean it as a tease, because that's what Vicks and I do. We tease.

But she says, "*God*, Jesse," and faces the window.

I'm stung. *And* I feel wrongly accused, because aren't I in fact bouncing along this crappy side road instead of heading toward I-10? I'm "living a little," dang it. Don't I get credit for tarnishing my stupid halo?

And she shouldn't take the Lord's name in vain. That's one thing I refuse to do, no matter how Goody Two-Shoes it makes me, 'cause otherwise I could end up in the bad place. That's what MeeMaw says. MeeMaw prays all the time about Mama, 'cause she's afraid that's where Mama's going to end up if she doesn't change her ways. Mama doesn't even go to church with us. MeeMaw and Pops pick me up each Sunday and Wednesday, and off we go.

"I'm not scared of Old Joe," Mel says in a tinyish voice.

I don't bother to respond.

Incubus fades out, and "Oops! . . . I Did It Again" by Britney Spears takes over. But despite the pull, I refuse to share a grimace with Vicks. She lost that privilege by being a jerk.

What kills me is she doesn't even seem to notice.

By seven, my belly is growling, but I don't say anything 'cause I don't want to be the one who has needs. "Wheat Kings" is on the stereo, some Canadian song Mel wants us to listen to. It's soft and kind of lonely sounding, and Mel starts telling us all about Canada, which is where she's from. Just as I've never known a rich person before, I've never known a Canuck, either. That's what Mel says Canadians are called. Canucks. Sounds like an insult to me.

She tells us that in Canada they have dollar coins instead of dollar bills, and that they're called loonies. They have two-dollar coins too that are called twoonies. They even spell things differently up there. *Color* and *favor* have a *u*; *gray* is *grey*. In Canada, everyone has free health care. In Canada, you don't have to take SATs. In Canada, the drinking age is eighteen or nineteen, depending on the province. In Canada, they have provinces instead of states.

She's kinda trying too hard, as if she thinks we're gonna like her better for being so sophisticated. Or maybe she's just homesick. But to my surprise, I don't mind her jabbering. It's interesting to hear about a whole different country where people have whole different spellings and hopes and dreams. I wonder if Epcot has a little bitty Canada stuck in there with the other countries.

In addition to the other Canadian stuff, Mel also talks about food, which is the part Vicks latches on to. Sometimes in my head, I imagine Vicks in one of those white poufy chef's hats, cracking eggs on the edge of her spatula while judges watch and a timer ticks away. What's that show called? *Iron Chef?* It's on the Food Network, which we get 'cause Mama loves her cable. I know it's a waste of money, but I don't complain. With cable, we get the Praise Network, which means I can stay caught up on all my talk shows.

Mama won't watch the talk shows with me, not even *Word!* with sassy Faith Waters. She prefers those Animal Planet shows, especially the one where some dog trainer comes in and cracks the whip with dogs who bite and pee all over the floor. Mama doesn't agree with his methods, but she has to admit he gets results. She wants to be a dog trainer someday instead of a dog groomer.

If someday ever comes, I think, and then I switch off that brain channel right there. No. Nuh-uh. I tune back in to Canada.

"*Poutine?*" Vicks is saying.

"*Poutine,*" Mel says.

"What is it? Sounds dirty."

"Fries and gravy and cheese curds," Mel says, as if that combination of words wouldn't make everyone and her brother want to gag.

"Nasty," Vicks says.

"No, it's amazing, trust me. The most fattening thing in the world, but worth every calorie. Even my sister loves it and she's *always* on a diet."

"I don't mean fries and gravy," says Vicks. "I mean

the word. *Poutine*—it sounds like Tully asking Penn about what he did last night." Vicks deepens her voice. "'Dude, you were out late with Liza. Were you getting yourself some *poutine* in the backseat?'"

"Ew," Mel says.

I laugh, like I always do when Vicks brings up Penn. Though I don't like the thought of him getting *poutine* in any backseat. That's just nasty. "He's not going out with Liza again, is he?" I ask.

"No. He's single. Why, you interested?" Vicks says.

I blush.

"Ooo, someone's blushing!" she crows.

"Oh, please!" Like Penn and me could ever be a couple. Penn is *not* the marrying type, and according to the scripture, I'm not even supposed to date anyone unless I can see the two of us joining in holy union. Which has limited my dating options, believe me. To like, zilch. I kissed Matthew Pearson at Vacation Bible School last summer, and that is it for my wild and exciting love life. And Matthew was *so* not Penn Simonoff.

I blush some more and fervently hope Vicks isn't a mind reader. But I'm safe 'cause, lo and behold, she's moved back to her favorite topic of food, food, and more food.

"Well, anything with fries and gravy is okay by me," she says. "But what I wanna know is, what's a cheese curd? Is it like cottage cheese?"

"More like hunks of soft cheddar," Mel says. "Hey, all this food talk is making me hungry. Should we maybe stop for dinner?"

"Here," Vicks says, tossing her a cellophane-wrapped pack of Ding Dongs.

"Do we, um, have anything healthier?"

"You want healthy? No prob." Vicks lobs back a mango.

"Ow!"

Vicks laughs. After a second or two of silence, she glances over her shoulder and says, "I'm not hearing any smacking sounds. Why am I not hearing any smacking sounds?"

"Mangos are too messy," Mel says in a small voice.

"Nooo, you did not just say that. Mangos are too messy?"

"Um . . . well . . . I don't want to drip all over the seat. Mangos are very . . . drippy."

"Girl, you have insulted the wrong fruit," I say. "Vicks is *all about* mangos. Ask her how to cut one—turns out there's a foolproof technique."

"Well, there is!" Vicks says.

"She about throttled me once for cutting one up like you'd cut a peach." I lean away to avoid her thwack. "Hey! No hitting the driver!"

"I learned it from Rachael Ray," Vicks says, meaning that lady who has her own TV show.

"Ooo, Rachael Ray!" I say.

"You have to peel them like they do in Cuba, with slices cut in so you can pull the flesh off the pit. It was on one of her 'Tasty Travels' episodes."

"Ooo, tasty travels!"

"Does peeling a mango count as cooking?" Mel asks.

I giggle, and this time I fail to avoid Vicks's thwack.

"I happen to be a gourmand," Vicks says. "Do we have a problem with that?"

"She's a *gourmand*," I say to Mel.

"A gourmand," Mel echoes seriously.

Vicks huffs. "It's only an hour to Carrabelle. We can eat there."

"What?" Mel wails. "No!"

"We can stop now," I say. "It's no big deal." I feel expansive, and I like it. I also like saying "It's no big deal" to Vicks 'cause Vicks is always telling me to relax and not be such a tightbottom. Though she doesn't say "bottom."

I take the next exit, which has one of those signs with a picture of a knife and a fork. But turns out there's no restaurant, just a trailer outside a Texaco with a wooden stand fixed on it. A hand-lettered sign says, GENUINE ALL-BEEF DOGS! GENUINE TOASTED BUNS!

I pull up to the pump, thinking we might as well top off the tank while we're here. Vicks and I get out of the Opel and stretch—it feels so good—and Mel climbs out less happily.

"Um . . . this is not really what I had in mind," she says.

"Uh-*huh*," Vicks says. "Who's the gourmand now?"

Mel plays with a strand of her hair. The hot dog guy is wearing a shirt that features a dancing dog in a bun, and his calf is tattooed with a faded red frank.

"Nice tat," Vicks calls.

"Ain't it something?" he says. He stands up from his aluminum chair. He's got an umbrella set up to give him some shade. "Tell you what, I love the hot dog."

"I bet you do," I say, unscrewing the cap to the gas tank and jamming in the nozzle. MeeMaw wouldn't like that tattoo one bit—*your body is your temple*, and all that—but I feel at ease with guys like this. Long as they don't ogle Mama in a wet T-shirt contest, I like good ol' boys just fine.

Hot Dog Guy scratches his gut. The gasoline chug-a-lugs and then clunks off. The nozzle jumps.

"Fourteen dollars," I marvel. "Dang, what's wrong with this world?"

Mel says nothing.

"Guess I'll go inside and pay," I say, giving her another chance.

Mel remains mute. I sigh. I go inside the Texaco, give the cash register lady more than half my funds, and then plunk down an extra dollar-fifty for a Florida state map. Since we're off the main highway, I figure we might need it. I return outside to find Mel *still* standing there while Vicks fools with her cell phone, probably checking for messages.

"You guys ordered yet?" I ask. To Hot Dog Guy, I say, "I'll take your combo special with a Coke."

"Make that two," Vicks says, snapping shut her phone. She jams it hard into her pocket, which tells me all I need to know. "So, hey, you been in the food industry long?"

The food industry. She kills me. Hot Dog Guy grabs the tongs and launches into his life story, and I bump Mel with my hip. "Aren't you going to get anything?"

She pales as Hot Dog Guy pulls two pink wieners from the steamer. They do look, well, awfully pink.

Hot Dog Guy says something to Vicks that involves the term "by-products," to which Vicks responds, "Me, I'm a waffle bitch. I'm no stranger to grease, believe me."

"I'll just . . ." Mel swallows, one of those big ones you can see. "Just a toasted bun for me, please. And a Diet Sprite."

"A bun?" I say. "Who orders just a bun?"

"I do," she says. She lifts her chin and meets my gaze dead on, and I grudgingly give the girl some respect. So she's ordering just a bun. Fine.

I pay for my combo—once again Mel does not whip out her wallet and say, "Oh, here, let me get that for you"—and sit on the curb. Mel follows with her bun and drink, since Vicks is still talking shop with Mr. Hot Dog. She's quizzing him about the different fixin's, and I'm thinking, *Fixin's? What could possibly be so fascinating about fixin's? We're talking ketchup and mustard here, not caviar.*

Then Mr. Hot Dog launches into a story about being on the *Today* show, because that's how famous he is, and I snort. Do I like this good ol' boy? Sure, why not. Do I think he's been on some big, celebrity talk show? *Yeah, right,* I think. *You and me both, buddy.*

But when Mel expresses her own disbelief, I play the devil's advocate.

"He is so full of it," she says to me. "Him? On the *Today* show?"

"Why not?" I say. "Just because he's a redneck, he can't be on the *Today* show?"

"I didn't say because he's a redneck."

"You thought it, though." So did I, but she doesn't have to know that.

"It just seems unlikely, that's all." She pulls off a bit of bread with her thumb and forefinger. She puts it daintily in her mouth. I take a whomping big bite of my hot dog.

"If he owned some fancy-schmancy five-star restaurant, then would you believe him?" I say with my mouth full. "'Cause, FYI, money doesn't make you a better person. In fact it usually makes you a worse person."

I think about Dr. Aberdeen, Mama's oncologist, who made Mama wait for two hours before going over her lab results. I know he wouldn't have made Mel's mother wait like that. I know it in my soul.

"Who said anything about money?" Mel asks.

"Huh?"

"Are you talking about *me*?"

"What? No!" My heart starts pounding, 'cause this isn't where I meant to go. "I just think it's wrong to label people, that's all."

"Jesse, you're the one who basically said that all rich people are jerks."

Me and my big mouth. "Um . . . well . . ."

"Guys, check this out," Vicks says. Mr. Hot Dog's holding a photo, and he and Vicks are admiring it.

I get up and brush the crumbs from my shorts. Mel folds her napkin into fourths and drops it in the trash can. We walk over to see the picture.

It's Mr. Hot Dog and Al Roker, the weatherman from the *Today* show. The black guy who lost all that weight. He's shrunken looking in the photo, with an oddly large head, and he's holding up a hot dog.

"No way," I say. I raise my eyes to the in-the-flesh Mr. Hot Dog. I can't believe I'm talking to someone who stood within millimeters of a TV star.

"Best day of my life," Mr. Hot Dog boasts. He shuts his wallet.

"Well, we gotta go," Vicks says. She sticks out her hand, and Mr. Hot Dog shakes it. "It was a pleasure."

"Don't forget what I said about relish," he warns. "There's an entire spectrum of relish out there."

"Spectrum of relish," Vicks says. "Got it."

The Opel is as hot as sin when the three of us climb in, and Vicks says, "Damn, somebody should have parked in the shade."

"Somebody should keep her opinions to herself," I retort. But she's right. I should have moved the car after filling it up. My fanny is being scorched even through my cutoffs, and I'm mad at myself for the mistake.

"Toasted buns," Mel says, giggling.

"What's that?" Vicks says.

"Genuine toasted buns," she repeats.

Ohhh—from the sign. "I think you mean genu-*wine*," I say. "It's all about the accent, Canada Girl."

"Genu-*wine* toasted buns," Mel says, stretching it out.

Vicks laughs, and just like that I feel better. I kinda want to glance at Mel, to tell her *thanks* or something.

Instead, I start the engine.

5

MEL

I'M NOT GOING to make it.

We still have a half hour of driving before we get to Carrabelle, home of the world's smallest police station, and I can barely breathe.

Vicks has . . . stomach issues.

And they're bad.

The two of them think it's hilarious.

"Don't you know it's unlawful to pass wind in Florida, after five o'clock, on Tuesdays, Thursdays, and Fridays?" Jesse asks.

Vicks laughs, her feet propped up against the dashboard. "But on Saturday it's okay?"

I think I'm going to be sick.

"I am so not lying!" Jesse says. "That is an honest-to-goodness state law. I learned it when me and Mama were playing Balderdash."

The smell returns in a second wave.

"You did it again!" Jesse shrieks, fanning the air.

"Silent but deadly," Vicks says, not the least bit embarrassed.

If it were me, I'd have to move back to Canada. I try to breathe through my mouth. I cough.

"Poor Mel has to sit behind me," Vicks says, shaking her head.

"No problem," I say, almost choking.

She shrugs. "It's not my fault. It was the hot dog. Al Roker had gas too."

"What, you're psychically in tune with Al's intestines?" Jesse asks.

"Me and Al Roker, you'd never know we had so much in common, would you? United by flatulence."

Flatulence. I'm in a car discussing flatulence. My family would rather die than discuss flatulence. *I* would rather die than discuss flatulence.

Vicks turns to look at me. "How'd the dog go down with you? You're looking green."

"Mel had her hot dog without the dog," Jesse says, when I'd just as soon she kept that bit of information to herself. I think she's mad at me because I didn't pay for the food. I should have paid for the food. The only reason I didn't offer was because, well, I thought that maybe they wanted me around for more than just my wallet. I was hoping that perhaps it was the excuse for letting me come, but that secretly they wanted me along.

"What?" Vicks shrieks. "Without the dog?"

"Without the dog," Jesse repeats "You missed it. You were discussing the finer points of relish."

"What is wrong with you, woman?" Vicks cries. "I thought you were hungry."

My cheeks heat up. "I don't like hot dogs."

"And why not?"

"I heard they're made from the leftover scraps of cows and pigs and stuff," I mumble.

"Says who?" Vicks asks.

"Says my sister."

"Is she a doctor?" Jesse asks.

"No, but I told you, she's always on a diet." I instantly feel dumb for using my sister as an expert. She's just obsessed with food. And how much she and I eat of it. I sink into my seat. Am I ever going to know the right thing to say to these girls to get them to like me?

"It's a sad life when you can't eat a hot dog," Jesse says. "If a hot dog comes your way, you eat it."

"Dude," Vicks says. She cracks up.

"What?" Jesse says.

"Not to burst your bubble, but when have you *ever* eaten the hot dog?"

Ew.

"Are you wigging?" Jesse says. "I ate my hot dog." Then she gets it. *"Ohhh,"* she says, rolling her eyes. "Very funny."

"What about you, Mel?" Vicks asks me. "You ever eaten the hot dog?"

First they talk about flatulence and now . . . that. "You guys," I say, my cheeks now on fire.

"Oh, come on. You look innocent but you're secretly a badass, aren't you?"

"Not quite," I say.

A third wave of *wind* sneaks through the car—Vicks most certainly *did* eat the hot dog—and I might really gag this time.

"Geez Louise, woman!" Jesse says. "For the last time: Stop pooting!"

Even with all the windows open, we're being asphyxiated.

"Al Roker! You are my kin!" Vicks cries.

"Feet off the dashboard," Jesse commands, swatting her legs. "Point that thing in another direction!"

Vicks cackles. Jesse speeds up to escape the fumes, and I'm relieved when she finally eases to a stop in front of an empty phone booth. We all spill out of the car.

Thank God, fresh air.

"This is it?" Jesse says, obviously disappointed. "The world's smallest police station?"

Vicks gestures at a neatly lettered sign on the glass, which does indeed say POLICE. But other than that, it's just a boring phone booth.

"Where are the police officers?" I ask.

"Police offi*cer*," Jesse says. "It couldn't fit more than one."

"Maybe he's off duty," Vicks says.

"Maybe the whole town's off duty," Jesse says.

There's no sign of life on the entire block, other than the deafening chirp of cicadas. There's a convenience store across the street, its faded wooden sign hanging from a single nail. No one is inside.

We stare at the vacant phone booth.

Vicks looks sheepish. She shifts her weight and another wave of grossness squeaks out. Jesse takes a step away.

I can't help but feel embarrassed for Vicks.

"Seen enough?" Jesse says at last.

Miss Indigestion smacks her fist into her palm. "*Now* we go see Old Joe the Alligator," she says. "He's only half an hour away in Wakulla Springs, and he's *got* to be better than this."

Jesse climbs back into the Opel, and Vicks folds her seat forward to let me in.

"Come on, come on," Vicks says.

"So Old Joe . . . ," I begin. I was kind of hoping that they might have forgotten about visiting the gator.

"Some jogger got eaten by a gator just last week," Jesse says. She turns the key in the ignition and puts the car in gear while Vicks scans the map. "In Pensacola. People say they're getting braver."

"Haven't there been, like, three alligator-related deaths in the last month?" Vicks wonders aloud.

"Guys," I say.

"The jogger lady's friend saw it happen, but there was nothing she could do," Jesse says. We pull onto the highway. "*Chomp*, and she was gone."

"In Orlando, a gator carried off a three-year-old," Vicks adds. "Now, that is so sad."

"Imagine seeing your one-and-only child be dragged off in the jaws of a gator," Jesse says. "Not even having a body to put in the coffin."

"*Guys,*" I plead.

They laugh, and Vicks turns up the music.

Old Joe here we come.

When we get there, the place Vicks wants to go to is just a little museum. Not a natural habitat with night tours, which is what I had pictured. This is nothing but a small building with a CLOSED sign on the front door, down the road from a Stop-N-Go and a Piggly Wiggly grocery store, also shut for the night. This town is even deader than Niceville; no, even deader than Carrabelle, which I wouldn't have thought possible. The street is dark except for our headlights.

Thank God.

"Oh, well," I say, trying not to sound too relieved. "We better get going anyway. It must be at least nine, and we still have a long way to go till we get to Miami, eh? We're not supposed to be on the road after one A.M., right? Since we're not eighteen? I think that's the rule in Florida. I don't want you guys getting into trouble."

"Damn," Vicks says, ignoring me. "I really want to see Old Joe."

"You can't always get what you want," Jesse says.

Vicks gets out of the Opel and strides to the museum. She tries the door. Locked. She disappears around the side, then fast-walks back into sight. "Hey, y'all," she whispers. "Come here."

Oh, no.

Jesse turns off the headlights, and darkness stretches around us. She climbs out of the car. I don't want to, but I don't want to sit here by myself, either. I scurry after them.

"What's the scoop?" Jesse asks her.

Vicks leads us to the back of the building and points up to a rear window no one bothered to shut. It's the type that cranks outward instead of being raised; there's

72

maybe a four-inch gap between the pane and the sill. The screen inside is torn. It's directly above the back entrance.

"Someone with small hands could reach through and jiggle the knob to the back door," Vicks says.

I clasp my hands behind my back.

"If that small-handed person so desired," Jesse says.

"I don't think this is such a good idea," I say, my heart pounding.

"I'm thinking it is," Vicks says.

I glance down the street. There is no one, absolutely no one, around. But what if we get caught? Arrested? What would people think?

That I'm a criminal? That I'm pathetic?

I would so lose my credit card privileges.

But if I don't? What are Jesse and Vicks going to think? That I'm a wimp? That I'm no fun?

I wish I didn't care what anybody thought.

"We're not going to fool with anything," Jesse says. "We just want to see Old Joe."

"Old Joe needs us," Vicks says earnestly. She presses her palm to her heart. "I can feel it."

"Come on," Jesse says. "Please?"

Vicks cups her hands below the window and nods, like, *See how easy?*

I close my eyes. I don't want to be a wimp. I don't want to be a wallet, either.

I want to open the damn window. I place my sandaled foot in Vicks's hands, and she heaves me up. I teeter. Oh, no. I'm going to fall. I'm going to fall. I'm going to bust my head open and die.

Jesse grabs my waist and steadies me. "Whoa, soft shirt," she says. "Like . . . super soft."

"Um . . . ," I say. "Thanks?"

"Can we focus here?" Vicks asks. "Do you have it?"

I worm my arm through the window, but I can't find the doorknob. "No," I say, my voice shaking. I touch something sticky. Was that a spiderweb? Oh, God.

"Now?" Vicks asks again.

Nooooooo, I want to yell, but I don't.

I can't do it. I just can't.

"You can do it, Mel," Jesse says, reading my mind.

I turn to her and she's nodding, and I think, maybe I can. I stretch my fingers out and I feel it, hard and smooth.

That's it! *That's it!* I turn the lock, and we all hear the click. "Got it!"

Light and laughing and giddy with pride, I free my jelly arm from the window. The girls lower me down.

Vicks runs up the steps and opens the museum's back door.

Jesse squeezes my shoulder.

I wonder if I've finally earned my seat.

6

VICKS

THE ROOM WE enter is dark, but a few windows let in light from a single street lamp outside. A wooden counter holds several racks of postcards, an old-time cash register, and a lamp like in someone's living room. The walls are lined with maps and old tourist posters. A model of the intracoastal waterway stands in the center of the room.

Not much to look at. More like some dad's boring collection than an actual museum.

We tiptoe around a corner into the front gallery, still seeing by the faint light through the windows. The place is mainly devoted to tourist dreck you can buy anywhere in the state. Bright blue T-shirts decorated with fish and oranges; mugs that say "Grandma and Grandpa went to Florida and all I got was this lousy cup"; toy license plates with kids' names on them (only never "Vicks," just "Victoria"); teddy bears wearing sashes that read "The Sunshine State."

No gator.

"Where is he?" whispers Jesse.

"He's gotta be here somewhere. The guidebook says."

"How old is that thing?" Jesse asks.

"The book?" I check the copyright. It's fifteen years old.

Damn.

"He's here, I'm telling you," I insist. No way am I going to let them down. Not when Jesse is finally acting like her old fun self and little Mel got the door open even though it's obvious she's scared out of her mind.

I go back into the model room and rummage behind the counter. Yep—a flashlight on the bottom shelf. I flip it on and scan the walls. Right next to the entrance we came in by is a small hallway leading to the bathrooms. And on the wall between the doors I find a small sign, black with red lettering: GATOR DOWNSTAIRS.

The museum basement is practically pitch-dark—it's only got those tiny windows up high at ground level.

I reach the bottom of the stairs and shine my light into the center of the room: Old Joe is sitting in a glass case—sixteen feet long, nose to tail—and grinning an enormous toothy smile that says, "I love you, baby," and also, "I could eat you alive if I felt like it," both at the same time.

Mel squeals as my flashlight shines into the gator's mouth, but Jesse walks straight up to the glass case. She kneels down and stares at him, real intent.

I stride up beside her and say, "Joe! How you doing there? Wow, you're a big boy, aren't you?"

Jesse follows my lead. "Aw, who's a giant reptile, eh?" she says. "You are! You are!"

"Come to Mama!" I coo. "What big teeth you have! And not a single cavity. What a good boy!"

I'm so happy, 'cause it's me and Jesse, like how we've been all summer, working at the Waffle. Us in sync, playing off each other's jokes. Like how it was up until she got so sour.

Anyway, the two of us are right up near old Joe, kneeling down with our faces close to his big, meat-eating grin—but Mel is hanging back, with a sick look on her face. Suddenly I feel sorry I pushed her so hard when any idiot can see that even a dead gator is making her nearly wet her shorts. "Come on," I say. "You don't have to pet him. I'll keep him away from you. Joe? Sit. Stay. Good boy. Stay. . . ."

I grab Mel's hand and walk her over to a spot about

five feet from the case. We sit down cross-legged on the floor, just looking at him, shining the flashlight along his bumpy green body. Jesse comes and joins us.

We admire Old Joe in silence. Mel's breathing a little hard, but otherwise she's okay.

"He may be dead," I say eventually, "but he's a *badass.*"

"He is," says Mel.

"He's like a god," I say. "He's like the god of badass. Look at him."

"You should watch your mouth, saying stuff like that." Jesse smacks my arm playfully.

"What?" I ask.

"He can hear you!"

"Who?" I ask. Then I get it. "God?" I say. "You're worried God can hear me?" She's such a Christianpants.

"Listen, I'm all for being a bad . . . *bottom—*"

I hoot. "You? *You?*" To Mel I say, "She said 'bad-bottom.'"

Mel giggles.

"But it's a sin to worship false idols," Jesse reminds me.

"I'm an atheist," I explain to Mel. "My family worships pretty much nothing besides the glories of the potato."

"The gator is not a god and neither is a potato," Jesse tells me. "You shouldn't worship them."

"I'm *joking,*" I say. "Hello? And besides, God—if he or she is up there—God is way more pissed about us breaking into the Wakulla Springs Museum than about me calling the gator a "god of badass." Any real god wouldn't get mad about minor stuff like that when there are actual laws being broken."

"I think God would be okay with us being in here," puts in Mel.

Jesse turns to her. "How come?"

"We're not hurting anything. We're just—well, *you* two are appreciating the gator. And that's what it's here for, right? To be appreciated."

"Tell that to the world's smallest policeman," I say.

"What?"

"The one who works in the world's smallest station. 'Cause you know no normal-size policeman could really work in that phone booth we visited."

Jesse smiles.

I continue, "God might be fine with us breaking and entering to appreciate Old Joe, but the itty-bitty policeman's gonna have a hissy fit."

"How tall do you think he is?" asks Mel. "Is he like, yay big? Four foot tall? Or smaller?"

"Oh, way, way smaller. He's the world's smallest," I say.

"I think he's like six inches tall," says Jesse.

"What?" says Mel. "That's not even human. That means he's a leprechaun."

For some reason this strikes us all as incredibly funny.

"Of course he's not a leprechaun!" I cry. "He's a human being! Give him some respect!"

"He's an officer of the law!" Jesse giggles. "He's six inches tall and he's like the policeman for cats, he makes the cats stop fighting."

"Cats and those—what are they called, those yappie dogs?" I say.

"Yorkies," says Jesse, child of a dog-grooming lady.

"Yorkshire terriers," says Mel, child of a rich man.

"Yeah, he's breaking up Yorkie fights," I say.

"And he hits them with a Popsicle stick if they don't listen to him," adds Jesse.

"Oh, and he doesn't eat doughnuts on his break," cries Mel. "He just eats the little doughnut holes."

"The Munchkins." Jesse nods. "That's so perfect."

I raise my finger in the air, dead serious. "He's gonna barge in here any second wielding a miniature club and pointing an itty-bitty gun at us and yelling, 'Put your hands on your head and back away from the gator!'"

Mel is wheezing she's laughing so hard.

"But when he does that," I go on, "we'll just pick him up and cuddle him to death!" More laughter. "I'll squash him between my boobs!" I cry. "He'll die happy!"

We can barely breathe.

"Not to death," Mel chokes out. "If you boob-squash him to death we could get life in prison for murder of an officer."

"Oh, he's like a twelfth of a full-size officer," I say. "They'll be lenient."

"You think?" Jesse wrinkles her brow.

"Oh, for sure," I say. "You saw the man's police station. It's a freakin' phone booth. He's got no respect in the community. They barely count him as a police officer. No way will we get life. And besides, we can say the death by cuddling was an accident. It'll only be, like, accidental manslaughter."

"Okay, then," says Mel. "We have a strategy." She says it with a completely straight face, and at first Jesse and I think she's missed the entire joke, but then we realize that's cosmically impossible and bust out laughing again.

When I get my breath, I want to make it up to Jesse. "I don't mean he's like a god," I say. "What I mean is, he's like a role model."

"Old Joe?"

"Or the smallest policeman?" Mel makes me laugh again, even though I'm trying to be serious. Because of course I wouldn't boob-squash my *role model* to death. "No, the gator. Look at him. He isn't afraid of anything."

"He's dead, that's why," says Mel.

"No, he wasn't afraid when he was alive. He's like a symbol. He was never scared a day in his life, he was ugly as sin, and he just rested in the sun, lapping up the goodness of the tropical air and knowing that he could bite clean through anybody who tried to mess with him."

"He didn't care what anybody thought." Mel puts her hand to her cheek.

"Exactly. Don't you kind of have to admire the guy?"

"Yeah," says Jesse, after a minute. "I do. We should sing to him."

"What?" Singing was not part of my plan. "This isn't a cookout. It's badass admiration."

"No," she says. "I mean we should do like a ritual. To show Old Joe some love."

"I'm not gonna sit here with you two and sing 'I love you, you love me,' like you do in Camp Fire Girls or whatever. That is way too hokey. Old Joe would not like it."

"No, no," Jesse says. "It'll be good. Mel, you'll sing with me, won't you?"

Mel plays with her fingers. "I probably won't know whatever you're going to sing."

Jesse pooh-poohs her. "You have an iPod with a two-thousand-song capacity. I think we can come up with something you'll recognize."

"I meant, I don't know any church songs or anything. I'm Jewish."

Jesse looks surprised for a second, but then says, "Shh. Let me think of something."

So we are quiet for a minute, and then Jesse begins.

From this valley you say you are leavin'
I will miss your bright eyes and sweet smile
For they say you are takin' the sunshine
That has brightened our pathways awhile—

And then Mel takes a breath and joins in:

Come and sit by my side if you love me
Do not hasten to bid me adieu
But remember the Red River Valley
And the cowgirl who loved you so true.

Mel has a real voice, a singer's voice. Bright and shiny—
like a sweet apple. Jesse stops singing to let Mel have a
solo.

"'Won't you think of the valley you're leaving—,'" Mel
sings, but then stops as soon as she realizes she's on her
own. "Jesse?"

She shakes her head. "You go."

"I don't like to sing alone."

"Oh, come on," I say. "Old Joe wants you to. Al Roker
wants you to."

She crosses her arms in front of her chest, closing
herself off, like she's about to say no.

"Please?" says Jesse. "You sing so pretty."

And Mel keeps going:

> *Oh, how lonely, how sad it will be—*
> *Oh, remember the heart you are breaking,*
> *And be true to your promise to me.*

I feel my throat closing up. The girl in the song, her guy goes away and takes the sunshine. He might not remember his promise. Hell, he might not even remember the valley he's leaving, once it's out of sight.

They say you are taking the sunshine. That's exactly how it's felt since Brady went to Miami. He took the sunshine.

Why hasn't he called me? How could his feelings change so fast? Why does he have to jump into my brain even when I'm doing everything possible to keep from thinking about him?

And why can't I make my own sunshine?

I don't want to start sobbing about my love life in the middle of our Badass Admiration Ritual, so I swallow hard, dig in my bag, and pull out a mango. "Let's leave him a token of our appreciation," I say, handing the flashlight to Mel. I walk forward on my knees, bow, and lay the mango at the foot of Joe's case. "Old Joe Gator, you great Badass of Wakulla Springs, fearless symbol of our road trip, we thank you. For your inspiration. You were uglier than a cactus and never sorry about it. You were fierce. And you had some honking big teeth. Yet you were peaceful and made people happy. Long may you rock."

"Long may you rock."

"Long may you rock."

"Oh, and we hope you like the mango. It looks like a juicy one."

By the time we leave the museum, it's officially night. The street is dark. From the shadows, a voice rings out to us. "Find anything good?"

There is a guy sitting on the hood of the Opel.

At first, a jolt runs through me. I think he might be a cop. But as my eyes adjust, I can see his face is smooth, barely shaven. His navy T-shirt is untucked and his jeans are frayed at the bottom, like he keeps stepping on them.

He's maybe seventeen. Just a teenager holding a bag of salt-and-vinegar potato chips. Built wide in the shoulders and narrow in the legs. Black hair and darkish skin; maybe he's Cuban or Puerto Rican. A flat nose, pretty brown eyes.

This guy is a Lotto ticket. Hello! Because if we're gonna be badass, a hot guy like him is definitely a place to start.

I know, I'm attached, and I love Brady—but that doesn't mean I don't have eyes.

"Can you get your butt off our car?" I hear Jesse ask. Mel is staring at her toes.

"Sorry," he says, though he doesn't get off. "But I'm curious why you ladies broke into the museum." He cocks his head to the side and grins. "You didn't take anything, did you?"

"Of course not," Jesse says quickly.

"Are you sure?" he says, still smiling. "They have some excellent postcards."

"Mind your own business," she mutters.

"Ignore her," I tell him, walking over to get a closer look. I lean against the hood of the Opel. "Can I have a chip?"

"Vicks!" Jesse snaps. "You can't just talk to strangers!"

Why is she so uptight? We were just downstairs bonding and singing folk songs and being badass *despite* singing folk songs—and now it's like The Return of Christianpants. A month ago, I swear she would have been flipping that corn-silk hair at him and adjusting her shorts to show a little more belly. Jesse might think that premarital sex is a guaranteed ticket to hell, but she never *used* to think the Lord was against flirting.

"He's not a stranger," I say. "He's . . ."

"Marco." He hops off the Opel and offers me the bag of chips.

"There you go," I tell Jesse, popping a chip into my mouth. "He's Marco. Hello, Marco. Thanks, Marco."

Jesse stomps over, leaving Mel gawking on the sidewalk. "Well, *Marco*, what are you doing, sitting on my car?"

Her hostility has got to go. God, we sit on the stupid Opel at least twice a week, eating toasted almond ice-cream bars in the 7-Eleven parking lot.

Marco shrugs. "I live here."

"At the museum?" Jesse asks.

He smiles, like she's being funny on purpose. "In Wakulla Springs."

Jesse crosses her arms. "And you perched yourself on my car because . . . ?"

He crumples the empty bag of chips and jerks his head down the road, where I can see a dingy cement building. "I was walking to the bus station when I heard a noise. Thought it was Morrison closing up. Turns out it was you three, doing some kind of stealth maneuver."

"We were just visiting the gator," I explain, holding out *Fantastical Florida*. "I read about him in my guide-book."

"Ahhhh."

"We didn't hurt a thing, took nothing," I add. "You can search me if you want."

He gives me a look that reminds me of Brady, like he knows I'm a professional flirt. But he's enjoying it. I can tell.

"Come on, you trust me, don't you, Marco?" I say.

"I don't even know your name," he says, but he's bluffing. I learned this from my brothers: If a guy thinks you're hot, he always remembers your name, even if he just heard it in passing.

"Sure you do," I say. "My girlfriend here called me by it just thirty seconds ago."

"Okay." He chuckles. *"Vicks."*

Ha! See, Brady? You're not the only guy who ever looks my way.

"We have to move," Jesse interrupts, pointing at me. "We're going to Miami to see *her boyfriend.*"

She thinks she's making me feel guilty, but I wasn't gonna *do* anything. I was being badass, that's all.

I know how to get her back. "Where you going?" I ask Marco.

"Fenholloway."

"Isn't that off 98?"

"Yup."

"Then it's your lucky day," I tell him. "Want a ride?"

"No way," Jesse snaps.

"Why not?" I ask her.

"Because I said so."

"What happened to Christian charity?" I give her a steely eye. "Don't worry," I tell Marco. "You can come."

"You sure?" he asks.

"No problem."

I glance at Mel, to see if I've got an ally or an enemy, but I can't quite tell. She's stopped staring at her feet, and now she's glancing at Marco with a weak, dizzy look.

88

Like she can't quite breathe around him. Like he's making her feel faint.

"Why are you going to Fenholloway?" Jesse wants to know.

"My boy Robbie's having an end-of-summer party. He wants me to come."

"That's gotta be at least an hour and a half away," Jesse says.

"I used to live there," he explains.

"Uh-huh."

"You know what?" Marco tells her, bending down to get his pack. "I can take the bus if a lift isn't cool."

"It's cool," I tell him.

Jesse gives me a dirty look. "We're not letting some random guy in our car. He could be a serial killer."

"Are you a serial killer?" I ask.

"I am not."

"As if he would tell us!" Jesse cries.

He gives Jesse a half-smile. His eyes crinkle. "I would. I'm very honest. You can search *me* if you like."

Mel laughs. Or rather, Mel giggles semihysterically, and Jesse turns on her, cheeks flushed. "Shut up, Mel!"

And for the first time, Marco turns and looks at Mel too. He smiles.

She smiles back.

That's it. I can tell Mel likes him, even if she's not saying anything. And I can see that he's looking at her—not exactly like he looked at me. More like he's *seeing* her as a person, not just as a cute girl.

"Hi, I'm Marco," he says, holding out his hand. "We haven't been introduced."

"Melanie," she says. "But everyone calls me Mel."

Mel wants him, so that means we have to take him with us, because I have worked a lot of shifts with that girl and I know for a fact Mel could use some love. "Get in," I tell Marco.

"Vicks!" yells Jesse.

"Jesse!" I yell back at her.

"It's my car!" she cries.

I roll my eyes. "Don't pull that. It's a road trip, you gotta relax. Let's take a vote. I say yes. You say no. Mel, you're the tiebreaker. What's it gonna be?"

Mel glances at me, then at Jesse. Her expression seems pained.

Then she looks at Marco. She blushes. "I think Old Joe would want us to take him," she says.

Ha! I knew she liked him.

Marco grins and we all pile into the car.

7

MEL

MARCO IS SITTING next to me in the back.

This should make me happy—and it does—but I'm also hot and unable to catch my breath. Something about him is making my stomach tight. Twisty.

From nine till ten, Vicks and Marco made small talk. It's so effortless for her. She just talks and jokes like she doesn't care at all what anybody thinks. I could never be like that. Even back home with Laurie and the other girls at my old school, I couldn't just *talk*. I didn't want them to think I was too chatty, too plain, too boring.

I guess I was myself around Alex, since he was always

hanging out at my house. He used to Rollerblade with Blake and fake-flirt with Nikki. We'd eat Pringles and have chess matches and listen to music and try to teach ourselves how to play piano.

I wonder if Laurie knows "Chopsticks."

Vicks and Marco seem to have run out of conversation, because now they're listening to "Drops of Jupiter" in silence. Like they're lulled by the mellowness of the song.

But not me. I desperately have to pee. Not that I'm going to admit that.

I do not talk about those types of things in public.

Especially not in front of Marco.

It's not that I like him or anything. Because I don't. I mean, I don't *not* like him, but I barely know him. He's just some random guy sitting next to me in a random car.

Meanwhile, I'm convinced Jesse is purposefully driving over potholes to cause me physical pain. *Bump. Bump. Bump.* She knows I have to go to the washroom because she saw me down that entire Diet Sprite. "How are we doing on fuel?" I ask in my most nonchalant voice. "Do we need to stop?"

"Are you kidding?" Jesse asks. "We've got three-quarters of a tank. Why, do *you* need to stop?"

It's because I voted against her. That's why she's punishing me. The swing voter strikes again. No matter which way I go, I always make someone unhappy. It's too bad, because when we were at the museum, she made me think that . . . I don't know. Made me think she'd started to like me.

Vicks likes me, I guess, but it's not like she'd notice if I was gone.

"No, I'm fine," I say, squirming. I can't be the only one who has to pee, can I? Damn that Diet Sprite.

Bump. Bump. Bump.

Ow. Ow. Ow.

Vicks is staring out the window deep in thought, oblivious to Jesse's unique form of torture.

And Marco is . . . Marco is sitting beside me, smelling like salt and peppermint. He's tapping his fingers against his knee. His nails are jagged and ripped up. He reaches into his backpack, takes out a pack of Certs, and offers me one.

"No, thanks," I say, noticing that he's inched closer to me now, closer than he was before, and his knee and my knee are almost touching.

"You don't take candy from strangers?"

I laugh. "I try not to."

He pops one into his mouth. "Safer that way. You shoulda searched me when you had the chance. Tested my Certs for poison."

"I see a sign for Fenholloway," Jesse pipes up. "Exit 382?"

This is it. Good-bye, Marco.

"That's the one." He picks at a piece of ripped cuticle on his thumb.

"That must hurt," I say, courageous now that I'll never see him again.

He wiggles it. "Sometimes."

"Bad habit."

"I know. One of many."

"So why don't you stop?"

He's watching me now and it's burning up my skin. "Don't you do anything you know you shouldn't do?"

"I'm in this car."

"You shouldn't be here?"

Well, you're not supposed to get into a car with strangers, yet here I am. All three of them—strangers.

No, I probably shouldn't say that.

"I, um, didn't tell my parents," I lie. "They don't know where I am."

"They probably think you're lost somewhere in your house," Jesse pipes up from the front.

I bite the inside of my cheek. I hate that she just said that. I want Marco to think I'm mysterious, not some spoiled rich kid. "It's not *that* big."

"Puh-lease," she says, laughing. "It's like a museum. Well, not Old Joe's museum, but, like, the Louvre." She pronounces it *Loo-vur*. "You can practically charge admission to get in."

I sink into my seat.

"So how long are you staying in Miami?" he asks, letting his knee fall all the way to the right, so his jeans are grazing my bare thigh.

"Just the weekend," I answer.

"Where are you staying?"

"A hotel, I guess? I don't know. We'll figure it out when we get there."

"It's already after ten. You're not driving straight there tonight, are you?"

"I don't think so. We're not supposed to be on the road after . . ." I let my voice trail off because I'm being a wimp again. "*Are* we driving straight there tonight?" I'm hoping no. Forget breaking the law; if there's not a bathroom break soon I'm going to burst. "How far is Miami from here?"

"It's a good five hours," Vicks says. "We need to find a place to crash."

"Mel's springing for a hotel," Jesse says. "Right?"

He's looking at me again.

"Right, Mel?" Jesse persists. "Unless you're going to go back on your promise."

"I can pay for a hotel," I say quickly. I turn back to Marco. "Do you know if there are any nice places to stay nearby?"

"Oh, yeah, there's a Hilton right off the exit," he says.

"Do you know if there's a Marriott?" I ask. "My dad's a frequent customer, so I bet I could get us a suite."

His cheeks redden. "I was kidding. There's no Hilton. There's a Super 8 Motel."

Vicks and Jesse burst out laughing.

"I knew that," I lie again, wanting to crawl under the seat.

Jesse is *still* laughing when Marco turns to me and says, "Why don't you guys come with me to Robbie's? You could crash there. He's having a house party."

I feel sick and then excited and then sick again.

"Oh, we are so there," says Vicks.

"We are not," says Jesse.

"Make a left here," he says. "You are not crashing or you are not coming to the party?"

She puts on her blinker and veers left. "No to both."

"Now make a right at the next light," Marco instructs.

"Let's go to the party and then decide," Vicks says. "We can always leave."

"Left here," Marco says.

Jesse turns and we can hear the party even before we see it. The *thump, thump, thump* of a heavy bass makes the road vibrate. My insides are thumping too, but not from the music. His jeans are still touching my leg.

"It's the house on the—"

"Yeah, I got it," Jesse says. "We'll just drop you off."

The one-story white house we pull up to has a wide front yard crowded with girls in short jean skirts and fluorescent halter tops, and guys with baggy jeans beginning at their knees. "Oh, just park," Vicks says. "We'll stop in for a second."

Jesse veers onto the wrong side of the street into an empty spot, but she doesn't cut the engine. She looks hard at Vicks. "I think you're forgetting what this weekend is about."

"I have to pee," Vicks tells her. "So if you don't want me urinating on your seat, you better park the car."

Ha! I knew I couldn't be the only one.

8

JESSE

"MARCO-MAN! YOU'RE HERE!" calls a waify-looking blond guy who's so pale he's almost see-through. He's sitting on the kitchen table next to a gum-chomping brunette. They're both drinking beer straight from the bottles, and my stomach goes down, down, down. I hate parties like this. I suck at parties like this.

"Hey," Marco says. He sweeps his arm at the three of us. "Everybody, meet Vicks, Mel, and Jess."

"It's *Jesse*," I say.

"Jesse. Sorry. Can I get you guys a brew?"

"Sure," Vicks says.

I shoot her a look. I thought we were here so she could pee, not so she could fill up again.

"I'll take one, thanks," Mel says in a shy little voice. She's such a teensy little thing, and she somehow seems even teensier around Marco. She's gazing at him with big eyes—big blue eyes in a teensy-weensy girl—and Marco pauses for a second and grins, just at her. She turns bright red.

One beer'll knock Mel flat—yet another reason to hit the road. A tipsy Mel is not something I need to see.

"I would kill for your hair," the gum chomper says. "Are your highlights real or out of a bottle?"

Nobody answers. Her words hang like bubbles. Then I realize she's talking to me, and I say, "Huh?"

She rolls her eyes. "Never mind."

"Real," I say. "They're real."

Marco grabs three beers out of the fridge and passes them out, starting with Mel. When he gets to me, Vicks says, "Don't bother."

"I don't drink," I say. It comes out stiff. I don't mean for it to, but it does, 'cause that's what happens to me in situations like this. I'm much more of a hang-out-and-watch-TV kind of girl. Or games. I do like games.

Tonight, for our weekly game night, Mama was going to make her sugar cookie cake with a layer of cream cheese and then cherry pie filling and then strawberries and kiwis and those baby oranges out of a can. R.D. was gonna bring his drink cart so we could all have icees.

I don't like admitting it, but there's a part of me that wishes maybe I was there instead of here.

Except, *no*. I'm off to Miami, thanks very much, just as soon as Vicks and Mel finish their stupid Buds.

"So, you guys up for staying a while?" Marco says. He looks straight at Mel, and I swear the girl stops breathing. Which is kinda cute. Only there isn't any point crushing on a boy you're never gonna see again.

"Sorry," I say. "We gotta go."

"No, we don't," Vicks says. She glances at Marco, then she glances at Mel, a smile dancing around her lips. "Hey, Mel, come find the bathroom, 'kay?"

She tugs Mel toward the hall, both of them giggling, and Marco is left with just me.

He shifts uncomfortably. "Well . . ."

I turn away, and Marco gets the hint. He says something pointless about catching me later, and in my head I'm like, *Yeah, sure, whatever. Go play beer pong or put a lamp shade on your head, I don't give a hoot.*

He leaves, and now I'm the one left with just me, miserable and alone.

9

MEL

"HE SO WANTS you," Vicks says, grabbing on to my arm and leading me down the hall.

"He does not!"

"He does. He was watching you the whole trip."

"He was not," I say, laughing. I love the way she's holding on to me. Like we're friends.

We spot a girl in pigtails waiting outside a closed door, assume it's the washroom, and join the line.

"You better go for him."

"Vicks, we don't know anything about him!"

She laughs. "We know he's hot."

"He could have a girlfriend."

"He didn't mention anybody."

"So? Doesn't mean there isn't one."

"A guy with a girlfriend doesn't invite three stylin' girls to a party. Trust me. I'd kick Brady's ass if he did that."

"I guess," I say, suddenly nervous.

"What's your problem? You don't like tall, dark, and handsome?"

"I don't like . . ." I don't like putting myself out there. I don't like feeling exposed. After all, I told Alex how I felt about him—no, I *showed* Alex how I felt about him—and look what happened there. "I've had some boy issues."

The bathroom door opens, a guy with a goatee comes out and the girl in front of us hurries in. Vicks takes a long swig of her beer, and I do the same. Gross.

I should have asked for a wine cooler.

"You should jump him. Drag him into one of the bedrooms and have your way with him." Vicks whistles. "I would totally go for it if I were you."

"Then *you* go for it." I take a long disgusting sip.

"Hello? Brady?"

"Right," I say, and remember how cute Brady was, how happy to see her he was, the few times I saw him at the Waffle House. For the first time I feel a question in my mind about Vicks. I mean, if we were on the way to visit my boyfriend, I wouldn't want to stop at some house party with a bunch of people I don't know. Not that I'm some expert on having boyfriends.

I hear a flush, and Pigtails comes out. I rush inside—I don't think I can wait another second—but Vicks follows me.

"Oh, um . . ."

I'm freaked out, but in a way I'm oddly flattered. She likes me! She's coming to the bathroom with me! We're *really* friends! But can I actually pee in front of her?

Vicks doesn't seem to notice my emotional ambivalence, and begins playing with her hair in the mirror. "Hurry, I really have to go."

Okay, then. I put my beer on the floor, tug at my pants, and crouch over the toilet seat.

"Are you squatting?" she asks, eyeing me in the mirror.

"Kind of?"

"At someone's house?"

"Don't you?"

"No. I mean, at a public toilet definitely, but not at a house."

"But it could be germy."

I wipe, flush, and then quickly cover myself with my clothes. I wash my hands while it's Vicks's turn, and then dry them on my hair.

She washes her hands and pulls a lip gloss out of her purse. "Want some?"

"No, thanks."

She laughs. "Too germy?"

"No, I'm just not into makeup," I admit.

"Why not?"

"My sister's the pretty one," I say, the words falling from my lips faster than I want them to. "She doesn't like when I get more attention than she does." As I say it, I realize how sick it sounds.

Vicks's eyes are the size of two steering wheels in the mirror. "That's crazy. We'll get Jesse to make you up; she's like a makeup artiste. I barely know what I'm doing."

Someone pounds on the door. "Hurry up in there!"

"Keep your pants on!" Vicks screams.

"Who are these people?" I ask, laughing. "Ready?"

"Wait, we need a toast." She picks up her bottle, and I do the same. "To strangers in Fenholloway," she says, and we clink.

It's not clear to me if we're drinking to Marco, to the other people in the house, or to us.

We slowly make our way back to the crowded kitchen. Jesse is going around picking up beer bottles and depositing them in the recycling bin, but Marco and the blond guy are gone.

As Jesse scowls and wipes up a spill, Vicks sneaks behind her back, opens the fridge, and takes out another beer. I stop myself from giggling and giving her away.

Vicks winks and twists off the top. We creep back out without Jesse even noticing.

We spot Marco on the front lawn. There are drunk people all over, some laughing, some hollering, and one attempting to do a handstand.

But I don't really notice them. All I see is Marco.

"Go talk to him," Vicks urges.

"By myself?" I ask, panicked.

She pushes me toward the front door. "I'll hang out for five minutes, and then I'm disappearing."

"Hey," he says, waving us over.

Vicks elbows me. "I'm off."

What? "That wasn't five minutes!"

She winks and backtracks into the house. I take a small sip of beer—gross—and walk over.

I ease myself onto the grass, so Marco and I are facing each other, sitting cross-legged and less than a foot apart.

"It's so hot; I miss the snow," I say, and kick myself inside. Why start with the weather—the most boring topic in the universe?

"Where'd you see snow?" he asks me.

"I'm from Montreal. It hits zero degrees, like, all the time. Zero Fahrenheit. It hurts to breathe when it's that cold."

He stretches his leg out in front of him. "I've never seen snow."

"You're kidding."

He shakes his head.

"My brother, sister, and I used to build these insane snow forts in the backyard," I tell him. "There'd be like five rooms with tunnels in between, and we'd haul our stuffed animals in there and bring hot chocolate in thermoses."

His eyes light up. "Do you ski?"

"No."

"I want to, if I ever get up North. I water-ski, though. You ever tried that?"

"No." I can't believe all the stuff about him I didn't notice in the car. The faint scissor-shaped scar on his square jaw line. The way he picks at his fingers when he talks, but keeps them still when he listens.

"It's wild. You should try it."

I'm about to say, *Sure, I'm up for anything*, but then I stop myself. Why lie? I'm never even going to see this guy again. "Um, that's probably not going to happen. In fact . . . can I tell you a secret?"

"Shoot."

I motion him toward me, and I feel a thrill at my own brazenness. He scoots over until his knee is touching mine. I lower my voice. "The only sport I ever do is Pilates."

He whispers back. "What's that?"

"It's a bunch of stretchy exercises," I murmur. "I'm

the most unathletic person in the history of the world."

He laughs. "Why are we whispering?"

"It's classified information. All these people"—I gesture at the crowd on the lawn—"they look very sporty."

"Okay," he whispers. "I'll tell you a secret back." He leans right in and I can feel his lips on my ear. "So am I."

I reply in his ear, inhaling his peppermint smell. "So are you *what*?"

"Unathletic." His breath on my neck sends a shiver down my back.

I bat him on the arm and speak aloud: "You just told me you water-ski."

"Yeah," he says, grinning, "but I didn't say I was any good at it." He picks up his beer and takes a swig. I'm sad the whispering game is over. "Hey, will you tell me something?" Marco asks.

"What?"

"Why are you the one in charge of paying for your posse's hotel? Why aren't they chipping in?"

My face gets hot. "Oh, it's no big deal. They were short on cash so I offered to pay for hotels and gaz—"

He raises an eyebrow. "Gaz?"

"Yeah. You know. Fuel. Gaz."

"Oh! *Gas*. I've never heard it pronounced like that."

I look down at my nails. "Whoops. It's a Montreal thing, I think. A French-English hybrid. I'll have to remember to say *gas* now."

"No, don't," he says, leaning back on his elbows in the grass. "It sounds exotic."

"Gaz?"

"Yes," says Marco. "It makes you sound like a French movie star."

"Gaaaaaz."

"Stop saying that or you'll blow your cover."

"Gaaaaaz."

"The paparazzi will descend on us! We'll be mobbed! Fans are going to swarm you!"

"Gaaaaaz!"

"Will you be quiet? You're causing a serious security breach!" He leans over, laughing, and puts his hand over my mouth. I am giggling and trying to push him away. Okay, not really.

"Just talk to me like I'm an ordinary girl," I tell him. "Don't be intimidated."

"It must be tough trying to find true friends when you're so famous."

"Oh, it is, it is. Ever since the James Bond movie last year, I can barely go out in public. I had to move to Florida just to get a break." I toss back my hair.

"I knew the ordinary-girl thing was a ruse." He reaches over and takes my hand. "You made up that stuff about the snow forts, too, didn't you? Your hands are too soft. That's what gave you away. That and the *gaaaaaz.*"

His hand feels cool from the beer and now my body is cold and hot and cold and hot and he's holding my hand, he's holding my hand, Marco is holding my hand.

"I soak them in buttermilk three times a week and sleep in gloves," I say with a straight face. "That's the secret."

"You're just full of secrets." He touches the back of my flip-flop with the toe of his shoe. "What else should I know about you, Melanie?"

That I have a huge crush on you? "My last name is Fine."

He shakes his head. "That's not a last name. It's an adjective."

"Ha-ha. What's yours?"

"Exceptional."

"Yeah, right."

"What's wrong with Exceptional? I mean, I don't like to brag, so I prefer just Marco, but my dad is Mr. Exceptional. My mother used to be Mrs. Exceptional but since they got divorced she went back to her maiden name, Ms. Prettygood."

I laugh again. His hand isn't cold anymore. It's warm.

I love that he makes me laugh. I love that he thinks I'm exotic. I love that he listens to me. I love that he makes me want to talk. I love that he's so hot. Sexy hot, not Florida-weather hot.

Maybe I should kiss Marco.

My lips burn. No, no, no. Can't kiss Marco. Too scary. Too hot.

"Mr. Exceptional and Ms. Prettygood," I say instead. "I'll have to remember all that when I meet your parents." It's only after the words leave my mouth that I realize what I've just said. *When I meet your parents!* As if I'm meeting his parents!

Way to get ahead of myself there. I've known him for, like, three hours, I'm probably never going to talk to him again, yet I'm practically sending out the wedding invitations. I drop his hand, fall on my back, and groan. "I'd like to take back that last line, please."

"What, now you don't want to meet my family?" he asks, his voice teasing.

"No," I squeak. I cover my face with my hands.

"Why not?" he says, grinning. "What do you have against my parents? They're nice folks. They're even Exceptional."

He moves closer to me, next to me on the grass, still smiling. "So if you don't want to meet my parents, what do you want?"

I want you to kiss me. I should just say it. Why not? I haven't held anything else back. I want you to kiss me. *I want you to kiss me!*

I want to say it. I think he wants to kiss me too.

But what if he doesn't?

"I want . . . a wine cooler" is what I finally say instead.

He nods. Pulls back. Pulls me to my feet. "Then let's go find you one."

SATURDAY, AUGUST 21

10

JESSE

I'M SICK OF cleaning up other people's messes. Why *am* I cleaning up other people's messes, especially for "my boy Robbie," who isn't *my* boy and who looks like an albino to boot?

It's past midnight. No one should be cleaning up someone else's kitchen after midnight, especially when it's so sticky with beer that your flip-flops make squelching sounds.

I leave two white plastic bags on the floor by the kitchen counter, one for recycling and one for plain old garbage, and hope Marco-man and his boys have the brains to figure it out. I'm restless, but I can't hunt down Vicks and Mel because Vicks is on her second round of drinks and already using me as comic relief. As in, "Don't tell Jesse, I'll get scolded." Does she honestly believe I didn't see her when she oh-so-slyly went to the fridge? She knocked a bottle of ketchup onto the linoleum, for Pete's sake. Which *I* put away, thank you very much.

I find a back room where the music is slightly less loud and the smoke slightly less thick, and I drop down on the carpet and try to be invisible. Three girls and a guy are clumped by a laptop on a desk made out of a door, and best as I can figure, they're using the laptop to take pictures. *Beep, beep, beep—click!* And then they whoop and says things like, "Dude, look at your nose!" or "You are such an *f-word* alien!" (except they don't say *f-word*) or "Omigod, you geezer! That's how you'll look when you're, like, a hundred!" Then they do it all over again: *beep, beep, beep—click!*

The carpet smells like dog. I check my shorts, and sure enough, dog hair. Great.

"What's wrong with you, girl?" R.D. has said more than once, referring to the fact that I don't love up every dog on the planet. He can't understand why I'm not a "dog person," what with Mama making her living brushing and washing dogs and clipping their dang toenails. We don't own a dog of our own, at least not anymore, but there's always two or three hanging around the trailer. Mama boards them when their owners go out of town, so they don't have to stay in the kennel with five thousand other yapping dogs.

Some of the dogs are sweeties, I admit it. Like how they nose your hand for treats and flop their heads on your lap when you're watching TV. But what R.D. doesn't get, when he sees me shoving them away and wiping the slobber off, is that you can't get attached to every mutt that comes along. What's the point? They're just gonna leave.

Vicks is a dog person. Dotty brought her geriatric labradoodle to the Awful Waffle one day, and Vicks was all, "Hey, girl. What a good dog. Oh, yes you are!" Dotty's old dog gazed up at her solemnly, prompting Vicks to call her "one dignified doodle," which made us all laugh.

Vicks was the same way with Old Joe the alligator, even though he was dead. She cracked me up cooing over his fine sharp teeth—she cracked us all up—and it made my heart lift. I thought, *Yes, this is what this trip should be.* And when Mel started singing . . .

Her voice was like a piece of sea glass, rounded and clear and pale seaweed green, and I had the crazy thought, gazing at that gator and hearing Mel sing, that that's what an angel would sound like. Then the even crazier thought: Maybe Mel *was* an angel. Maybe that's why she came on this trip. To save me, or—*don't, it hurts*—to somehow save Mama.

Stupid. Miracles don't happen to folks like me. And if one did, it would happen in a manger or something. Not in the basement of a podunk museum, with a stuffed reptile grinning in the dark.

Anyway, Mel's Jewish. Can angels even be Jewish?

A guy with a fro sticks his head into my-boy-Robbie's room, which reminds me that I am at a party, and people at parties aren't supposed to be thinking about angels and being saved.

"Todd!" the guy cries. "The *Todd*ster!" He jabs his finger at the guy parked in front of the laptop, who looks up.

"Wayne," he says, jerking his head. "Get over here, you gotta see this."

"No time, my man," Wayne says. He's holding the door frame. "You are needed in the den. SpongeBob. Drinking game. *Now.*"

"I *love* SpongeBob," one of the laptop girls says wistfully, as if she really is heartsick in love with Sponge-Bob's yellow spongy self. "He's so *nice*, you know? Even to Mr. Krabs. Even to *Plankton*."

The Toddster stands, and he and the three girls file into the hall.

Wayne spots me with his bleary eyes. "You in?"

"No, thanks," I say.

"You sure?"

"I'm sure."

"All right, then," he says. "Keep it real." He shoots me a point-and-wink, and I point and wink right back. I even make the cheesy *tchh* sound. It makes me think of Vicks's brother Penn, who's also a fan of the point-and-wink. Penn does it with such delight that it's funny, though. Like he knows he's being a goofball.

If Penn were at this party . . .

Well, that's a crazy thought, since he's not. But me and him hung out once at a Fourth of July bash Brady threw. Penn felt bad for me, that's what I figure, 'cause Vicks and Brady were pretty much the only people I knew and they ended up in Brady's bedroom doing something that I preferred not to think about. *Don't ask, don't tell*, that's pretty much what me and Vicks have worked out when it comes to her and Brady in the bedroom.

Anyway, Penn came and found me out on the patio.

"Hey," he said. He jerked his chin at the hammock where I was sitting and said, "You mind?"

"Huh?" I said. "Oh, no. I mean, that's fine." I scooched over, and he joined me. Our bodies touched. That's just the way hammocks are.

We lay there for a while, and I worried I might be sweating, and that my heart might be beating really loud. But I also liked it, just being there with him.

"I went to the train tracks this morning," he said at last.

"Oh, yeah?"

"Had coffee and a doughnut and watched the train come through."

"I love trains," I said. It was true; I've always loved trains. I love the sound and strength and power of them.

"Me too," Penn said.

There was a whole bunch more silence, and then he shifted his body and pulled something out of his pocket. It was a penny he must have laid on the track, 'cause it was all smushed and flattened.

He handed it to me, and I said, "Cool." I turned it over in my hand, thinking, *A penny from Penn*. I liked how those words connected, how the penny was, like, a symbol of the Penn sitting beside me. Penn's penny. A mini bit of Penn.

And then I did something I'm still embarrassed about. I put it in my pocket.

He chuckled, and the sound of it told me I'd misunderstood. Blood rushed to my face and I dug it out quick and tried to give it back.

"Here," I said. "Omigosh, sorry. Sorry!"

"Nah, keep it," he said, standing up from the hammock. He grinned, and I know what he was thinking. He was thinking, *Vicks's little friend Jesse. What a card.*

He stretched, and I saw the muscles of his tummy. And then he left. Later I saw him making out with a girl wearing a tube top.

I still have that penny, though.

* * *

Eventually I start feeling pathetic, so I get to my feet and brush the dog hair off my cutoffs. I approach the laptop just for the sake of something to do, and staring at me from the screen is the Toddster. Only he looks like a Martian, or Jack Nicholson, or a bulging-forehead combination of both. His eyes are too close together, his nose too pinched.

I sit down in the swivel chair and skim my finger over the touchpad. I click a button that says "Photo Booth," and all of a sudden there *I* am on the screen. Only I'm a bulgy-headed Jack Nicholson clone too. I move my head to the right, and my computerized image slides with me, making my forehead grow pointy and my left cheek stretch like taffy. I move to the left: Now the right half of my face whooshes out.

As Vicks would say, this is seriously wacked. I move closer to the screen, and my eyes swell into saucers. I pull back, and my head turns into a tiny pinhead floating on a creepily long neck.

I scan the toolbar and see that there are other options for my entertainment. I've been using "Bulge"; now I click on "Twirl." *Whoa*—now that is just wrong. My face dips and twists like a Picasso painting, or whoever that guy was who lopped his own ear off. Vicks is good at that artsy stuff. She would know.

I click another icon, and I'm hit with the telltale *beep, beep, beep—click!*

Ah, crud. There I am, frozen in time looking like a

mess of scrambled-egg eyeballs and loosey-goosey lips. At first I panic, and then I giggle. What is Robbie going to think when he sees this picture of a girl he doesn't even know? He'll think, *Thank goodness that freak show cleared out of here,* that's what. Though he probably won't use the word "goodness."

I move the cursor from the snapshot button, which I now know to stay away from, and click on "Squeeze." Ew—this must have been the one the Toddster was using when one of the girls called him a geezer. My cheeks cave in and my eyes turn to wrinkled slits and my teeth, when I grimace, grow long and skinny. I *do* look old. Or sick, like I've got some terrible wasting disease.

I hold still. I stare.

People always say how much me and Mama resemble each other, which I hate, because I'm like, "Do I wear stretchy aquamarine bra tops? No, I do not. Stop saying we're two durn peas in a pod!"

I glance at the door, and then I swallow and hitch up out of the chair. I position my upper body in front of the tiny red dot at the top of the computer, which I've figured out is the camera. My boobs wither before my eyes. I pull farther back, and my boobs collapse in on themselves, like smushed-down cupcake liners.

This is what she'll look like, I think. *No more aquamarine tops.* And then, *What is she going to do?*

Voices sound in the hall, one guy's raucous laugh and

a second guy's response, and I stand and jerk away from the laptop.

"I'm telling you, she wants it," the first guy says. "I heard her with my own two ears. She was like, 'Ooo, he's so hot. Ooo, he's so sexy.'" He pitches his voice high the way guys do to make fun of the female sex.

"Shut up, Robbie, you drunk fool," guy number two says.

They're coming closer. I edge up against the wall.

"Ah, you want the other one," Robbie says. "The one with the big titties. I get you, bro!"

What a slime.

They're outside the room, they're passing right by, and I can't help glancing their way. I take in Robbie's underbelly whiteness, and why, look, it's Marco at his side. I *knew* he was bad news. Then Robbie makes a comment about "big titties' skunk stripes," and suddenly I put it together.

They're trash-talking Vicks and Mel.

I burst out of the room without thinking.

"Don't you dare," I say. "Don't you *dare* talk about my friends that way!"

"Whoa, whoa, whoa!" Robbie says, holding his hands up.

Marco stops short. "Jess," he says. "We weren't . . . I wasn't . . ."

"It's *Jesse*," I spit. "And Mel doesn't . . . what you said.

She's not that kind of girl. And Vicks has a boyfriend, you turdball!"

"'Turdball'?" Robbie says. He's amused, and my anger flames higher. "You've got to be fucking kidding me."

"Jesse . . . chill," Marco says. "Nobody's slamming your buds."

"*He* is," I say, jutting my chin at Robbie.

"Baby, you're reading me all wrong," Robbie says. "I'm not slamming them. I'm complimenting them!"

I storm past, purposely ramming his shoulder. He laughs.

"Get a fucking life!" he calls to my back. "Fucking buzz-kill!"

My heart races. We shouldn't have picked up Marco, and we shouldn't have come to this . . . this . . . cesspool of sin. I'm going to find Vicks and Mel, and we're getting out of here. Even if it is one in the morning.

I find them in the crowded TV room. Vicks downs a shot as Plankton orders a Krabby Patty; then she lets out a burp like a foghorn. The guy with the fro slaps her a high five.

Mel is draped in a C shape on the sofa. Her feet are on the coffee table, a wine cooler is in her hand, and she's crooning softly to herself. As I push through to her, I make out her slurry words.

Which are about Marco.

And which are not pure.

And there are two other empty wine cooler bottles on the coffee table, plus a couple of empty beer bottles, and maybe she didn't drink all of them, but it's obvious she's had her share.

"Oh, Maarc-o!" she says to the ceiling. "Vicks says I should jump your bones, but how can I if you're not here? Where *are* you, Marco?"

She is beyond trashed, and so is Vicks, who cracks up.

I back away before either of them sees me. I should have known they weren't going to stop at two beers—or in Vicks's case, even three. What did I think they were doing down here, knitting tea cozies for the elderly?

My face is hot, and I don't like how I'm feeling toward them right now. I don't like them for *making* me feel like this, all tight and flushed. A buzzkill, as Robbie so kindly put it.

And yet, I clearly am.

Equally clear is this: Mel's sure as heck no angel.

11

MEL

I AM DRUNK.

Drunk, drunk, drunk. Drunk as a skunk! I am a rhyming drunk. I am holding on to the wallpapered wall because otherwise I will . . . fall.

Another rhyme—go, me.

"Where is sexy Marco?" Vicks asks me from her sprawled position on the sofa. "You should find him."

"Yes!" I exclaim. "I should. You stay here."

"I think I'm going to stay here," she says.

Good idea, I say. I think. I hold on to the wall and feel my way through the party. Are you Marco? Nope. You?

Nope. He was here before. But now he's gone. Gone, gone, gone. Gone as a . . . prawn?

"There you are," I hear.

"Marco!" I cheer. I grab on to his arm. His hard arm. Hello, muscles. He's so lying about being unathletic. I lean over to whisper a secret to him. "I need to talk to you in *private*."

"Mel, you're wobbling. You okay?"

"I have another secret," I say, trying to enunciate. "Not about Pilates or moisturizer gloves," I clarify in case he's confused.

"Okay, let's hear it."

"I have to show you," I say. I am going to have sex with Marco. It's perfect. He is sweet and adorable and we are going to do it.

Now. While I'm brave. And drunk.

He likes me. He must.

The wine coolers have made me much smarter, eh? They've made me more like Vicks. Less afraid.

Bye-bye to Scaredy-cat Mel. Hello to Brave Mel. I love Brave Mel!

"Are you okay?" he asks me again. He looks concerned. He looks sexy when he's concerned.

"I'm wonderful." I pull him into a room, but it's a closet.

"I think you need to lie down," he says.

He gets it! "Exactly! We need to lie down."

He leads me out of the closet and into a brown bed-room. Brown walls, brown bedspread, brown brown brown. "Your eyes are brown," I tell him. Then I throw my arms around his neck. "Let's do it, sexy brown eyes!"

Brave Mel is invincible. She's Super Mel. And nothing scares her. Not a bird, not a plane, not the brown-eyed boy. She deserves a cape.

He somehow untangles himself from my superhuman grip. "Mel, this isn't a good idea."

"It is!" I flop backward on the bed, and pull him down on top of me.

He smiles at me for what seems like forever, but then the smile gets a little sad. He looks sexy when he's sad. He heaves himself back off the bed. "You need to rest, okay? I'm going to get you some water."

I kick off my flip-flops. It's not polite to wear shoes on Robbie's bed. I sit back up. "I am not going to sleep! You said I could meet your parents!"

"Yes, but not tonight." He gently pushes me back down. "Close your eyes. I'll be right back."

La, la, la. Robbie's room might double as a disco. It's starting to spin. "Do you like to dance?" I ask, but no one answers.

Nikki and I used to dance all the time when we were kids. We'd blast Britney and make up our own dance routines that we'd do over and over and get our dad to videotape. Until she got to high school and stopped wanting to hang out with me. Nope. I am not good enough for Nikki. Or Alex. Nope, nope, nope.

I bet I still remember those routines.

Arm up, arm down, spin, turn, kick . . . no, turn.

"Here you go," Marco says. Oh, there he is. "Sit up and take a big gulp."

I do as I'm told, or try to, but now there's water on the brown sheets, turning them almost black. "Whoopsies," I say, and then kiss him.

Or try to. I might have licked him by accident. I gulp down more water.

"Now I want you to take a nap," he says.

"Are we not going to do it?"

He doesn't answer.

Maybe he didn't hear? "Are we not going to do it?" I ask again, raising my voice.

"Go to sleep, Mel. I'll come check on you in a half hour."

Oh. I am kind of sleepy.

He pulls the comforter over my arms and legs and then kisses me on the forehead. Damn! I wasn't ready for that. I pucker my lips in case he tries again, but I think he's already closed the door.

Robbie's bed is quite comfortable. I wonder if he has a pillow-top mattress? That's what I have. It's very good.

"Can someone get my pillow?" I ask. "It's in the car!"

Maybe I should call Vicks. I take out my phone, and scroll through the measly five numbers I've accumulated since I got to Florida. Old Mel was Pa-the-tic. "Vicks?"

It's not dialing. I don't think I'm doing this properly. I wish the phone would stop moving. "Hello? Anyone?"

No one answers.

"Let her sleep!" a voice in my dream says.

"I want out of here."

"What's the problem? Let's just sleep here."

"I'm not sleeping in Robbie's bed!"

"So sleep on the floor."

"Fine. I will. But Mel sucks."

I don't suck, I want to tell my sister. When did she get a Florida accent?

"The only reason she got to come on this trip was because she promised to pay for a hotel."

"I get points at the Marriott," I say before rolling over and going back to sleep.

12

VICKS

MY CELL BLEEPS. It's 1:34 in the morning. A text. From Brady.

Hey there U. All good here. Stay cool.

About freakin' time, I think. And then I think, *Stay cool?*

I walk out of Robbie's bedroom into the empty hallway and press my speed-dial.

"Stay COOL?" I say when Brady picks up.

I can't believe he picked up. He hasn't picked up since he left for the U.

"Stay COOL? That's all you've got to say?"

"Vicks! I didn't think you'd be up. I didn't want to bother you."

"I'm up," I say. "I'm stayin' cool."

"Okay, you got me. That was lame."

"Forget it. What's new?" I say to Brady, thinking, *Don't cry. Don't complain. Don't become a flowery needy girl on him, or he'll leave.*

"Oh, God." He sighs.

"Oh, God, what?"

"It's just—it's different hearing your voice live, on the other end of the phone. Vicks, I miss you so much right now."

Then why haven't you called me? I want to scream. But instead I say, "How come you're up so late?"

"I went to a party, but it sucked."

"Oh." What party? I want to know. Who with? "I have practice at 6 A.M. too," says Brady. "I'm going to be whupped."

What *party*? I want to know. With cheerleaders?

"Coach runs us really hard," Brady is saying. "And classes started on Wednesday, so I've gotta study too."

Why do you have to be secretive? What *freaking party*?

"The only morning we get off is Sunday," he continues. "But the twice-daily workouts do make a difference. You can feel it."

Fine.

132

"Maybe you should go to sleep then," I snap, interrupting. "If you've got such important things to do."

"What? No, I want to talk to you."

So why did you just text me, then? Why did I have to call you? I want to shout. But I rein myself in and say, "Wonderful. So what would you like to talk about?"

"Nothing. Just talk. Aren't we talking?"

"You're telling me about early-morning football practice. If you call that talking."

"Isn't it?"

"Sure, if you think so," I say. "Why don't you tell me about your classes, next? How are they going for you? Do you like your teachers?"

"Vicks, you sound weird."

"No I don't," I say, knowing full well that I do, only I can't make it stop. "Aren't you going to tell me about your classes? How's freshman comp?"

Brady sighs. "Um. I got my in-class essay back with red pen all over it this morning. And I have a quiz already on Monday."

"How fascinating. What's your quiz on?"

"Um. Intro to Anthropology. Categories of early humans."

"Whoop de do."

"What?"

"Nothing. I'm dying to talk about anthropology."

"I didn't say I wanted to talk about anthropology."

"Oh? I thought you did." Don't complain. Don't cry.

"Vicks, are you drunk?" Brady asks. "Where are you?"

I can't tell him I'm halfway to Miami, 'cause I can't tell for sure if he's going to be happy to see me. Can't bear to hear him say, "Oh, baby, that's sweet that you're driving down, but I've got football practice twice a day and I'm really busy, and we talked about you coming down to see the game Thanksgiving weekend, so maybe you shouldn't go to all that trouble." So I say, "It's Friday night, Brady. I'm not gonna sit home."

"You sound kinda drunk."

"So? I'm at a party with Jesse and some guys we met."

"What guys?" Brady asks. "And with Jesse? Really? She hates drinking parties."

"Well, I'm changing her mind," I say, ignoring his first question. I can be secretive too.

"Oh."

"It's kind of a bad time to talk, actually," I say. Thinking, he doesn't deserve to get hold of me after midnight anymore. I'm not his puppy; I'm not leaping up and down every time he knocks on my door. If he's not thinking about me enough to even text me back until now, I'm not going to—

"Can I call you later?" I say.

"Aw, come on, Vicks."

"We can talk about football and anthropology some more next week."

"Baby, I know something is wrong. Tell me."

I cannot tell him, *I miss you, I'm lost without you, I'm lonely, you're off meeting other girls, I'm jealous, I need you to call me, I can't stand being apart if you don't call me.* Because if I say any of that, I'm just going to push him away—and if Brady doesn't want me, then I'm not going to know who I am. I already don't know who I am with him gone, with my brothers gone too, and me just rattling around in that big empty house with only my parents, and . . .

Three beers and a shot is obviously too much if I'm getting all emotional like this. Reminder to self: Two is your limit. Retain some dignity.

"What do you mean?" I ask Brady. "Nothing's wrong. I just don't have time to talk right now. Heart you! Bye!"

"Vicks—wait!"

"Yeah?"

"What guys did you meet? Who's driving you home?"

Oh, like he's not meeting girls every second there at college. "Just some guys. I think a couple of them are lifeguards," I lie. Because lifeguards are always hot.

Truth is, I am dying to tell Brady about busting into the museum and celebrating Old Joe and Mel's beautiful voice and "Al Roker, you are my kin"—which is all the kind of stuff Brady would love. It's almost like it

135

hasn't really happened, since I haven't told him about it. I've told him about everything that's happened to me all year.

But he's not really asking me what I've been doing. He just doesn't like the idea that I met some other guys and went to a party with them.

"Do you have a ride?" Brady wants to know.

"I think we're staying over, but yeah. Jesse's the driver. And you know she never drinks."

"What? You're staying over at the party?"

He's probably right to be worried, now that I think of it. It's a bit of a dumb situation to have gotten into. But no guy who doesn't call me for two weeks gets to tell me what to do. "Don't be so possessive."

"Vicks, are there people you know there?"

"You sound like one of my brothers." Why won't he say he's sorry? Why doesn't he explain why he hasn't called me?

"I just don't want you doing anything stupid," he says instead. "You should have Jesse take you home. I want you to be okay."

Exactly. He just wants me to be okay. He doesn't want anything to be wrong, ever. Doesn't want to hear about it, doesn't want to feel guilty.

I'm not okay. I'm drunk at a strange party and we can't leave 'cause Mel's so trashed she can't even walk and Marco's nice but some of these guys are obviously skeevy. I want to say, *Brady, drive up and get me. Now.*

Brady, talk me through this dizzy drunk feeling until morning.

Brady, take care of me.

But he wants me to be okay without any help from him, and he hasn't called me, and he's only sent me two stupid texts and he's talking about football practice instead of about anything real and he's probably bonking some cheerleader and that's why he's being so weird with me and fake and all, *Oh, I'm taking anthropology.*

I can't go on like this. It's too lonely, too terrible to check my phone all the time and never hear from him, too sad to live in that empty house and get off work with no one waiting to pick me up and no one to hold my hand during movies and before I even think it through, I blurt, "I don't think this long-distance thing is working out."

"What? It's only been like a week."

How can he not know how long it's been?

"It's been two weeks," I correct him.

"Okay, two. It feels like forever, what do I know?" Brady sighs.

"Well, it's not working out," I say, trying to sound strong. "Since you can't even count or make a phone call."

"Vicks!"

"Let's just say it's over," I tell him. "It's better that way."

137

"How can you say that?" Brady is nearly shouting.

Don't shout at me, you stupid, weird-acting, football anthropology boy. You're going to make me cry, and I am *not* going to cry. "You say it just like this," I tell him. "It's over."

"Vicks, wait!"

"Over," I repeat and hang up the phone.

It rings not three seconds later—Brady again—but I hit "ignore," then turn it off and shove it in my bag.

Down in one corner of the backyard Robbie's folks have an aboveground pool. It's not big, maybe ten feet across. No one's in it. People are sitting on the back steps with bottles and the bright dots of cigarettes in their hands. Someone's lit some citronella candles to keep the mosquitoes away. A girl is sitting on the grass, playing guitar.

I don't want to talk to anyone, so I walk over to the pool and dip my hand in. Trail my fingers through. Then I climb the rickety ladder and step into the water wearing my shorts and T-shirt. It's only slightly cool, and a number of bugs have drowned themselves. They float sadly on the surface.

I duck under. Wash the heat of anger and humiliation off my face. Try to get away from my thoughts, but they're spinning through my head, muddled by the beer.

I was right to dump Brady.

I was right. I was right. Steve, Joe Jr., Jay, Tully, and

Penn—they would all say I was right.

My brothers—well, except for Penn, he did worship Liza Siegel and never cheated on her even when Tiffy Gonzaga took off her shirt in front of him—but my brothers showed me again and again that it's "out of sight, out of mind" with guys. My brothers, as soon as their girls go out of town, they're flirting with someone else. And probably fooling around, though I don't know for sure. Yes, fooling around, because Tully started going with that redhead—what was her name, Jewel?—when Katelyn went to summer camp.

Brady's at the U, which has a competitive cheerleading squad, for God's sake. He's a football player on a major college team surrounded by hot and bouncy blond girls. And older women. And girls who've traveled somewhere beyond the Waffle House parking lot in Niceville, one trip to Disney World, and Grandma Shelly's retirement complex in Aventura. Girls who never smell like fryer grease and never fart and probably shave their whole bodies and never do stupid things to their hair.

Brady's a guy. Of course he's gonna be fooling around on me. I'm better off without him. Right?

I duck underwater and when I come up, Marco's standing next to the pool. "There you are," he says.

"You were looking for me?"

"I just wanted to ask you if Mel's okay."

"She's plastered, but Jesse's in there with her," I say.

He nods. "I didn't want to barge into the room."

"Probably better not to. But thanks for letting us stay."

"No problem." He tilts his head at the pool. "Mind if I get in?"

"Knock yourself out."

He's changed into blue swim shorts and he pulls his T-shirt over his head. The muscles of his chest ripple. "I always come out here when Robbie's parties get too crazy," Marco says as he eases himself into the water.

He's not big—I probably outweigh him by a few pounds—but his body's not bad, either. Nice skin. Big eyes like an antelope's or something. And a good sense of humor. I could tell when he was flirting with Mel in the backseat.

"Robbie and Jesse had words," he reports. "That's the other reason I wanted to check in with you."

"Sorry about that," I say. "She gets uptight when people drink."

"No, he was being a jerk. The guy is a maniac sometimes. He doesn't mean any harm, but he's always getting girls mad."

"So why are you friends with him?"

"Known him since fifth grade. He let me stay in his house last summer, when I wasn't getting along with my stepdad."

"Huh." My head is spinning from the beer and the swimming; everything feels floaty.

"Your friend Mel," says Marco.

"What about her?"

"She with anyone?"

I shake my head. "Not now. I think she's got a complicated love history, but I don't know the whole thing."

"Huh." He shrugs. "She doesn't seem like the type."

"No? How does she seem?"

"Simple," he says.

"Ha!" I laugh. "If you think that's a compliment, let me tell you why you're still single."

He splashes me. "I meant, simple like honest, not simple minded."

"Okay."

"She's not like the girls at my school, all attitude and putting other people down. She's funny, once she gets going. It's easy to talk to her."

He's right. "Did you know she's been on safari?" I say. "Like to real Africa, the continent."

Marco smiles, wide and open. "I know what Africa is."

"Oh, do you?" I say, liking his smile.

No guys ever smile at me, they never do. I mean, no guy has smiled at me, really smiled at me, in . . .

Well, fine, the hot dog guy smiled at me, and that cute guy at the gas station. And also that guy at Waffle House this morning who tried to chat me up while I was on my smoke break.

But Brady is off smiling at some other girl, multiple girls, and I need that smile from Marco to go on flashing at me the way it is right now.

"Yeah, it's the one shaped like this." He makes an Africa shape with his hands in the air. "Where all the zebras live."

"Mel saw a zebra," I tell him. "With her naked eyes."

I get the smile again.

He's into Mel, I can tell by the way he blushes when I say the word *naked* about her. "Her *eyes* were naked," I say. "Not the rest of her."

"The zebras were naked," says Marco.

"Oh, yeah, those zebras are total nudists. The giraffes, too. Would you believe it? There they were on the savannah, just lettin' it all hang out."

The smile flashes. I am so grateful to think about anything but Brady, I set a little goal for myself to get that Marco smile over and over, like getting lights to blink on a pinball machine. "Zebras are so unbadass," I continued. "We saw this stuffed alligator in a museum—"

"Old Joe."

"What? How did you know?"

"Vicks. I met you outside that place."

Oh, wow. Too much beer. "Okay, Old Joe. So he was naked too, like the zebras, but he was so badass he didn't look naked, you know what I mean? Like he's got this hide that's leather—they make shoes out of alligators—it's so tough he doesn't need any protection but his own skin."

"Uh-huh."

"But we, people, we kill the gators and make them into shoes and boots and whatever else so we can be protected, you know? Keep our feet safe. Hide our nakedness. We're a lot closer to zebras than we are to alligators," I say. "I bet that's true. Biologically speaking."

Marco laughs. Jackpot! "Do you always talk this much about nakedness?"

I shake my head. "Only when I'm with naked people."

"I'm not naked."

"You look naked," I tell him.

"You wish," he says.

And suddenly, it seems clear to me that Marco is Brady is Marco is Brady, because both of them will flirt with other girls when the girl they really want is out of the picture, and both of them will leap on whatever's nearest that has boobs and a heartbeat, and I was right to break it off with Brady 'cause he'd do just what Marco's doing, eyeing my chest in my wet T-shirt, only he'd do it to some cheerleader, is probably doing it to some cheerleader right now, and if Marco makes a pass at me, that'll prove I'm better off without Brady and . . .

I slip underwater and swim across the pool, surfacing next to Marco. "Maybe I do wish," I tell him. "You know,

I meant it when I said you could search me."

"What?" he asks.

"Outside the museum. I said you could search me. Like for concealed weapons."

"I—"

"Shut up." I press my chest up against him and put my lips on his.

13

MEL

ow. ow, ow, ow.

Obviously, a truck has driven over my forehead. Where am I?

Flashes from yesterday pop into my brain like a strobe light. Pop: I told Marco I wanted to have sex. Burst: Marco turned me down.

I think I'm going to be sick. Literally. I'm upside down on a roller coaster. I lunge over a body in the fetal position on the carpet—Jesse?—toward a waste basket. I dry heave.

"That's revolting," Jesse mutters, pulling a pillow over her face.

"Good morning, you badasses!" Vicks says from the other side of the bed.

When nothing comes out, I blindly reach for the glass of water I spotted earlier and down it.

Jesse pushes herself up. She has crease marks on her cheek. "So can we go already? Or did you want to throw yourself at some other perfect stranger?"

She knows? Does everyone know?

"Let's go," I say. I can think of nothing I want more than to get out of here immediately. Except brush my teeth. I definitely want to do that. Too bad my stuff is in the car.

I wobble over to the door, creak it open, find the coast clear, sneak into the washroom, wash my face, pee, and feel sick all over again.

Hello, hot dog bun. Good-bye, wine coolers.

Eventually, I start to feel better. I find Crest in the medicine cabinet and gargle a squirt of it with water.

By the time I get back to the room, Jesse has already made the bed.

Vicks is rubbing her hands together. "I had a great sleep. Do you want to know my antihangover secret?" Her voice is extra loud and chipper.

Or maybe it just sounds that way to my broken head.

"Shhh," I whisper. I just want to get out of here. Fast.

"Okay," Vicks says, smirking. "But you look like you need it."

"Don't you want to tell your boyfriend we're leaving?" Jesse says to me.

"Marco? I'm sure he's sleeping, no?" I'm way too humiliated to ever speak to him again. "Can we just go?"

Vicks shrugs, and then we sneak through the house, and out the front door. I squint as the brightness spears my eyes. The street is silent, except for the sound of early-morning birds, and the air is cool and dewy. It's a beautiful day.

"Oh, crap," Vicks says, pointing to the car.

A blue piece of paper flaps on the dashboard.

"No way," Jesse says, running over to her car. "A ticket! I got a ticket!" She tugs it free. "Fifty bucks!"

"What's it for?" Vicks asks, blinking in the sun.

"For facing the wrong direction. Mel, this is so your fault!"

"How is it Mel's fault?" Vicks says. "You're the one who parked the car."

"We were only supposed to be here for a second! There weren't any other spots!"

Could this morning get any worse? I mean, honestly. "I'll pay for it, I promise," I tell them.

"Just like the hot dogs?" Jesse huffs.

"Let's just go," Vicks says. She opens the door and pushes down the front seat. "I'll sit in the back this time."

"You will not!" Jesse says.

147

Vicks climbs into the back. "I need to stretch."

I take the front seat, and slam the door shut. Is the weekend over yet?

Jesse starts the car, makes a U-turn, and then hits the gaz. I mean gas. I do up my seat belt. Every time she turns a corner, I feel sick again.

I expect her to go straight back to the highway but just before it, she pulls into the parking lot of a Dunkin' Donuts. "You," she says to me. "Get us a box of blueberry muffins and three large coffees."

I unsnap my belt. "What do you like in your coffee?"

Vicks is lying across the seats with her eyes closed. "Black. Like nature made it."

"Two creams, two sugars," Jesse orders.

"Be right back."

"But wait, Mel?" It's Vicks.

"Yeah?"

"Make it six muffins, half blue half cran-orange, and then the rest doughnuts. Two glazed twists, two jelly with powdered sugar, and two with chocolate frosting. Nothing with sprinkles."

"Okay."

"Remember that about the sprinkles. They have chocolate with and without, but the sprinkles are nasty." Vicks puts on her sunglasses and it's clear the conversation is over.

So I do what they say. I am too embarrassed to do anything else.

There's no line, so I walk right up to the counter, rehearsing the order in my head. An older woman in a blue apron is saying to a younger one beside her, "I told my daughter in Cocoa Beach that with Harriet fixin' to hit today, she better pack up the kids and get up here."

Three coffees, one black . . .

"Uh, *yeah*," the younger one says, then turns to me. "What can I get ya?"

"Three coffees, one black, two fully loaded." I order the rest, just as Vicks told me to. "No sprinkles," I emphasize.

Then I imagine my sister beside me, eyes bulging, asking me if I know how many calories are in a doughnut. "And can I get that?"

"This?" the woman asks, picking up the bran muffin I just pointed to. The droopy, deflated, beige, fat-free, carb-free, flavor-free bran muffin.

"You know what?" I say. "Forget it."

"No prob." She turns back to her older colleague. "At least Harriet shouldn't head up here. I can't deal with that this year."

I reach into my purse for my wallet and realize that I don't feel my phone.

Oh, no. I rummage around . . . come on, come on. Where is it?

149

I vaguely remember trying to call Vicks last night during my drunken stupor.

I must have left it at Robbie's. And I'm definitely not going back there.

Damn.

14

JESSE

SOMETHING'S UP WITH Vicks. She's been hyper all morning, which Mel might think is normal, but it isn't. Not for Vicks. Not this early, without even half a cup of coffee in her.

"You talk to Brady last night?" I ask, thinking that might explain her mood. "Is that why you're such a Mary Sunshine?" I pull into traffic, balancing my muffin on my thigh.

"Brady who?" Vicks says. And laughs.

It irritates me, that laugh, 'cause it feels like she's making fun of me—or maybe making fun of Brady, which is just plain rude since he's the whole reason for this trip. Kinda.

Or maybe I'm still put out about how she acted at the party. Drinking and flirting, while Mel was passed out in Robbie's room after getting into all kinds of trouble of her own.

So I say, "Brady, your boyfriend? Who loves you and wants to marry you, and who one day in the far, far future you might even lose your virginity to? After you become Mrs. McKane, of course."

I didn't plan on throwing in the "virginity" bit like that—unless maybe I did. Maybe I wanted to remind her—and Mel too—that life's not one big party, much as they might want it to be. Or maybe I'm just being mean, since I have a pretty big hunch that Vicks and Brady didn't wait for no wedding vows.

"Jesse, you're wacked," Vicks says. "Do you seriously think—"

"Do I seriously think what?"

She doesn't answer. I glance in the rearview mirror, and she's scowling.

"What?" I say. "Do I seriously think *what*?"

"That I would take Brady's last name?" she snaps. "Or anyone's? Uh, *no*. Maybe you want to be someone's chattel, but not me."

"Geez, don't bite my head off." Now that I've stirred Vicks up, I wish I hadn't. I don't do so well with fighting, not the out-and-out kind where you actually say what

152

you feel. I glance at Mel, but she's facing straight ahead and pretending she's not listening, like *La la la, nobody here but me and my good buddy the windshield.*

"And babe?" Vicks continues. "For your info? My 'virginity,' as you so quaintly put it, was lost long, long ago. So you can say good-bye to that little fantasy, 'kay?" She waves into the mirror. "Buh-bye! *Sayonara! Adios!*"

Well, she doesn't have to be so sarcastic! My heart's all poundy, but I don't know what to do about it, so I chomp off a big chunk of muffin. Then I'm stuck with the mess of it, 'cause I can't seem to force it down.

"Jesse?" Vicks says.

I shake my head. I can't come up with any words for her right now. Through the speakers, Fergie's singing all nasty about her London Bridge going down every time her guy comes around, and I say to Mel, "Will you switch the dang song? Please?"

Mel registers the badness of her music selection and looks aghast. "Sorry," she says, punching at her iPod. "Sorry!"

A new song fills the car: Marvin Gaye's "Let's Get It On." My jaw drops, and Mel hyperventilates.

"No, wait!" she stammers. "Not on purpose. Wait!"

"This is *exactly* why I didn't tell you," Vicks says, and she's being unfair, 'cause I've shut up and there's no reason for her to keep going off on me. "Because you freak out about the dumbest stuff. Because you'd have lectured me about premarital sex and how *sinful* it is. Admit it!"

"Where Is the Love" by Elvis Costello replaces "Let's Get It On." I know this song. Penn played it in his car once when he was giving me and Vicks a ride. It's sad and beautiful, all about truth and forgiveness and looking deep into your own heart. Not that I'm in any mood to appreciate it.

My voice is pinched when I say, "Maybe yes and maybe no, but we won't ever know now, will we?"

"Oh, *God*," Vicks says, like I'm wearing her out. Like I'm the problem here, when she never gave me a chance. Never even *tried* saying, "Brady and me . . . and it was special . . . and I know it goes against your faith, but Jesse, *I am in love with this boy*!"

"Let's just drop it, all right?" she says.

"Fine," I say. She might not know it, but I could tell her a thing or two about "where is the love." Could tell her how my gut says Brady's one of the good ones, so different from R.D. and Mama's other losers, who never in a thousand lifetimes would kiss her all sweet at the movie theater and say "anything for my girl" if she asked him to refill the popcorn tub right at the most exciting part.

"Anyway, I don't know why you're playing all innocent," she mutters, still carrying on. "I asked you to go to Planned Parenthood with me."

"Which you *know* I couldn't, because all that place does is—" I break off, realizing that any talk of teenage

154

sex and immorality is just going to bear out her own position.

It's with a sinking feeling that I realize something else. I guess maybe she did try to tell me about her and Brady. Okay, fine, she did. It was before the actual deed (at least, I hope it was before the actual deed), but by asking me to go with her to that place, she was bringing up the subject, one friend to another.

And what did I do? I shut her down and we never talked about it again, not in any true way.

"At best you are a cruel coward," Costello sings in his woeful way. *"At worst you are a worthless hypocrite."*

I peek at Mel. I need to know how she's taking this. She's in a scrunched-up ball on the vinyl seat, iPod clutched like a Teddy bear, and I can tell from her expression that she thinks I'm a jerk.

"It's not that big a deal," Vicks says. "It's just sex."

Whatever. I accelerate to pass a white Pontiac, and Mel's coffee sloshes onto her fancy shorts, which is just great. Now she's got even more reason to hate me. Only all she does is curl up tighter and hide the stain with her hand. Why? 'Cause I'm Freaky Religious Girl, apparently. Freaky Religious Girl who isn't worthy of being told secrets and who terrifies spoiled rich girls in their million-dollar shorts.

There's something sticky in my hand, and it's the remains of my durn muffin. I scowl and peg it out the window.

15

VICKS

STUPID ME, STUPID Brady, stupid beer.

I am so unbadass right now.

Just bad bad bad.

I am a bad person. How could I be such a wench to Jesse? And last night—ugh. Mel is the nicest little person and I go hurling myself at the guy she likes. What kind of a friend does that?

Thank God Marco pushed me away and jumped out of the pool, or I'd have a whole lot more to regret right now.

I am not drinking any more beer for at least two months. Beer is not my friend.

Beer made me not a friend to my friends.

Beer made me not my own friend.

I wonder if I'm still a little drunk. That would explain me, maybe. I know I should tell Jesse to turn around, to head back home to Niceville, since I don't have a boyfriend anymore, but somehow I can't bring myself to say it.

My phone vibrates, and adrenaline shoots through me. I've ignored two calls from Brady this morning already—because of course, now that we're broken up, the guy remembers my number. Well, he doesn't get to talk to me just 'cause he suddenly wants to.

I hesitate before opening the phone. I don't want it to be Brady.

No, actually, I do. I do.

I don't.

I do.

I check the name. Unknown number. Could be Brady calling from a hall phone, or a friend's cell, couldn't it? I answer. "Hello?"

"Vicks, it's Dotty from the Waffle."

"Hey, Dotty." Why is she calling me? She never calls me. She must have got my number from the staff sheet. "What's up?"

"That's Dotty?" says Mel, turning around from the front seat. "Did Abe find a sub for me? Ask her if he found a sub."

"Good grief, Mel," Jesse says. "Didn't you get someone to cover your shifts?"

"I left Abe a note that I wasn't coming in," Mel explains.

"Quiet, you guys!" I bark. "Sorry, Dotty, Mel wants to know if Abe found her a sub."

"Pearl came in last minute so I don't think she's fired," Dotty answers. "But Abe had a right old fit, I'll tell you that." Her voice changes. "Listen, Vicks, where are you?"

"I don't know, on some road past Gainesville. Why?"

"You with Jesse?" she asks.

Jesse glances back at me. "What's she asking?"

"Yeah," I tell Dotty while motioning for Jesse to shut up.

"Jesse's got her mama's car," Dotty says.

"Yeah, I know," I say. "In fact I am enjoying the majesty of the Opel as we speak. Wasn't Ms. Fix a sweetie to let us borrow it?"

The car jerks to the right and we fly over a pothole and bounce hard on the road.

"Jesus," I exclaim. "Watch it, will you?"

When I get the phone back to my ear, Dotty's saying, ". . . and Harriet is why I'm calling you. She *is* not and she *did* not and she's worried as all get-out."

"Huh?" I say.

"Twyla didn't give Jesse the car. Jesse took it without asking."

I don't get it. "She what?"

Now Dotty's voice goes sad. "Twyla came by the Waffle this morning, and she's fit to be tied. Jesse didn't even leave a note."

I can't believe it.

Saintly Jesse. She took this car and left town without telling her mother? And dragged me along with her?

"So you tell her to call her mama, 'kay?" Dotty says. "She's out of her mind with worry."

"Yeah, I'll tell her," I say, noticing how tense Jesse's shoulders are as she drives us farther into nowhere.

I take the phone off my ear and snap it shut. Maybe I'm not the worst person in the car after all.

Liar.

Liar.

Fine, steal a car if you have to, if you're mad at your mom, if you're trying to knock yourself out of whatever slump you've been in that's made you such a pain to be around. Not that it's good to steal a car, but damn, Jesse's been acting so holier-than-thou this whole trip, cranky about drinking, cranky about flirting, cranky about virginity. How can she act like that when she stole this stupid car and tortured her mom with worry and sadness? How can she give me all that attitude and dump the silent treatment on me and be such a martyr at that party when she stole the freaking car?

"Lookit," Jesse says to Mel, pointing out the wind-shield. "A pelican—do you see?" Her words come out jittery and pitched all wrong, and I think, *Yeah, you're nervous, aren't you?*

As she should be. Liar. And anyway, it's not a stupid pelican. It's a darter. We had a Florida bird book when I was a kid and I used to look at all the pictures. "Not," I say.

"Not what?"

"Not a pelican," I tell her.

She swallows. "'Course it is."

"No, it's a darter. You're not *always* right, you know. You're not *always* little Miss Perfect."

A shadow passes across Jesse's face, and now she knows for sure what Dotty said to me. I can tell. Her breaths are shallow and she speaks only to Mel, saying, "It really is a pelican. See how long its wings are? And the pouched bill?"

"It's *not* a pelican," I snap. "And you're driving too fast. And you have no idea where we are, do you? Or wait. Don't bother answering, because why should we believe anything you say?"

We veer off the road, and I grab on to Mel's seat as Jesse hits the brakes.

"Jesse?" Mel squeaks. We jolt to a stop.

"What the hell was that?" I shout.

Jesse gets out of the car, her face tight and scared. She

flips her seat forward and takes a step back, like she's making space for me to climb out. "You drive!" she says. "Since you think I'm doing such a crappy job!"

I climb out, stepping over empty coffee cups and the box of doughnuts. "Did you steal your mom's car?" I demand when we are face to face.

Jesse stammers.

"*Did* you?" I persist.

"*No,*" Jesse says. "Heck no! What do you take me for?"

I just look at her.

"I *borrowed* it," she continues. "The keys were right there on the counter!"

"'Thou shalt not steal,'" I spit at her. "Isn't that one of the ten commandments?"

"Why are you getting on me like this?" she says. "You're the sinner. Not me!"

What? I knew she thought it sometimes, but I never figured she'd actually call me that to my face. "You don't get to use that on me," I tell her, narrowing my eyes. "I'm not the one stealing other people's property and making them crazy with worry. All I did was sleep with my boyfriend. Consensual, protected sex. No harm done."

"Yeah, but . . . but—"

"You are so full of crap. You make me sick."

"I didn't steal from you, so what's the big deal?" Jesse asks. "You're acting like it's a personal betrayal!"

"Because it is," I tell her. "People should be *true*. People should be who they say they are."

A splat of rain hits the roof of the Opel. Then several in a series, *plop plop plop*.

I gesture to the backseat. "You want me to drive? Fine. Get in. I'll drive."

I am a little surprised when Jesse does what I tell her without saying a word. I push the front seat back into place and drop down into it.

"Pelican my ass," I say, and slam the door.

16

MEL

AWESOME. NOT ONLY have I lost my phone and unknowingly conspired to commit a felony, but I am now trapped in said stolen car with two people who won't stop fighting.

I hate that they're fighting.

The first day I saw Jesse and Vicks was the day I spent job hunting, looking for anything that didn't mean working for my dad. They were in their gray and white Waffle shirts and bow ties, and Jesse was pulling Vicks by the hand through the restaurant, howling with laughter. Right that second, I decided I wouldn't mind working at the Waffle.

It was so good to see a friendship that was based on something more than matching sheepskin coats.

But is it possible they don't really have that?

No. No way. They love each other. They need each other. They just have to apologize to each other and move on.

I scroll through my iPod, find the Feist song I'm looking for, and press "play."

"I'm sorry . . ."

Oh, yeah. How can they not feel sorry when they're listening to this song? It's psychologically impossible!

"—When I realize I was acting all wrong—"

Vicks has one hand on the steering wheel, blasé. Jesse is staring out the window in the back. Why are they *not* apologizing?

Maybe it's too low-key. I need something more dancey. Something to get them pumped up.

Aha! I know! I find Will Smith's "Miami" and press "play." Oh, yeah. C'mon. We're going to Miami!

Party in the city where the heat is on,
All night on the beach till the break of dawn—

No acknowledgment, except for a big sigh from Jesse.

"Do we have any Ho Hos left?" Vicks asks, like she doesn't even hear the music. "Oh, never mind. I'm not really in the mood."

Not in the mood for fun, obviously.

Fun! That's it! That's Plan C. Silly me, why didn't I think of this before? New song. *Great* song. A classic. I crank the volume on baby-voiced Cyndi Lauper. *"I come home in the middle of the night—"*

I start grooving in my seat, just a little, because how can anyone hear this song and not dance? *"'But girls, they want to have fun,'"* I sing. *"'Oh girls—'"*

"Not Jesse," Vicks says. "Other girls maybe. Like me, for example. I *love* fun."

I sneak a look back at Jesse, and she looks pained. I glance over at Vicks. She's not happy, either.

I press "stop."

I adjust my shorts, which are riding up a bit. I pick at a chapped spot on my lip.

But I've got to do *something*. We can't just drive like this forever, all doom and gloom and hot hot hot.

Hot! Weather! It worked so well last night, when I was sitting outside with—

No, my brain says.

So I don't.

But still, weather is . . . weather. It's multipurpose.

"So," I begin. "Sure is hot here, eh?"

"It's *Florida*," Vicks points out.

Jesse lets out another epic sigh. "It's fixing to pour."

"Is it?" I say. I peer through the windshield, and see that, yes, there are a whole bunch of dark clouds cluttering the sky. "We need to be optimistic," I say, try-ing to keep my voice peppy. "Oh! I know just the song. A little 'Walking on Sunshine,' ladies?" I scroll through my music, press "play." As soon as the words kicks in, I sing along.

Jesse swivels her head to look at me. Her expression is forlorn. "Mel, can you turn it off? Please? My head is killing me."

I hit the power button and slump against the seat.

I miss the snow.

17

VICKS

THERE'S THIS THING the rain does in Florida. It trickles for a few minutes, and then the sky goes suddenly black and before you know it, you're standing in a waterfall. It's not even cold out; the water can be warm. Buckets and buckets pour onto you and you forget the sun ever shone. Forget the sun shone on you that very morning, heating up your skin until you were dying to escape into some air-conditioning, shone on you till you squinted your eyes and put on your shades. It's like all that never happened, and the world is just wet and black and loud with the weeping sound of tires going through puddles. I'm crawling the car through sheets of water that seem to stretch forever down this blank stretch of asphalt Jesse's got us on. I don't even know what road we're on, but when I see something that looks like a highway and the sign says SOUTH, I pull onto it.

I'm not a great driver. My brother Tully, who taught me, was always telling me I drove "like a girl," which was the biggest insult in his book. I'd spit back and say, "Then the way a girl drives is awesome, as you can see from my mad skills, so up yours." Or, "Thank you very much. Then I know I'll pass my test the first time around." But then his meanness kind of sapped my confidence when I was learning, because he'd laugh at my parking and say I looked over my shoulder too much and I shouldn't be so fussy about my blind spot. I got my license, but the mad-skills thing was just a front. I never get to drive my parents' van because one of them is always using it, and when I do drive, I get nervous, and hear Tully's teasing voice in my head: "Ugh, Vicks, don't be such a woman! Just change lanes!"

But I don't want Jesse and Mel to think I'm anything less than stellar behind the wheel—especially since Jesse herself is an annoyingly good driver. Usually. And I don't want to question where we are because I don't want to get into it with Jesse about what turn she made or didn't make. We don't need to get to Miami anymore anyway, because Brady doesn't really want to see me and

I don't want to see Brady; so driving one way is pretty much the same as another.

We are all silent. We just listen to the rain, which hammers the windshield with little relief from the sluggish wipers.

Great. A toll booth. The signs never say how much you need until you're right up next to that little metal basket and then you're digging around in your pockets and the guy behind you is irritated because you're so slow, and besides, I've only got three bucks left after the hot dog yesterday.

"Toll thing," I say, to get Mel's attention.

She seems to have gotten the hint after we made her buy the doughnuts this morning, and hands me two quarters from her change purse. It's so wet out, I wait until we're under the roof of the toll booth to try and roll down the window.

Ugh. The window won't go down.

"Bang it under the handle," Jesse says from the back. She says it like I should know it.

I bang.

It still won't go down.

"*No*, you gotta wiggle waggle it before you turn it."

I try. No luck.

A guy in some monster-size pickup has pulled up behind me, and he's honking.

"No, you've got to bang, then right away wiggle

waggle. No pause in between."

I bang, wiggle waggle, roll. The window opens. But we are way too far from the metal bucket where you're supposed to throw your change. And I cannot do crap with my left hand. Really. Tully and Jay are always teasing me about it. "Throw past Vicks on the left," they'd tell their buddies when we all played basketball. "She'll never block it." It's even evident in the kitchen at Waffle House. T-Bone can pour pancakes with his left while he flips eggs with his right. But not me.

The toll is fifty cents. I toss the first quarter in the direction of the metal basket. It hits the pavement. Damn.

I unhook the seat belt, open the door, and look for the quarter on the ground.

Can't see it.

"Just throw another one," says Mel, handing me another quarter while looking at the truck behind us. "It doesn't matter." How can she be so calm?

I close the car door and throw the next one, which goes in. But the third one hits the edge and bounces out again. I am starting to sweat.

The guy behind us honks again.

Damn.

I open the door a second time to scout around the ground for those two quarters that didn't go in. Where did they go? I can't see them. Just asphalt and a few cigarette butts. Are they under a wheel?

Honk. HONK.

I'm not asking Mel for yet another quarter. Even though she said she'd pay for stuff, it's another thing to keep giving coins to a person who is throwing them into the middle of the road like a complete fool. So I step out of the car, get down on my knees, and look underneath it.

Honk. HONK.

I can't stand it. I get back in the car, slam the door, step on the gas, and drive through the red light.

"What are you *doing*?" screams Jesse. "We can't go through without paying!"

"That guy was honking at me," I explain.

Damn. Maybe Tully was right about me. Maybe driving like a girl is as lame as he thinks it is, and maybe I do cower in the face of monster pickups. Hell, I can't even toss a quarter into a toll basket.

"Stop driving. Pull over," Jesse commands. Although we are back in the torrents of water, I do what she says. The honker in the pickup drives past us. "Since when do you run through a toll booth, Vicks?" Jesse barks. "What are you thinking?"

"We tried to pay," I say. "We left three quarters instead of two, even."

"But they're not in the basket!" yells Jesse. "I'm going to get a ticket! We're gonna get in even more trouble than we already are. What if my mom calls the police and has them trace the license plate for a stolen car and now we're caught on the hidden camera?"

"I tried to pay the toll," I say. "I didn't run through on purpose. That guy was honking at me." It sounds stupid, even as I say it.

"Look," says Mel calmly. "Let's go back and pay it now."

"I can't reverse on the highway!" I cry. "There's like no visibility. Someone's going to drive right into me while I'm going backward!"

"Well, if you just walk back there and pay the toll," Jesse says, "they won't know what license plate it's for."

"Use your cell camera," says Mel. "Take a picture of the car and of you paying the toll, that way you'll have proof you went back and paid if they send you a ticket."

"What planet are you on?" I say. "I don't have a cell camera."

"Oh." Mel looks startled.

"Do you have one?" I ask her. "Use yours."

"I lost my phone," Mel says.

Since when?

Jesse's breathing fast. "I can't get two tickets in less than twenty-four hours. Mama's already going to kill me."

Mel has a new idea. "I know. We make the security camera work for us!"

"How?" I ask.

"We run out, find the camera, look at it, hold up a little sign with the license plate number on it, and put in a quarter."

"Do we even have another quarter?" I ask.

Mel roots around in her purse and hands me three nickels and a dime. Jesse finds a pad of paper and writes the license number on it in lipstick.

I pocket everything and step into the downpour.

We are silent again when I'm back in the driver's seat. Mel thoughtfully put a towel underneath me, but I'm shivering and damp and I can hardly see the road.

"I need another doughnut," I say, squinting through the windshield.

"Me too," says Mel. "Can you please just call a truce and eat doughnuts for a few minutes without any more arguing?"

"All right," says Jesse. And if she can say "all right," then I can too.

"All right," I say.

Jesse hands up doughnuts from the back and we all three eat, driving ten miles an hour through the storm.

"Wanna play a car game?" Mel asks.

"Like what?" I ask.

"Um . . . free association?"

"Explain."

"I say a word, then Jesse says the first word she thinks of, then you say the first word you think of, and we go around."

"Yeah, okay," says Jesse.

"Can I start?" I ask.

"Sure."

Me: "Doughnut."

Mel: "Naughty."

Jesse: "Sticky."

"No, Jesse," Mel interrupts. "You're still thinking about *doughnut*. You have to clear your mind and only think about *naughty*."

"Okay," says Jesse. "Sorry. Do-over."

Me: "Doughnut."

Mel: "Naughty."

Jesse: "Repent."

Me: "Regret."

"Wine coolers," Mel says. "Yeah, I know that's two words, but it's my game so I make the rules."

"Ooh, *wine coolers*, huh? Now where did you get that idea?" I ask.

Mel bites her lip. "Unfortunately, last night was not the first time I've had more than is good for me."

"Do we get to hear that story?" I ask.

"No." She laughs. "We're playing the game! Jesse, your turn. Wine coolers."

Jesse: "Bad breath."

Me: "Garlic."

Mel: "Vampires."

Jesse: "Bite marks."

Me: "Hickeys."

Mel: "Band-Aids."

"You did *not* cover your hickey with a Band-Aid!" I shriek.

"I had to! It was so obvious," Mel confesses. "But I've only had one hickey."

"Let's move on," Jesse says. "Peroxide."

Me: "Hair."

"Did you really peroxide your hair?" asks Mel. "I hear that's so bad for it."

"I tried," I tell her. "But it didn't work. I ended up getting the frost-and-tip and leaving it on for twice as long as the box told me to."

"Wow." She fingers her own brown hair. "I would never have the guts."

"It's just hair," I tell her. "It grows back."

A silence follows. "Hey, you guys?" I say eventually. "I'm sorry I messed up the toll booth thing."

"S'okay," mutters Jesse. "I'm sorry I stole the car."

My cell vibrates. We're only going ten miles an hour, and I can tell it's not Brady. It's some number from Niceville, but one I don't know. I hit "accept." "Hello?"

"Is this Victoria?"

"Depends who's asking."

"This is Twyla Fix, Jesse's mama."

"Hello there, Ms. Fix," I say.

Even though I know she's probably pissed as shit, her voice still has that bounce in it, the one that makes Abe at the Waffle House blush. I'm tempted to hand the phone to Jesse, because I'm still mad at her, car game or no car game. But then I look back over my shoulder and see her waving frantically that she won't—she can't—speak to her mama, and she's my best friend even if she did call me a sinner.

"Is Jesse with you?" asks Ms. Fix. "I need to talk to her real bad."

"Oh, she just went off to pick up stuff for lunch with our friend Mel, you know, the hostess at the Waffle? And my boyfriend, Brady," I lie, my voice sounding like a straight-A, student-government good girl. "Brady's taking us on a tour of the school."

"Where are you?"

"Brady goes to the University of Miami, you remember, I told you when you took me and Jesse to Applebee's? He's on the football team and he's taking anthropology," I say, to make him sound respectable. "We're going to have a picnic down by the ocean, if the weather holds. Doesn't that sound nice, Ms. Fix?"

"You girls okay in that car with the storm?" she asks. "Where are you sleeping?"

"We're okay. We got a hotel across the street from campus," I tell her. "Mel's mom and dad gave her money for it. She has a credit card and everything. Don't worry, it's a nice clean place. Parents stay there when they come visit their kids at college."

"I really gotta talk to Jesse. You know when she's coming back?"

"The sandwich shop is kind of a ways from here. Could be half an hour, an hour? I can have her call you back if you want."

"Do you know she left me without any way to get to my job?" Ms. Fix says, beginning to sound irritated. "Do you know I had to catch me the bus going all over town to look for her, and then was late to work and got docked an hour's pay? Do you know I was up half the night, waiting for her to come home?"

"No, ma'am," I say. "I did not know that. I'm so, so sorry if I caused you any problems. You know I begged her to take me down to see Brady. I miss him so much now that he's in college, I just begged her and begged her to take me here. Jesse's the loyalest friend, Ms. Fix. You should be really proud of her. She took off work to help me and everything."

Mel is giggling into the fabric of her T-shirt and Jesse is staring out the window with her hand over her mouth, looking like tragedy just struck.

"Well," says Ms. Fix. "I'm not happy with her. Do

177

you understand me, Vicks?"

"Oh, I do," I say. "But really, I take responsibility for everything. I just missed my boyfriend so bad and I had to, had to see him. You know how that is, don't you?"

I say it like I'm lying. But it's true.

Ms. Fix sighs on the other end. I can hear a dog barking. "My break's over," she says. "I gotta go." She pauses. "You're young and in love, huh?"

I swallow hard. "Yes, ma'am."

"That's a great thing, first love," she says. "You treasure it now, you hear?"

"I sure will." I was trying not to giggle before, but now I'm trying not to cry.

"I want Jesse calling me the second she gets back."

"I'll tell her," I say.

Ms. Fix hangs up and I wipe my eyes on the bottom of my sodden T-shirt. "She's off your back for an hour or two, at least," I tell Jesse.

"I owe you," she says.

"That's for damn sure," I say. "Hey, do we have any water?"

"You're kidding, right?" Jesse says. She gestures out the window at the deluge.

"Hey, I'm thirsty," I say. "Lying for your friends takes it out of a girl." Really, I just want to get rid of the lump in my throat.

Mel looks around on the floor of the front seat and

shakes her head. "Anything in the backseat?"

"Just a half-empty bottle of orange juice that's been sitting here since yesterday," Jesse reports.

"Gross."

"Isn't there anywhere to pull over and buy something?" asks Mel.

"Nope. All I can see is rain. Rain again. And then more rain," I answer. "At least it's not another hurricane."

"What letter are they on now? *G?*" Jesse wonders.

"Nah, we had Greg offshore a few weeks ago. Didn't make it inland. Now we're on *H*."

"Um, guys?" Mel interrupts. "Could Harriet be the name of a hurricane?"

"Sure," Jesse says. "They name 'em in alphabetical order. So the next one'll be Harriet, or Helen. Something like that."

"They were talking about a Harriet in Dunkin' Donuts," Mel says. "Saying she was headed for Cocoa Beach and they wanted their relatives to leave town. But I just thought—"

"We're in a hurricane?" I interrupt.

"Mel." Jesse is serious. "Are you telling me you knew we were driving into a hurricane and you never said anything?"

"I didn't realize what they meant," Mel explains. "I thought they were talking about a cousin or a nasty old

179

aunt or something. Mean Auntie Harriet."

"You are so clueless," moans Jesse. "This is dangerous. People's houses get knocked over. Whole neighborhoods flood. Hello? Katrina?"

Mel starts blinking repeatedly, like she's about to start crying. "I'm sorry," she says. "I didn't realize."

"We have to get off the road," says Jesse. "We can't keep driving in this."

And I want to do what Jesse says—but the water is coming down so hard I can't see more than a foot in front of me—and the roof of the Opel is starting to leak.

18

MEL

EACH RAINDROP IS like a bomb against the foggy windshield, exploding into a circle of water. *Kabam!* I've never seen rain this gray, this hostile. This everywhere. It's like being underwater with your eyes open. I am a jerk for not paying more attention to the Dunkin' Donuts ladies. But how was I supposed to know?

Jesse has scooted over to the middle of the backseat and perched herself on the edge so she is practically sitting in the front row with us. "Vicks, get off the road."

Vicks's hands are stiff and white and glued to the

steering wheel in the ten and two position. She's shaking her head, back and forth and back and forth. "And go where? I don't even know where I am."

She's driving about two miles an hour. The wipers are barely even crawling across the windshield. They slush one way, then they slush back.

The sound of thunder rips through the sky and the whole road feels like it's shuddering. Next comes a bolt of lightning. I hold my breath when the sky lights up and for a brief second we see the gushing water. Then it's dark again and a gust of wind whips my side of the Opel. It looks like it's the middle of the night instead of eleven in the morning.

I try desperately to see through the foggy window. "Um, stay straight. I'll watch for a sign."

Jesse reaches over to Vicks's shoulder and pats it. "Just go slow." Her words are soft, like she's putting a baby to sleep. "Straight and slow. I'm sure we'll see somewhere to stop."

We keep driving. No one talks. The only sound is the rain pummeling the car.

"Wanna play free association some more?" I ask, trying to slow my speeding heart. I turn back to look at Jesse. "Where were we? Peroxide?"

"Mel, please," Vicks says. "Not now."

"Sorry."

"You should have told us about the hurricane, Mel,"

Vicks finally says. "It was really irresponsible of you not to."

"I'm sorry," I repeat, sinking back into my seat, blood rushing to my head. "I honestly didn't know." I try to sink back farther but the seat won't let me in. My eyes are getting watery—great—so I turn to the side window. My throat is closing up. I stare out the side window and watch the fat raindrops slide sideways like they're running away from the front of the car.

"I just don't understand what you were thinking," Vicks continues, her voice rising. "I mean—"

"Come on, enough," Jesse says. I notice that it's my shoulder she's now patting. "Mel didn't know. She said she was sorry."

Vicks lets out a throaty laugh. "Sometimes that's just not enough though, is it?"

Silence.

"Hey, look!" Jesse says. "A sign!"

I see it! I see it! It's a big green sign! I press up against the window to try to make the words out on said sign. But the windshield keeps getting slammed with water. I can't see anything. How useless am I?

"It says . . . Disney World is up ahead," Jesse says. There's wonder in her voice.

"We can go if you want," I rush to say. "I'll buy the tickets."

"Really?" she says. Then she reins herself in. It's

weird: I can sense her doing it, like Disney World isn't something she's allowed to want. "It's raining," she says. "We need a hotel, or at least a restaurant where we can sit for a few hours."

"Of course," I say. "I meant, like, tomorrow. Or whenever it clears up. I love Disney parks. I've been to the one outside Paris."

I wish I would shut up. Not only am I babbling, but I sound like I'm showing off. I don't mean to show off. And how do I know Jesse hasn't been to Paris? "Have you been to that one?" I ask. Shut up, shut up!

"Can you forget about your fancy life for a second and focus on finding a place we can be indoors?" Vicks retorts.

I turn back toward the side window and follow the running raindrops. "I think I see a hotel. Maybe. See? It's a building, anyway. Do you think it's a hotel?"

Vicks sighs. "How do I know? Does it look like a hotel?"

"Um . . . I think." It's hard to see anything. It has flags on it, I think. Black flags.

"We'll wait in the lobby until the rain lets up. Someone tell me how to get there?"

"Take the next exit," Jesse says. "Just take it super slow on the off ramp."

Vicks flicks her turn signal. "My phone is vibrating. Will someone get it?"

Jesse reaches into Vicks's purse for it. "If it's Mama, I'm not answering."

"Five, five, five, two, one, five, eight," Jesse reads out. "Not Mama."

Those numbers sound familiar. Wait a sec. "Hey, that's my number!" I twist around to the backseat.

"Yeah?" Jesse answers Vicks's phone. "Who am I speaking to?" Her eyes widen. "Ohhh. Hello, *Marco*. Mel did what? She did? Ah."

I try to catch my breath. Marco is calling Vicks from my phone? What does that mean? That he regrets not kissing me? And then I realize that all it means is he found the phone and saw my Canadian maple-leaf sticker and he knew it was mine and then he found her number in my contacts list and now he's calling to tell me that he has it. He is being nice. He *is* nice. Just because he didn't find me attractive doesn't make him not nice.

"Is anyone paying attention to the road?" Vicks asks. "I need help finding the turnoff."

I turn back toward the front, my heart thumping. "Sorry. Keep driving, I see a sign. I think it says . . . Treasure Chest Hotel?" I twist back to Jesse, who is making smoochy Marco faces at me.

To Marco, she says, "What? I can't hear ya. What? Yeah, we were in a bit of a rush to hit the road. What? Speak up! Yeah, we realize that *now*. Thanks, genius."

She rolls her eyes at me. "But we're already in it."

Vicks is following a narrow lane up toward the hotel.

"Do you want to talk to him?" she mouths to me.

No. Yes. I take a deep breath and put out my hand.

But then Jesse's forehead wrinkles. "Did I tell Mel about what? What pool?"

What pool indeed? I didn't go into a pool. Did I go into a pool?

The car swerves to the left.

A weird strangled expression takes over Jesse's face. "No, Marco, I'm not kidding. This is Jesse, not Vicks, and I want you to tell me what the heck happened in the pool with you two."

Vicks was in a pool with Marco? My Marco?

"Oh, I will," Jesse says dangerously. "Only why don't you tell her yourself?"

The rain is now pounding against my head. Inside my head.

I look at Vicks and she is pale. Jesse's face is a mask of stone. I wonder what I look like. I examine my outstretched hand. It looks stupid and small. My nail polish is chipped.

I drop my hand and put it in my lap.

"Fine," Jesse says. "You know what? The reception here sucks." She *pings* the cell closed.

My throat is on fire. My tongue is on fire.

Jesse returns her hand to my shoulder.

"Vicks, anything you'd like to tell us?" she says. Her voice is soaked in acid. The acid drips through her fingers and into my shoulder. Now my arm is on fire.

"I . . . did something dumb," Vicks whispers.

I imagine that I'm a windshield wiper who can slosh her words away. I can't believe it's happening *again*. I can't believe what an idiot I am. I can't believe I thought she was my friend. She's not a friend, she doesn't care about me. She doesn't even care about her boyfriend, the great and wonderful Brady. I shouldn't care, she's nobody to me. Just some girl I met at a stupid job. A stupid job I don't even want. She can be a slut if she wants because it shouldn't matter to me. None of this matters to me. I don't even know why I'm here. I don't want to be here.

I open my mouth to breathe. But there's no air. I need to get out of this car.

I search for my voice. "Can you stop the car, please?"

Vicks snaps her head toward me. "What?"

"She *said* stop the car," Jesse says. There is a fierce glee to her anger.

"No," Vicks says.

I need to get out. Now. "Stop. The fucking. Car!"

The car jerks to a halt. When I get out, the rain digs into my face and arms, soaking me, my shirt, my shorts. My feet slosh in my sandals.

It hurts to be outside. The wind whips my hair into

my mouth. The car crawls along beside me.

There is no sidewalk, only road. I plow through the puddles until I reach the hotel driveway. Three curving buildings loom side by side, each at least thirty stories high. In front of the middle building are massive gold-plated letters set against black sails that scream TREASURE CHEST DELUXE HOTEL AND CONVENTION CENTER. Giant pirate ship replicas are docked in front. It is beyond cheesy.

The slut pulls into the parking lot and I find refuge under the hotel awning.

A bellhop in a white satin ruffled shirt, black pants, and an eye patch looks me over. "Do you need a towel, miss?"

"No, thank you."

He opens the heavy door for me and I step inside the huge pirate-themed entranceway. Treasure maps are framed on the walls. I wipe my feet on the gold welcome mat but it doesn't help. I leave footprints on the aqua-tiled floor with every step. Gold chests stuffed with glass jewels clutter the lobby. Parrots squawk in gilt cages, and the ceiling is draped with fishing nets.

Forget waiting out the storm in the lobby. Maybe the rooms will be less hideous?

The young woman behind the reception counter is wearing a red corset, a black choker, and a fur-trimmed pirate hat. "Hello!" she chirps.

"Hello!" chirps the parrot on her bare shoulder.

"I'd like a room, please."

"For tonight?"

"Yes, please. For three people." I'm on autopilot. Why am I getting a room for three? Vicks doesn't deserve a room. Maybe I'll let Jesse inside but make Vicks wait it out in this pirate cheese-fest.

The pirate types something on her keyboard. She has fake pirate nails. Long black talons with tiny skulls on them that are clicking against the keyboard. Each click sends a bullet into my brain. *Click, click, click.* "Unfortunately, we're full tonight."

I snap in half. "What? How can a hotel this size be full?"

"Due to construction we're only using the south side of the complex, and I'm afraid all of those rooms are committed. However, it's possible we might have some cancellations due to the weather. Would you like to wait by the cannons or visit the Jolly Roger, and then check back in an hour or so?"

No more explosions. No more drama. What I want is a nap. "You're telling me there's nothing available?"

Click, click, click. "Only suites. There is the Golden Coin Suite on the twenty-eighth floor for three hundred and fifty *dollars*, and the Black Pearl Suite on the thirtieth for five hundred *dollars*." She emphasizes the word *dollars* in case I'm confusing her currency for pesos or Monopoly money or something. Her lips are sealed in a disbelieving, I-feel-sorry-for-you-because-you-obviously-can't-afford-a-suite smile.

"They both have one king-size bed, as well as a separate living room and sofa bed," she says, overly polite. "Would you be interested in one of those?"

I no longer care about Vicks or Jesse thinking I'm a princess. In fact, I want to show them both. Show them what I have and they don't. Show this pirate how wrong she is. Look here, ladies, at what I can do. Charge five hundred dollars to my credit card because I feel like it. I don't need anyone.

I give her a big fake smile and press my mother's AmEx on the desk. "I'll take the Black Pearl Suite, please."

19

JESSE

I BOUNCE ON the huge bed—it's king-size! I wish I had a king-size bed! I wish our trailer could fit a king-size bed!—and watch the rain pummel the window. From up here on the thirtieth floor, with nothing but swirling gray as far as the eye can see, it's like we're smack in the deepest part of the ocean. Only we are safe and dry in the Black Pearl. I love the Black Pearl. I would like to live in the Black Pearl for the rest of my life.

I use my arms to score more air as I jump. The mattress is incredible. It feels so good to move.

"'Who did, who did, who did, who did, who did

swallow Jo Jo Jo Jo,'" I belt out.

Mel watches. I can see her in the living room, slumped in a red velvet chair. Oh, yeah, this place even has its own living room, velvet chairs, a velvet couch, another TV, and a glass coffee table. The coffee table is etched with a fleet of ships.

"Shut up," Vicks calls from the bathroom. But I don't have to listen to her, 'cause she's being punished. When Mel marched out of the lobby and over to the Opel, she told me we had a room and to pop the trunk, grab our stuff, and come on. *Me*, as in no acknowledgment whatsoever of La Cheater.

Vicks tossed the keys to the valet (who looked at the dripping Opel as if it were, well, the dripping, soggy, malfunctioning heap it is) and followed us with her army green duffel bag. She acted the teeniest bit cowed, but jutted her chin out like, *What are you going to do about it?*

"I didn't say—," Mel began. Then bit her lip.

"You want me to stay in the car? Sleep in the car like a homeless person?" Vicks said. "Because I will, no problem."

The valet looked hopeful, like maybe Vicks would drive that heap away and he wouldn't have to deal with it.

"But then you won't hear my explanation," Vicks said.

"So?" I said.

"Fine, you can come," Mel said. "But *don't* talk to me."

I personally thought Vicks was being overdramatic. It was barely noon. She was going to sleep in the car like a homeless person at noon?

"Mel . . . ," Vicks had said, following her toward the hotel doors.

"No," Mel replied, surprisingly fierce. "Not. One. Word."

So the three of us filed silently through the lobby, up the elevator, and into this *suite*, which let me tell you is friggin' *sweet*. Even the bathroom is amazing, with a Jacuzzi bath, a separate glass shower stall, two sinks, a closet bigger than my trailer, plus heated towel racks decorated with doubloons. Yes, doubloons.

Vicks is camped out in there now, probably hogging all the heated towels.

"'Who did, who did—'" I sing.

"Could you stop singing that stupid song?" she calls.

"Not one word, remember?" I say. I'm going to sing all I want, as loud as I want. "'Who did, who did, who did swallow Jo Jo Jo Jo!'"

Vicks stomps out of the bathroom. Or skulks, more like. Something between a stomp and a skulk. She doesn't make eye contact with either of us.

"I'm going for a smoke," she mutters as she strides past me and then through the living room.

"They're your lungs!" I say.

The door leading to the hallway shushes shut, ending

with a solid click. I am so glad to have that girl out of my hair. She was giving me a headache—I just now realized it, 'cause now it's gone. It's gone 'cause she's gone. And here I am, me and Mel and no mean Vicks, in our Black Pearl suite with a big honking treasure map hung on the wall. It's even signed by Lord Matteo Crowley, whoever he is.

This place is so not the Sunny View Motel, where I stayed with Mama once when we drove to Gulfport, and where the doors were made of particle board. There were roaches in the bathroom, and the whole place smelled of pee. The mustard-colored comforter was stained. I pushed it off the bed with my feet and used only the scratchy blanket.

This place has four-hundred-thread-count cotton linens—a creamy card up near the pillows says so—and mahogany furniture that gleams. In the sitting room there's a wide-screen TV on a pull-out shelf inside an armoire thingie, so that you can be classy and have no TV (when the armoire is closed), or be life-of-the-party and On-Demand-here-I-come when the doors of the armoire are thrown open. I myself would love some On Demand action, but I figure I'll let Mel make that call, since she's the one footing the bill.

For real, I could live here forever. Even the air smells good, like ocean spray. I drop onto my fanny and flop backward on the bed. *Ahhhh*.

"So . . . ," Mel says, coming into the bedroom.

"Yeah?"

"Who *did* swallow Jo Jo?"

I laugh. "Not Jo Jo. Jonah." I roll onto my side and prop my head on my hand. "It's from *Veggie Tales*."

"*Veggie Tales?*" Mel repeats.

"Larry the cucumber?" I prompt. "Archibald the asparagus?"

"I have no idea what you're talking about."

"Oh, come on. Bob the tomato? You *gotta* know Bob the tomato."

Mel blinks, and I take pity on her.

"It's a cartoon, only the characters are all veggies," I explain. "That particular song is from their very first full-length feature film, which is about Jonah and the whale."

I hesitate, because maybe they don't have Jonah and the whale in Canada. Then again . . . she's Jewish, and Jewish people would have Jonah, wouldn't they? I realize how little I know about this whole other religion that Jesus Himself came from.

"You do know Jonah and the whale, right?" I ask.

"Um, *yeah*." She says it like she's not sure why I'm asking, like I'm quizzing her on what color the sky is or something. "Jonah's the guy who got swallowed."

"Yes!" I say with too much enthusiasm. "Good!"

She regards me curiously. I blush.

"In the film they call him Jo Jo, but that's who he is," I say. "Jonah. He's played by Archibald."

"The asparagus."

"Bingo!"

Mel isn't appropriately appreciative. If anything, she seems a little freaked out, in that way of being stuck with a batty bag lady spouting off about UFOs. Or in this case, produce.

"No, it's a really funny movie," I say. "*Veggie Tales* in general is really funny—and I'm not just saying that 'cause I'm a Christian."

Mel's still giving me the bag-lady stare, and I'm kind of wishing I hadn't started this.

"What I mean is, even normal people like the Veggies. Not just me." I laugh. "Not that I'm not *normal*."

"Oh," Mel says. She sighs. Then she sighs again.

Okay, enough sighing: It's time to snap into action. I'm up and off the bed with this crazy energy I've been possessed by, and I rummage through my purse, which is on the floor. I pull out eyeliner, powder, mascara, blush. Body glitter. Lip gloss. A three-pack of eye shadow: green, pale green, and neutral beige.

"I know what you need: makeover," I announce. I straighten up and pat the edge of the bed.

She looks dubious, but comes over and sits beside me.

"Close your eyes."

She does what she is told, and it strikes me that either

she always does what she's told, or she's so depressed about the whole Vicks-Marco thing that she doesn't have the energy to protest.

"I'm sorry Vicks did that," I say, stroking translucent powder over her skin. "With Marco, I mean. Especially after y'all . . . you know."

"No, what?"

I fidget. I don't want to go there again, to the topic of sinning with boys. "In Robbie's bedroom? At the party?"

Her eyebrows come together, and I see there's a little plucking to be done there. Only I don't think I brought my tweezers.

"Jesse, nothing happened between me and Marco," she says. "He wouldn't even kiss me."

"What? Y'all didn't even *kiss*? But . . . I mean . . ."

"He thought I was revolting."

"Oh, nuh-uh," I say. "I saw the way he looked at you—there's no way he thought you were revolting."

"Then why'd he pick Vicks instead of me?" she asks with such a miserable expression that I have to put down my powder brush altogether. "What's wrong with *me*?"

I hug her and say, "Nothing! It makes no sense. But just . . . don't even waste your time thinking on it, 'kay? Vicks shouldn't have let him. Vicks messed up big-time."

"She was drunk," Mel says.

"Doesn't matter." I squeeze her skinny shoulders, then release her and uncap the blue eyeliner. I use feathery strokes to draw a line above her lashes.

"People aren't themselves when they're drunk," Mel says. "Maybe . . . I don't know. She was probably missing Brady."

"So she hooked up with Marco to ease her pain?"

"It's not like I owned him," Mel says. "It's not like we were going out. I can't be mad at Vicks for doing the exact same thing I wanted to do."

"Yes, you can," I say.

"I just feel so *dumb*. When he called? I got so excited. I was like, 'Omigod!' Because I thought he'd called for me. I thought he wanted to talk to *me*."

"But he *did* want to talk to you," I say. I realize this twist has escaped me, what with all that's been going on. "He thought I was Vicks . . . but he asked to speak to *you*."

"He did?"

"'Can I talk to Mel?' Those were his exact words. And I would have let him, too, if the whole whoring-around business hadn't come out."

Mel lifts her eyes to mine. They're bluer than ever, thanks to the eyeliner. Then she looks down. "That's okay."

"No, it's not," I say. I *really* want to stay bouncy and flying, but dang it, it's starting to slip away. "Not everything's 'okay,' Mel. People cheat, people lie, people *die*. And sometimes people treat their friends like crap. But that doesn't mean you sit back and take it."

She shifts her posture in a way that makes my gut throb 'cause I haven't exactly been treating my friends so well myself. But I'm not the one on trial here. I'm not on trial, and I'm not calling Mama, and I'm not going back to the old buzz-kill Jesse now that I'm dry and warm and safe in the belly of the whale. *Heck* no. Nothing can touch me in the belly of the whale.

"Time to turn that frown upside down," I say to Mel. "Look up, please."

She does, and I line her lower lids. I apply pale green shadow at the inner corners and the bright green farther out and in the creases. Not everybody can pull off green eye shadow. Mel can. I stroke on mascara with a big, fat brush, and her eyes look amazing.

"Jesse—" she says.

"Tch," I say. "Hold your mouth still." I use my pinky to smooth on a dab of strawberry "Lip Burst" and it's unsettling, touching her in such an intimate way. It's not like, *Oh, Mel, I want to kiss you*. It's just . . . oh, I don't know. She's so different from me.

"There," I say, after brushing just a smidge of baby pink blush onto the apples of her cheeks. "Go look."

Any normal girl would dash to the bathroom mirror, which is what I want her to do. I want her to see my handiwork and be delighted. Instead, Mel draws her legs to her chest and wraps her arms around her shins. She rests her cheek against one knee and gazes out the window.

"Is it ever going to stop?" she asks.

"The rain? Yeah, of course."

She doesn't look convinced, so I hop off the bed, grab the remote, and flick on the TV to the Weather Channel. We watch as the man points at maps and talks about miles per hour, and then I click it off.

"See? We're going to get dumped on, but we'll be okay."

She sighs.

"Did it never rain like this in Canada?" I ask. What a concept—no rain. I could so totally get behind that. Except then I'd probably miss it.

"It rains," Mel says. She rests her cheek on her other knee, so that now she's facing me. I mimic her position without thinking about it. We're two monkeys on the bed, legs pulled up, faces inches apart. The rain drums against the glass. Lightning flashes, followed by the crack of thunder.

"Have you ever been in a real hurricane?" she asks.

"Sure," I say. "Live in Florida long enough, and you will too."

She grimaces, like *great*. "What was it like?"

Okay, I don't really want to go there . . . but I also

don't want to shut her down.

"In the worst one, our trailer flooded," I tell her. "Not the trailer we have now, but before." I blow out air in a *pffff*. "Yet another piece of crap, so no big loss."

"Were you inside? When it flooded?"

I shake my head. "There'd been warnings all day, so Mama had MeeMaw pick me up from school and take me to her place."

"How old were you?"

"Nine," I say. *Fifth grade. The year Sissy Roberts said I had ugly toenails. The year Mama broke up with Earl, who stank, and started going out with Darren, who had five zillion guns. R.D. with his truck stop wasn't even a fleck in her eye.*

"Were you scared?" Mel wants to know.

"Nah," I say. "I mean, yeah, but mainly for Mama, because she got stuck in PetSmart. They did that lockdown horn. Have you heard it? Which means nobody's allowed to leave till they sound the all-clear. Anyway, Mama couldn't call 'cause the electricity was out, so MeeMaw and me couldn't help being worried, even though we knew she was most likely fine."

"And was she?" Mel says.

"Yeah. She called when the phone lines got patched up, wanting to know . . ." Oh Lord, here it comes.

Mel waits.

My throat tightens, which is dumb. This is old news— so why do I still have to get choked up?

"We had a dog," I tell her. "A cocker spaniel with 'abandonment issues,' that's what Mama said. The owners moved to another state, so she was ours, clean and clear."

"Oh, no," Mel says.

"She was in her crate, 'cause she chewed up stuff something fierce when we weren't there."

"Oh, Jesse."

"So . . . yeah." I remember the water marks on our wallpaper, when me and Mama went to clean everything up. The marks were above the oven, above the fold-out couch where I slept. All that junk. Wet magazines and cereal boxes. Thick, sodden clumps of toilet paper.

Mel puts her hand on mine. "Did she . . . ?"

I've seen it in my mind too often: her claws scrabbling, her nose seeking the uppermost corner of the crate. Scared and alone. The water rising.

I drag my hand over my face, 'cause there's nothing to be done about it now. "It's fine," I say. "It's okay."

"No," she says, shaking her head. "Not everything's 'okay,' Jesse."

She's throwing my own words back at me. This itsy-bitsy girl in designer flip-flops, who's scared to death of a stuffed alligator and who doesn't know a hurricane from a doughnut—she's throwing my own words back at me. She's got to feel as awkward as heck, but she lets that awkwardness exist and doesn't try to act like, *Oh,*

202

let's just pretend that awful thing never happened.

"What was her name?" she asks.

"Sunny," I say.

She winces.

"I know," I say.

"That is *so* sad!" she cries. "Everything about it is so sad!"

I nod.

"Does Vicks know?"

"Huh?"

"Never mind. I was just wondering."

I think about it, and I realize that, no, I've never told Vicks about Sunny. I guess it's always been easier to tell her the easy, fun stuff than the hard stuff. Is that my fault, or Vicks's?

There's a *zzzzt* and a click, and the hotel door handle twists open. *Speak of the devil.*

Vicks walks in, takes one look at Mel's made-up face, and says, "Dude, what happened to *you*?"

I get up quick from the bed, 'cause I am *not* letting Vicks see this almost-teary me.

"I'm hungry," I say. "You hungry, Mel? I think I'll go get us some snacks."

"Oh," Mel says. She looks anxious at the prospect of being alone with Vicks. "Okay. Or we could just order room service."

"Get some salt and vinegar chips," Vicks instructs.

203

"And some cherry Coke."

I say neither yes nor no. I slip past her and out the door.

"Well, um . . . be sure to charge it to the room!" Mel calls.

In the hall, which is spacious and pale gold and has pirate flags all over, I take a moment to get a grip. My face is hot. I try to blame it on Vicks, but I can't make it stick. Not as well as before.

Vicks's phone is still in my pocket from when Marco called. It's a hard, unnatural bulge, and I wonder if I'd get used to it if I ever get a cell phone of my own. I also wonder what Marco actually wanted to say. To Mel.

The *Veggie Tales* movie about Jonah drifts back to me. I saw it one Sunday when I was volunteering in the church nursery, and I wasn't lying when I said how good it is. And clever, like when Jonah tells the sinners from Nineva, who are played by French peas, to stop slapping one another with fish.

"I bring you a message from the Lord!" Jonah proclaims, and the peas gasp in fear. Jonah cocks his head toward the heavens, quivering with excitement at the prospect of informing the peas that they're going to be smited, and then his face falls.

"Oh," he says, all glum. "It's a message of encouragement. Sounds like a standard turn-and-repent to me."

204

Now that's good humor. Instead of getting to damn the peas to hell, he has to be all nice and help them do better, and it kills him. And the peas—and the fish-slapping—it's awesome, that's all. Even Vicks would like it, I just know it. She'd poke fun at how the veggies have to hop about, since they have no feet, but she'd be amused despite herself.

Eventually Jonah gets a little humbler, of course. He figures out he isn't quite as perfect as he thinks he is, and guess what? God just keeps loving him. He just keeps on loving him.

Well. If an asparagus can let go of his self-righteousness, then surely I can too. I pull out Vicks's phone and scroll through to "incoming calls." I select the most recent number, and I avert my eyes from the familiar PetSmart number above it.

"Hey, Marco," I say. "It's Jesse."

He stammers, expecting me to go off on him again, but that's not what's going on here. Mel's a good girl, that's all. She deserves some mercy.

20

VICKS

AS SOON AS Jesse's out of the room, I talk. "I know you said don't talk to you, but you didn't let me explain," I say to Mel. She starts to put her hand up like she wants me to be quiet, but I barrel on: "You just heard Jesse say something on the phone, and then I said I did something dumb, and then you jumped out of the car in the pouring rain without even letting me tell you how I *broke up with my boyfriend last night.*"

"What?"

"I broke up with Brady."

"No."

"Late last night. Jesse was so huffy over us being drunk and then she got her stick up her butt about virginity, I couldn't even start to tell her."

"But you sounded so happy about him when you talked to Ms. Fix."

"I'm a good liar."

"Did he call you, or what?"

My eyes are starting to fill. "I knew I shouldn't go on this trip. He never wants to see me again and he's running off with some cheerleader probably."

"Did he *say* he never wanted to see you again?" Mel asks.

"He didn't have to."

She looks at me straight on. "How long has he been your boyfriend?"

"It woulda been a year September sixteenth." I start to sniffle because I know Mel is so mad at me right now that she almost left me in the rain and here she is, dropping all her feelings and being sympathetic and I can barely stand her being nice to me when I'm such a wench.

I throw myself facedown on the bed for a minute and press my nose into the blanket, breathing its smell and trying not to weep.

Mel is silent.

"Would you mind—" I choke out.

"Oh, sorry." She stands up as if to go.

"No, would you mind buying me a steak?" I ask her.

I'm shaking from too much sugar and caffeine on top of a hangover. "I could use something real to eat."

"Um. Sure. Let me get my wallet. We can go downstairs."

"You can still be mad at me," I say jokingly, as I head into the enormous bathroom to splash some cold water on my face. "I just need you to feed me."

"It's fine. I shouldn't be mad. I have no right to be mad." Mel grabs her bag and the room card. "I'm not mad."

"You are mad. You jumped out of the car. You practically got a room without me. You wouldn't let me talk to you."

"Wait," says Mel. "I want to leave a note for Jesse." She grabs a pen and writes on hotel stationery.

"You are mad," I say again.

Mel doesn't react.

"Can I explain something?" I say.

"Let's not talk about it."

We leave the room and walk down a long hallway to an elevator.

I can't not talk about it. "Nothing happened with me and Marco."

"Oh. Okay." Her voice is flat.

"I couldn't explain with Jesse in the room." The elevator comes and we ride down to the lobby. "It's like, ten minutes before Marco called she was all grateful to me for getting her mom to back down, but then she turned on me. And once Jesse turns on you there's no way she's going to listen to anything you've got to say until she's good and ready. You saw how pissy she got about me not being a virgin. It's so fucked up. We should all be worrying about hurricanes and money and world hunger for God's sake if we've got to spend our time freaking out. Not other people's virginity when there isn't anything you can even do about it anyway."

While I'm talking, Mel and I walk through the hotel lobby, following signs that say JOLLY ROGER, FINE DINING. We step through a pair of double doors and enter an enormous atrium, slightly steamy, and a large indoor lagoon. Floating on the water is a sizable pirate ship, complete with a skull-and-crossbones flag and large trunks overflowing with fake booty. I can hear crickets, and look down to see a small black speaker, hidden in a bush.

It's beautiful. We can hear the storm, beating hard on the roof of the atrium, but in here it's 70 degrees and the lagoon is sweet and calm. We walk in silence across a small wooden footbridge and a hostess with a hook instead of a left hand gives us a seat right on the deck of the boat. I can look over the edge at the water.

I'm still waiting for Mel to actually seem interested in my explanation.

For her to yell at me or ask a question.

How can she not be interested?

How can she not be mad?

"Nothing happened with me and Marco," I say again.

She nods. But she's looking at her menu like the choice of appetizers is very engrossing.

"After you went to bed, I talked to Brady and we broke up—" I rush over that part, it's so hard to even say. "Then I did make a play for Marco. I tried to kiss him."

"Oh." Mel sets her menu down. "I thought you said nothing happened."

"It didn't. I was so mad at Brady. I mean, it wasn't about Marco. It wasn't about you, either. It was—I was trying to get back at Brady. Or prove to myself that all guys are skanky, or something. And I was so, so drunk, you know how much beer and wine coolers we had. And we didn't have anything to eat since those hot dogs. Anyway, I was talking to Marco about how you went on safari and—"

The waiter shows up. He is like ninety-five years old and wearing a green-and-yellow-striped vest, a black pirate hat, and an eye patch. His name tag reads ELI WEINBERGER, HOSPITALITY. He talks to us about a lunch special and promises to bring us bread. Mel orders Pellegrino for the table, instead of tap water.

Then Eli leaves, and I just stare at her.

When the bread arrives, Mel takes a piece but doesn't eat it. "What happened after the safari?" she finally asks.

"I did make a play for him, I did, which is so bad.

Because I knew you liked him, but I never planned to go after him, I would never plan something like that, like moving on the guy my friend likes. I wanted us to go to the party 'cause I could see he liked you too. But then I don't know what came over me."

"Oh."

"He pushed me off. We didn't even kiss, Mel. I swear, we didn't. It was just a stupid drunk move I made and it didn't lead to anything. I am really so, so sorry." I look at my hand and I have scrunched a bread roll into a tiny, tight ball. "I'm not usually such a horrible friend, I just got so drunk and I was so unhappy . . ."

Eli Weinberger returns and we order. I get a New York Strip steak with a baked potato and a side of garlic spinach. Mel gets a house salad and a diet soda.

"I don't think I'm ever having beer again as long as I live," I say. "Not even wine. Not even light beer."

"It's okay," Mel says.

"It's not okay. I feel terrible."

"I can't be mad at you for doing what I did myself."

"What?"

"Going after him. He was cute. I mean, he *is* cute. Girls must go after him every day."

Mel is being way too nice. I mean, I feel like a bad friend and a slut for doing what I did, even though there were *reasons*, and I don't expect her to just lie down and take what I did like it's the normal course of things.

211

Not one of my brothers would do that. If one of Jay's friends hit on a girl he liked, he'd storm around and throw things at the wall. Steve or Joe Jr. would yell in the guy's face. Penn would look daggers and give him the silent treatment. And Tully would haul off and hit the guy across the jaw.

"I knew you liked him," I tell Mel. "It was a shitty thing to do. And I know you're upset about it, because you jumped out of the car."

She shrugs and looks down at her bread plate, and I know she's telling me it's okay—but if I believe her, we're not going to be friends after this. She's going to quit the job at the Waffle and that'll be the end of it.

"Hit me," I say—surprising myself.

"What?"

"Hit me. Come on, right now."

"Vicks, you're crazy."

"No, I'm not. If you were a guy, you'd hit me. For messing with the girl you like. The guy. Whatever. If you were a guy, you'd sock me on the jaw. Wouldn't you?"

She wrinkles her forehead. "If I were a cowboy, maybe."

"Not a cowboy. Just an angry guy."

"If I were a *pirate*, maybe. Not a regular guy."

"Okay, so be a pirate-cowboy. You just said you were angry."

"I did not."

"Yes, you did. You said you'd hit me if you were a

212

pirate-cowboy. So you should hit me."

"I said, maybe. I'm not mad at you, Vicks. I'm just . . . mad at myself."

"For what?"

Mel sighs. "For thinking you were my friend. For trusting you."

"Don't give me that," I snap. "That's the most back-handed bullshit insult I ever heard."

"No, I—"

"You're telling me I'm untrustworthy. Fine, I probably deserve it. But don't tell me I'm not your friend anymore and at the same time pretend you're not mad at me, be-cause that's just stupid." I take a deep breath. "I just fucked up, Mel. Seriously. But that doesn't mean I'm not your friend. God, will you just hit me and stop with this fake 'mad at myself' shit?" I get up, and walk over to her side of the table. "Come on," I say. "Stand up."

"Vicks."

"You're not going to get over this unless you hit me. I can tell."

"I'm not hitting you," she says.

"Come on, pirate-cowboy. I'm twice your size. You're not going to do any serious damage."

"We're in a restaurant. Will you sit down?"

"No. Hit me."

"Stop it!"

"I'm not going to stop it. You need to do something

about this bad thing that happened." People are looking at us. "Come on," I say. "Old Joe would hit me. Old Joe would *want* you to hit me."

"Sit down!" Her face is turning red.

"No!" People are now actually pointing at us, but I don't care.

"Vicks!"

I'm yelling now. "I'm not sitting down! Stand up for yourself!"

And just when I don't expect it, Mel stands up and hits me. She's little, so it's more like she punches up at my jaw from underneath, and my teeth bang together and my head jerks back and the sound of the punch rings through my head. I stumble backward, and bump into the empty table behind me, scattering silverware.

I look over at Mel and she's looking back at me with wide eyes. She covers her mouth and I think maybe she's going to cry—but then I see she's laughing, and I start to laugh too.

Eli Weinberger toddles over, trailing a pimple-faced young woman with a bandanna tied around her forehead and a fake parrot on her shoulder. Her name tag reads ASHLEY HARRISON, MANAGER. "I'm going to have to ask you to leave now," Ashley says. "We have a no-violence policy in the Jolly Roger."

My mouth tastes like blood. Am I bleeding?

We're being thrown out of a restaurant.

That is so badass.

True, we're being tossed by a great-grandpa and a girl with a fake parrot on her shoulder, both wearing striped vests.

But still.

"Okay," I say. "Mel, we gotta go."

She nods, wiping tears of laughter from her face.

"We're going," I tell Ashley Harrison. "Just let her get her purse."

Mel wipes her eyes, digs her bag from under the table, then stands tall. "Don't cancel the order," she says to Eli Weinberger. "Would you mind just sending it up to the room?"

"Certainly," he says.

"Actually," says Mel, "would you change it to three New York Strips, medium rare, and add an order of potato skins? With sour cream."

"Yes indeed," says Eli.

"Thanks. We're in Suite 3012." Then she lifts her little chin in the air, and walks out of the restaurant.

I follow, holding my jaw.

As soon as we're out, we run across the lobby and collapse against the double door of the elevators, laughing in semihysteria. "I can't believe I hit you!" Mel says finally. "I'm sorry."

"Don't be sorry," I say.

"Okay, good . . . because I'm really not that sorry."

"I didn't think you were." I shake my head.

"You're okay, though?"

I rub my jaw. "I'll live. It's not like I've got a boyfriend to impress anymore, anyhow. No one's gonna care if my face swells up."

"I can't believe she actually said, 'We have a no-violence policy in the Jolly Roger.'" Mel giggles as we get into the elevator.

"We got thrown off a pirate ship!"

"I know!"

"Jack Sparrow, you are my kin!" I cry.

"We are so badass," says Mel, wiggling.

I sigh. "Poor Eli Weinberger."

"Yes, poor Eli," Mel repeats. "But I left him a tip on the table."

"You look pretty with the eyeshadow," I tell her. "I was only snarky about it earlier because I knew it had to be Jesse's handiwork."

"You guys have to make up. You're lucky to have each other," she says, her voice wistful. "You should just get over your sex-God fight already."

"If we're fighting about who's a bigger sex god," I joke, "I don't think it's any kind of contest."

"Oh, shut up."

"Anyway," I say, "I prefer the term goddess."

"Not stylin' pirate/sex goddess?"

"Or that."

Mel's lips twitch. "With a heavenly booty?"

I laugh. "With an extremely heavenly booty. Thank you so much for noticing."

21

MEL

I CAN'T BELIEVE I hit her. I mean really. I *hit* her. Vicks. In the face. *Pow!* It was like I was in a comic book. Pow to the jaw! Stars flying!

Okay, fine, there were no flying stars.

But it felt good. Both getting the anger out—and knowing how much my forgiveness mattered. How much *I* mattered.

Anyway, it's hard to be angry at her for hitting on Marco when I know how upset she was about breaking up with Brady. It's hard to see people as bad when you understand their reasons, I guess.

And maybe friends, even real friends, make mistakes.

Vicks and I are lying on our stomachs on the king-size bed watching HBO on volume ten to drown out the hum of the pounding rain, when there are three loud knocks on the door of the suite.

"Excellent," Vicks says, hitting mute on the remote control. "Hope they sent up steak sauce."

I slip off the bed, pad over to the door, and ask, "Who is it?" I look through the peephole, expecting our waiter, Eli. Or if not Eli, *someone* dressed like a pirate.

It's not Eli. It's Jesse. And her face is red, her eyes are slit, and she is scowling.

Uh-oh. I quickly open the door.

She pushes past me with three soft drinks between her hands and a bag of chips balanced on top of them. "Thanks a lot," she mutters and then dumps the food on the coffee table in the living room.

"For what?" I ask.

"For what?" she mimics. She drops into one of the red velvet chairs. "For taking off! What happened to you guys? Where did you go? I went to get snacks and I come back and you're gone!"

Vicks turns off the bedroom TV and relocates to where the food is. She claims the couch and rips open the bag of chips. "We left you a note," she says and then pops one in her mouth. "Why did you get barbecue? Didn't they have salt and vinegar?"

"Didn't you see the note?" I squeak. I point to the side

table where it's sitting in the exact same place I left it.

Jesse's arms are now crossed in front of her chest. "How could I have seen it from outside the door?"

"Why didn't you come inside?" I ask.

"Because I don't have a room key!"

Oh.

"I was standing out there knocking, like an idiot," she says, her voice getting higher and higher with every sentence, "and no one was answering. So then I thought you couldn't hear me so I knocked louder and then I thought maybe you went out for a few minutes. So I sat by the door. And waited. And then I went downstairs to ask for an extra key, but they wouldn't give me one. So I called upstairs and left you a message—"

I spot the flashing red light on the phone.

"—where I told you I would be waiting in the gift shop so come and get me. Which you didn't. Thanks. Thanks a lot. Thanks for ditching me."

"We're so, so sorry," I say quickly, walking to her side. "We didn't mean to ditch you. Vicks wanted a steak—"

"You went for food? When I was getting food?"

"We're sorry, we're sorry, can you just relax?" Vicks asks.

That was probably not the best thing to say, because Jesse picks up a Coke and throws it at her, narrowly missing her head. The can lands with a thud on the carpet.

Whoa. I think someone may need a little trip to my therapist, Dr. Kaplan.

"Are you crazy?" Vicks shrieks.

The three of us stare at one another—me and Vicks at Jesse, and Jesse at Vicks. It's some sort of showdown.

"I punched Vicks in the face," I say.

Jesse turns and looks at me blankly, apparently unable to understand what I have just said.

"It's true," Vicks says, putting her hand to her jaw. "She did. I told her to. Do you want to punch me too? Or did you just want to lob the Diet Sprite at me now?"

Jesse has the grace to look embarrassed.

"Your loss," says Vicks. "One-time-only offer."

"Vicks wanted me to express my anger," I explain.

Jesse gets up out of her chair. "Maybe . . . maybe I need to express my anger too."

Vicks puts up her barbecue-stained hand. "Too late. Offer expired."

"Fine, I'll just stay mad at you," Jesse says. She sits back down. "Cheater," she mutters.

"Well, guess what?" Vicks says. "I no longer have a boyfriend to cheat on. I broke up with Brady."

Shock registers on her face. "You did? When?"

"Last night."

"Why?" Jesse blinks repeatedly.

"Because it wasn't working. I don't want to be *that* girl."

"What girl? The girl with the great boyfriend?"

"No, the girl who chases a guy when he couldn't care less and makes an ass of herself."

"Oh. Wow. Okay. Are you—"

A double knock from outside interrupts her.

"Room service!" a man calls.

I jump to open the door, and a guy in red pants, knee-high boots, and a black pirate hat tilted rakishly on his head rolls a white linen–covered table into the living room. On it are three silver place settings with matching coverings. The scent of red meat makes my mouth water.

He wheels the food in. "Just leave the tray outside and someone will pick it up."

I sign for it and add a 25 percent tip.

"Thank you." I close the door behind him.

"What did you get?" Jesse asks.

"Three steaks. One for each of us."

"Oh. That was—"

The lights go out. Along with the sound of the TV and the hiss of the air conditioner.

I scream.

"It's just a power failure," Vicks tells me. "Because of the rain."

The room is black. I look at the red numbers on the clock to get my bearings—it must be backed up by batteries—and then slowly make out my surroundings. There's the couch, with Vicks on it. The wheeled-in table. The door to the bedroom. Light slithers through the openings in the drapes.

"Maybe it's a sign from God," Jesse says.

"Do you really think that?" I wonder. I fold myself into the seat next to her.

"Do I really believe it's a sign?" Jesse asks.

"Yes," I say. "Do you believe the lights going out was a sign from God?"

"Maybe. He might be trying to tell us something." She pauses, then adds, "You believe in God, right? I mean, Jewish people do believe in God." Uncertainty flickers across her face. "Right?"

I almost laugh, but I stop myself. "Yes, Jewish people believe in God, I just—I don't know what I believe." I consider. "I don't *not* believe in God. I don't know. It's just that . . . a lot of bad things happen in the world for there to be a God, no?"

Like hurricanes so bad they flood people's trailers.

Jesse shakes her head. "God has a plan for us. I know He does. But we could be on the wrong path without even knowing it, which is why sometimes bad stuff happens."

Wow. She's really sure of things. I hug my knees. "I don't know if I believe in a grand plan," I say tentatively.

"Then what do you believe?" she asks.

"Um. Maybe in free will? I mean, if I hadn't gotten

drunk, then I wouldn't have made an ass of myself and I might still be on speaking terms with Marco." I make a face. "My bad. Not God's."

Vicks laughs. "Well said." She opens the drapes to let in what little light there is with the storm. "Now, can we eat?"

"Yes!" Jesse exclaims.

I wonder if this means they've called a truce. A Vicks-broke-up-with-her-boyfriend-and-we-have-no-power truce.

I remove the silver coverings and pass along the plates of food and cutlery. The knives are miniature cutlasses, which is hilarious. Vicks brandishes hers and says, "Arrrr!"

But I'm still thinking about God. I wish I believed in signs from God. I wish I believed in God the way Jesse believes in God. Although Jesse's idea of God sounds kind of . . . harsh. Still, life would be a lot less scary if I believed there was someone looking out for me.

I spread my napkin onto my lap, and Jesse does the same.

"Will someone pass me a Coke?" she asks.

"Go find the one you threw at me," Vicks says.

"Careful," I say. "I know someone who opened a Perrier bottle that had been shaken and it exploded and pierced her eye."

Jesse winces. "Ouch. A friend?"

"A friend of my housekeeper's." I feel dumb as soon

as the words leave my mouth.

"You have a housekeeper?" Jesse asks. She uses her cutlass to cut into her steak, then brings a bite to her lips.

"Yes." Now she'll probably start again with her all-rich-people-are-going-to-hell speech. "She lives with us," I add, just to get it all out there.

She chews, swallows, and then says, "Lucky."

"Does she cook?" Vicks asks, her mouth full.

"Yes. She's good."

"Not as good as me though, I bet. At least not with a waffle iron." Vicks makes a show of getting off the sofa and reaching to retrieve the can Jesse threw. "Look: aluminum. Should be safe. But I'll open it over the sink."

I cut a piece of fat off the tip of my steak, and push it to the end of my plate.

When Vicks returns, she makes a show of handing the opened and intact Coke to Jesse. "Here you go, matey. Mini-explosion, but I contained it."

"Thanks."

I cut off another bit of fat.

Vicks scoots back to her spot on the couch. "Mel, are you going to eat or play with your food?"

I stare down at my plate. "Eat. I'm just getting rid of the gross parts."

"I like the fatty part," Jesse says, skewering into a bit of marbled meat. "Mmm."

"Yuck," I say.

"Try it," she says. "It's juicy."

"Pretend it's foie gras," Vicks says.

Yuck. "I never eat foie gras. My dad loves it though."

Jesse takes a gulp of her drink. "What's foie gras?"

"Pieces of fat," Vicks says, stuffing a handful of chips in her mouth. "Technically, goose liver. But basically, just really expensive pieces of fat." We're chewing in silence when Vicks says, "So, Mel."

"Yes?"

"Are you going to call Marco back?"

"What? No." I poke my fork into a slice of potato skin and hold it out. "Anyone want?"

"Sure." Vicks reaches over and takes it. "But he does have your phone."

Damn. Right. "Maybe we'll stop in on the way back. You'll wait in the car and I'll run in and yell, 'Hey, what's up! Remember me? Crazy drunken girl?'"

Vicks snorts.

Jesse shakes her head. "Why do you think you got so drunk?"

"Four wine coolers have that effect," I say.

"I realize that, thanks. What I meant is why did you let yourself get so drunk? And in the car you said that it wasn't your first time having too much to drink. So why is that? I think you're insecure."

No kidding.

"Hello, do we need a lecture now?" Vicks says, rolling her eyes.

"You're trying to bolster yourself with alcohol," Jesse tells me.

"Why, thank you, Faith Waters," Vicks quips.

"You're welcome," Jesse says.

I nod. "I know that's what I'm doing. But, see, without booze it's not so easy for me to just talk to people, you know?" I mean Marco, but I also mean the two of them. I watched them laugh and mess around all summer, and I remember how much I wanted to be in on the joke.

"That's bullshit," Vicks says. "You were flirting with Marco in the Opel. So unless you snuck some whiskey from the Wakulla Museum, you're full of it."

I think about what she said as we finish our meals. I was flirting with Marco in the car. I was definitely flirting with him on the grass. And I liked the girl on the grass. She was flirty, funny, confident—and pretty sober. Until she freaked out and ruined it.

When we're done, Vicks stretches her arms over her head and says she needs a nap. I place the mostly empty plates back onto the trolley, and roll it outside. The hallway is brighter than the room because of the pink emergency lights that line the floor.

When I get back, Vicks and Jesse are both in the bedroom, lying on opposite sides of the bed, like parents in a sitcom.

I close the drapes and then crawl into the spot between them and put my head on the flattish corner of Jesse's

226

pillow. She moves over so I can share.

The gesture makes me so happy, tears prick the back of my eyes.

Instead of speaking, we listen to the sound of the rain crashing against the windows.

"I wonder how long it'll last," I say eventually. Then I start to worry. "What if we're stuck here for days?" I ask. "Without power, without AC, with only barbecue chips to eat?"

"We'll sacrifice Eli Weinberger," Vicks says. "And eat him."

"What if," I continue, "when we finally get outside the place has been destroyed and turned into some sort of wasteland? What if—"

Vicks yawns. "What if we take a nap?"

The yawn is contagious, and soon Jesse and I are yawning big and loud and I'm feeling full and lazy. I bury my face into my half of the pillow.

At some point the power comes back on. Instead of waking up Vicks and Jesse, I quietly make my way off the bed and turn off the lights and TV. I close the drapes. When I go back to the bed, I see that Jesse has somehow rotated 180 degrees and Vicks is kind of cuddling with her feet. They look cute. And they can't fight when they sleep.

I worm back in and close my eyes.

22

VICKS

"WHAT TIME IS it?" Mel moans. "It feels like midnight."

"No way," Jesse says. "It can't be midnight, can it?"

"Brace yourselves, kids," I tell them, looking at my watch. "It's only four in the afternoon." I woke up about an hour ago and have been staring at the ceiling, trying not to think. But I let them keep sleeping, 'cause that's the kind of stylin' pirate/sex goddess I am.

"Are you kidding?" says Mel.

Jesse sits up. "Listen."

"What?" I am out of the bed, shoving my feet into my Vans.

"The rain has stopped!" Jesse runs over and pulls the drapes. Sun washes the room with light. All three of us shield our eyes.

Goes to show. We were expecting an enormous disaster—and now it's just over. We ate steak and slept through the worst of it.

"So what happens now?" I ask.

Mel starts bouncing on the bed. "Disney World!"

Jesse bolts up. "For real? Oh my gosh. Can we go to Epcot?"

"Sure," says Mel.

"Yay!" Jesse's face breaks into the first real smile I've seen in a long time.

Personally, I would be more up for Universal, but Jesse's got an Epcot dream and who am I to squelch it? My posthurricane resolution is: no more spats with Jesse. No teasing, no baiting her with comments that bring out the Christianpants. "Epcot!" I yell, and I start jumping on the bed too.

Jesse gets up and jumps, and we're all three jumping on the beds like we're five years old, yelling, "Epcot! Epcot!"

Then Jesse leaps off the bed and heads for the hall door. "Only—ooo, that means we're leaving the hotel, right?"

"Well, yes," I say. "That's the way it works."

Jesse giggles. "Okay, in that case I just need to make one quick call. Two minutes. I'm using your cell."

"What?" I ask. "You are being weird."

Jesse turns and winks—actually winks—at me. "Never you mind," she says, and then trots through the living room and disappears into the hallway, closing the door.

"I hope you're calling your mother!" I yell after her. But she can't be. She wouldn't be winking if she was calling Ms. Fix. I look at Mel, who shrugs and goes into the bathroom. Because she's Mel, she also shuts the door, and there I am, surrounded by doors and not a single answer.

I march into the hall.

"Uh-huh," Jesse's saying. "It has big pirate ships in front of it with black flags; you can't miss it."

"Who are you talking to?" I whisper.

She winks again.

"Sure, Marco," she says. "See you then."

She clicks shut the phone, and I piece it together. Jesse called Marco. He's coming here to surprise Mel.

I'm so glad, I squeal. "Yay, you!" I say, squeezing Jesse's arm.

"I know—yay, me!" she says. She hands the phone back to me. "He's like an hour away. I called him after I gave Mel her makeover."

"You did? That's so . . ." I don't know what it is. Sweet? Romantic? Totally old-school Jesse?

"He really likes her," my friend says, giggling. The friend I know and love. The friend who's full of funny little secret plans and ideas. The one who hangs lists in the staff bathroom. Buys armpit hair. Arranges for possible boyfriends to show up, a hundred miles from where last detected.

"That's so great," I tell Jesse.

"Yeah, I know," Jesse says. She stops giggling and kind of sucks her lips in. "So you're not, you know, going to be all weird about it?"

Because of my slutty Marco ambush, she means. A hot flush come to my face.

"Vicks, don't," she tells me. "I have a good scheme going here. You've spoiled enough; I don't want you spoiling this."

And F you very much, I think. Only, she's right. I might spoil it.

"He must think I'm the biggest bitch," I say. "How am I gonna look him in the eye?"

"Just be Vicks," says Jesse.

I'm wary. "Meaning what?"

"Meaning stand up tall like you always do and act like nothing ever happened. You've toughed out half a million things worse than this. "

Actually, that is entirely true. Like I toughed out my hot-dog gas.

Jesse says, "Remember when Abe walked in on you in the staff bathroom and your pants were down? You lived through that, right?"

231

"Don't remind me," I say.

"You didn't just live through it, you *rocked* through it. You made jokes; you didn't act embarrassed; you made the whole thing perfectly okay for Abe and everyone else, just by holding up your head. 'Cause Abe was just about to die of humiliation. I mean, geez Louise, he saw your hoohaa!"

"Okay," I tell her. "Enough with the memories. I'll be fine."

"Promise?"

"I promise. I'll just pretend I can't remember a thing. But help me if I suddenly go silent. If I go silent, you know I'm weirding out."

"Got it."

"Guys?" Mel sticks her head out the door. "What's up?"

Jesse bursts into the hotel room. "We're going to Epcot!" she cries. "What else?"

"Oh, excellent," Mel says. "Let me just grab my purse, eh?"

"No, no, no, no, no," Jesse says. "Not so fast, missy." She makes a show of sniffing Mel. "Um, you need to take a shower."

"I do?"

"You do." She propels Mel back inside the room. "We *all* do, but you first."

"Oh. Okay." Mel is cowed.

"What, you want me to lie?" Jesse says. "This is *Epcot* we're talking about. We can't go stinky to Epcot."

"I'll shower, I'll shower," Mel says, and disappears back into the bathroom. Jesse looks at me, and I look at her. We collapse into giggles.

23

MEL

A HALF HOUR later, the three of us have showered, changed, deodorized, and are finally ready to go.

"Wait, let me do your makeup again!" Jesse says.

What? "You already did my makeup," I say.

"I know, but you washed it off."

Jesse glances at the clock. "Please? Just a little. I want you to try it out in public."

"Yeah, Mel," Vicks says. "You definitely should."

Why are they being so weird? "Okay, sure. If you really want to. Thanks."

I kinda liked the makeup. I still felt like me . . . just

more defined. Less invisible. My eyes were more blue, my smile shinier.

Maybe Nikki doesn't have to be the only pretty one.

Jesse does a quickie application, and then we finally leave the room and take the elevator down to the atrium.

And I see him.

Marco.

Sitting on the lobby couch. The same smooth skin, black hair, brown eyes. A new rumpled and untucked black T-shirt, clean jeans. He's looking around the marble and gold lobby with a slightly baffled expression on his face.

I feel sick.

Happy.

Confused. Embarrassed.

Fluttery. I don't know what to do with my hands. "What is he doing here?" I ask. I notice Jesse and Vicks are nudging each other and grinning.

"He came to bring back your phone," Jesse says.

Vicks slaps her arm. "Don't tell her that, she'll believe you. He came to see you."

"But how did he know—"

"Jesse called him."

Jesse smiles at me. I don't know what to say. I want to turn around and go back to the room and hide under the covers. Then Marco spots us. Spots me. His face breaks into a huge smile.

He came to see *me*.

He likes me. Marco likes me. Me.

They called Marco. For *me*.

I straighten my shoulders. "Um . . . could you guys maybe give us a minute?" I say.

"Take your time," Jesse says. "We'll go get a glass of water. There's a pirate restaurant somewhere around here. . . ."

"Yeah, no, that's not going to happen," Vicks says. "We'll go to the gift shop. We can browse the gum."

I can barely hear them anymore because all I can hear is a *rush, rush, rush* in my head. Marco. Marco.

Marco.

"Hello there, Marco Exceptional," I say, trying to sound calm and sitting down beside him on the couch. Inside, I'm all twisty again. "I can't believe you're here."

He smiles. "I would have been here earlier but I had to wait till the hurricane was over. You're not really supposed to drive through those, you know." He bumps me with his shoulder, on purpose. "But yeah, I'm here."

"How come?"

He whispers, "That's classified information."

"It is, eh?" He's here. Even though I made a total fool of myself—he's here. How is that possible? "How did you get here? Is that classified too?"

"No, that's public," he says, smiling. "I took Robbie's

car. He felt bad about what he said to Jesse, so I guilted him into loaning it to me."

"What did he say?"

"You don't want to know. He can be a really ugly drunk."

I take a deep breath. "Yeah. Me too."

He raises his eyebrows. "Melanie Fine."

"What?"

"You might get drunk, but you could never be ugly."

I smile. "Well, I'm sorry I had too many wine coolers and slobbered all over you."

He laughs. "You didn't slobber."

"Drooled, then."

"Well, I'm sorry about not . . ." His cheeks turn red. "I just . . . I didn't want you to freak out this morning. Regret anything."

"I know," I say. "You were being a gentleman." I look up at him. "I heard about what happened with Vicks."

He twitches. "I figured. *Nothing* happened, though."

"I know. She told me."

He nods. "Good."

I look at my nails. I don't know what to say.

"See, hooking up with Vicks would have been something *I'd* remember the next morning and regret," Marco says.

"Yeah?"

"Yes." He leans over and whispers in my ear, his

breath warm. "I would have regretted ruining my chances with you."

I catch my breath. And then I turn my face to his—and kiss him.

His lips are soft, and he tastes sugary, like Certs. The sweetness goes right to my head, and the room is swirling and I'm smiling, we're both smiling and kissing and then kissing some more.

I nuzzle my head into his neck. "So," I say.

"So."

"What happens now?"

"You meet my parents?"

I giggle. "Very funny."

He laughs and then traces his finger up my arm, giving me the shivers. "I'm always getting ahead of myself."

"Really?"

"You still have a lot to learn about me, Marriott Mel. So where to?"

I kiss him once more. Then I stand up and pull him to his feet. "Ever been to Epcot?"

24

JESSE

OKAY, I KNOW the Eiffel Tower is in France. The real one, that is. But here I am in front of an exact replica, and weird things are happening in my chest. Because it's so big, and I'm so small.

All of Epcot is so big—there's Japan and China and Italy, Morocco and the United Kingdom. There is indeed a Canada, where Mel's from. (Poutine is not on the café menu.) There's Norway and Germany and France. There's pretty much any country you can think of, each with its own restaurant and place to walk around in and music that's foreign and strange, with instruments I can't identify.

"Goodwill Ambassadors" wave and smile from fake street corners, and I know from their name tags that their real homes are thousands of miles away. And they're, like, my age. They left their homes and families to come work at Epcot, and they don't even speak English. At least, the girl from Japan didn't. Her name tag read, HI, MY NAME IS YUKI! and when I asked her where the bathroom was, she said, "Excuse?" So I said, "*Bath*room. Toilet. Pee-pee wee-wee?" And she said, "Excuse?"

Thinking about it makes a well of loneliness open inside me, even though here I am at Epcot, a place I've wanted to come to since forever. I'm supposed to be having fun, and instead I'm worrying about a girl whose name is the same as "yucky." Then I wonder what *Jesse* means in Japanese. *Cabbage*, maybe. Or *bladder*. That would totally suck if you went somewhere far, far away, and your name turned out to mean *bladder*.

Over by the Eiffel Tower, but not right up next to it, is Vicks. She's positioned her body with one hand balanced in the air and the other planted on her hip. Her expression is animated and false, like, *Look at me, I'm a tacky tourist!* My job is to capture the moment with Mel's camera phone, making it look like she's propped against the tower itself.

"Take the picture!" she calls.

I'm trying, but I'm not sure I've found the right button.

240

She's leaning too far, losing the pose. "Take the picture, dammit!"

I click, and the screen captures a flailing Vicks, her sideways body blocking the tower. She lands smack on her butt, and I quickly snap that shot too.

"Jesse!" she complains.

I giggle. Then I want to cry. My emotions are nutso, going from one to the next to the next. I'm in Epcot, surrounded by colorful banners commanding us to "Experience the Magic!" and I'm coming unhinged.

Vicks gets to her feet and dusts off her butt. She tries to look mad, but she cracks up instead. Things are better between me and her, but they won't be totally right until there aren't any more secrets between us. I do kinda know that. Maybe 'cause of talking about Sunny.

"Let me see," Vicks says, walking over. She scrolls through the pictures and groans. "Jesse, you are worthless."

"I know," I say.

She looks at me oddly, and I get nervous. First she was smiling, and now she's all solemn, and I wish I'd kept my mouth shut. Or—and this is closer to it—I wish she could just know everything without me having to say it: about me wanting to be a better person, about all the ways I *do* feel worthless.

Mel and Marco head toward us through the crowd. They're holding hands. It's so dang cute. Marco ducks in to give her a kiss—it's like he can't get enough of her—and I think to myself that mousy little Mel's scoring a lot of kissing action all of a sudden. I saw the two of them going at it in the hotel lobby too.

"Any luck?" Vicks asks when they reach us. They'd gone on a mission to find funnel cakes, but there are no funnel cakes in their possession and no telltale powdered sugar smears on their mouths.

Mel shakes her head. "Alas."

"Alas," Marco echoes, teasing her. They smile at each other, and this—the two of them—is something right in the world, no matter what else is going on. I'm proud of my girl.

I'm also a little in awe of her, 'cause she's the one who bought our ridiculously expensive day-passes to Epcot. Seriously, they were like seventy dollars apiece! I was like, "Can't we get a one-hour pass?" But the ticket lady said no, and she wasn't even sorry.

Marco bought his own ticket, though. Mel offered, but he wouldn't let her. I'm warming up to him, the bum.

"Oh, well," Vicks says about the funnel cakes. She tosses Mel her phone.

Mel looks at the Eiffel Tower shot on her screen, grins, and shoves the phone in her pocket.

"We scored easy passes for Soarin', though," Marco says. "It starts in ten minutes—you guys want to come?"

"Is it one of those rides where you get jerked all around?" Vicks asks.

"It's like you're hang gliding in California," Marco says. "It looks awesome." He looks at Vicks when he talks to her, but his manner's not the slightest bit flirty. It's not mean, either. It's more like he's putting all the party stuff behind them, for Mel's sake.

Vicks is doing her part too. She's been acting as normal around him as she can, even slugging his shoulder when he made some boy-sports comment about the Marlins.

"I'll pass," she says. "Rides like that make me sick to my stomach."

"Really?" Mel says. She, like me, probably figured Vicks had an abdomen of steel.

"I am a delicate flower," Vicks informs us huffily, which makes Mel laugh.

"What about you, Jess?" Marco says.

I start to correct him—it's *Jesse*, not Jess—then stop myself.

"Nah," I say. "I want to watch the Chinese dancers." There's a sign on a wooden post that announces a six-o'clock performance of YEAR OF THE ROOSTER, PERFORMED BY THE ROYAL CHINESE DANCE TROUPE.

"Cool," Marco says. "Enjoy."

We make plans to meet up later in Morocco, and then Marco leads Mel toward the space ride. She smiles and gives us a backward wave.

Vicks and I stand there after they're gone. There's

noise all around—a guy hawking glow sticks, a woman talking in a too-loud voice about fireworks, a toddler squealing, "Mommy! Where's Ariel?"—but Vicks and I are mute.

Finally I say, "Want to watch the dancers with me?"

"No, thanks," she says. But she doesn't leave.

"You sure?"

She stares at nothing in particular. I want to talk to her about Brady, in a way that counts and isn't just words. But I can't, not till I've cleaned my own plate.

"Vicks," I begin. "Listen." She turns toward me, and my heart thumps. "I'm sorry, for being such a . . ."

"Tightass?" she supplies.

It stings. She reads it on my face and says, "Sorry. *Sorry*. I don't know what's wrong with me."

"Is it Brady?"

She doesn't respond.

"What happened that made you break up with him?" I press. "You catch him with someone else?"

"And how would I do that?" she says. "He's in Miami, remember?"

"Then what *did* happen?"

She sighs. "He felt tied down."

"Why?"

"'Cause he just did. I don't know."

"Did he *tell* you he felt tied down?"

"Indirectly," she says.

Yeah, I'm not buying it.

"Well, when you broke things off," I say, "did he just *let* you? Or did he say, 'No way, I'm not letting you go'?"

Vicks won't meet my gaze. "He doesn't care about me anymore. Otherwise we'd still be together, wouldn't we?"

"That's stupid," I say.

"Tell that to Brady."

"No, I mean *you're* being stupid."

Her cheeks color, and I'm immediately mad at myself, 'cause that didn't come out the way I meant it to and here we go again. Sheesh. If Mel hadn't come with us on this trip, Vicks and I would have killed each other by now for sure.

I touch Vicks' arm. "I'm sorry," I say. "Let's stop."

Her lip trembles, and she gives me a great big bear hug that throws me off balance. When she releases me, I stumble.

"What was that for?" I ask.

"'Cause I love you, even though you are a tightass."

She is shocking me on purpose.

"I am not—what you said I am," I say.

"Oh, you so are. But are you ever going to tell me why? I mean, seriously. This whole trip, you've been even worse than normal."

"Ha-ha," I say.

"Is it because I told Mel about Brady not calling me? Before I told you?" she says. "Because that's kind of pathetic, you know. Kind of fourth grade."

I swallow.

"*Kid*ding," she says. "Kidding! Because I probably . . .
I wouldn't have liked it if you did that to me." She puffs
out a breath. "So . . . sorry."

"Nah, it's not that," I say. "I mean, it was, a little—"
A lot, I think.

"So what is it? What's going on?"

My lungs tighten up, which is ridiculous, 'cause in my
heart of hearts I know I should tell Vicks about Mama,
that I *want* to tell Vicks about Mama. I should get it off
my chest, open up, reach out to others—isn't that what
Faith Waters would say?

But my thoughts are glue inside my brain. I *want* to
say it—*My mom has cancer*—but I can't. And it isn't 'cause
saying it out loud will make it true, because it already
is true. Which is the problem. At best, Mama will have
part of her body chopped off. (And where will they go,
those lumps of flesh? Into an incinerator? Into the hos-
pital Dumpster? And it won't be "lumps of flesh." It will
be lumps of *Mama*.)

And at worst? She'll die. *Mama. Could. Die.* People do,
every day.

Vicks is waiting.

"Um . . . ," I say.

"Yeah?"

I make a deal with myself. If the next person who

246

passes us is wearing Goofy ears, then I will tell her. There are a *lot* of Goofy ears in this place. Whole families have strolled by wearing Goofy ears.

"Jesse," Vicks says. "Whatever it is, it can't be that bad."

An old man slow-steps by. He's got a tube attached to his nose, and he's lugging a canister of oxygen. He's also smoking, which I'm sure is against Epcot policy. But he isn't wearing Goofy ears.

"What an idiot," Vicks says, taking him in. She pitches her voice louder. "Want a stick of butter with that? How about a nice blow to the head? It would be quicker!"

"You smoke too," I say to Vicks.

"I'm not on oxygen," she retorts. "*And* I'm not smoking at Epcot." She harangues the man some more. "I'm gonna call the Epcot police on you! I'm gonna do a citizen's arrest!"

"Stick it, girlie," the man rasps. He shoots her an arthritic bird, and Vicks gasps. Then she covers her mouth and does a giggle-snicker combo. She loves it that the old geezer shot her the bird. She *loves* it.

As for me, I blow out my breath in a slow exhalation. I am stuck in this body, just like Mama's stuck in hers and that old man is stuck in his. There is nothing I can do.

The dancers are going to be performing outside, that's what one of the Chinese Goodwill Ambassadors tells

247

me. Her name tag says NUYING, which in my head I say as "New Ying." Vicks and me have parted ways, and now here I am struggling to understand Nuying's English.

"Sit," she says, gesturing at the pavilion. To my right is a domed temple, and in front of the temple is a reflecting pool. Except for the tourists slurping frozen lemonades, I could honestly be in China—at least as far as I know. Nuying is nodding and smiling and saying some more things that seem to mean she truly wants me to sit down, so I plop my butt on the concrete. As I wait, I watch the people going by. I notice all the different body types. I read their T-shirts.

A guy with stringy hair wears a red one that says, "Fat People Are Harder to Kidnap," and it makes me think of Vicks, who would laugh.

A burly dad-type wears one that says, "My Horse Would Buck Your Honor Student," and this one makes me think of Mel, who I'm sure gets straight As. I scowl at the man 'cause that isn't nice, making fun of Mel like that. The man's wearing a cowboy hat, and he swaggers.

Next comes a rash of expensive Mickey Mouse shirts, followed by a sparkly Tinkerbell on an army green pre-faded tank. I like that Tink shirt. If one just like it fell out of the sky and into my lap, I'd wear it in a jiffy. Then I change my mind, 'cause I see one I like better. The girl wearing this new one is maybe twelve. Her skin is pale, and her shirt is black. In glittery pink letters, it reads, "Gone to My Happy Place. Back Soon."

A series of silvery chimes ring through the air, and the dancers come parading out. Except it turns out they're not exactly dancers. They're more, well, jump ropers. There are five of them: all guys, all lean, all Chinese. The youngest looks to be ten; the oldest, seventeen or eighteen. He's my age, and a guy, and he spends his days jumping rope. Ha.

On the edge of the pavilion, a stern Chinese lady controls the music. It blares from a boom box, its melody calling to mind dragons and a whole drawer of silverware dropped on the floor. The two oldest dancers turn the rope while the three younger ones jump together, all in a line. Then the three form a pyramid. They keep jumping, with the littlest guy perched on the shoulders of the other two. He grins. Everyone applauds.

I marvel as they pull off more and more complicated formations, like twists and throws and backbends, while all along the rope goes *thwap thwap thwap* to the beat of the music. If any one of them messed up, it'd be ugly. There'd be falling, very possibly broken bones. They're performing on concrete, after all.

I wonder what it would be like to be one of them, to have to trust folks with your life like that. On the plus side, there'd be someone to catch me when I backflipped over a swishing rope. On the minus side, I'd have to wear

a unitard. White spandex in this case, with green spar-
kles at the wrists and ankles. I can see their underwear
lines beneath the fabric. I'd have thought the manager
lady would have found a way to avoid underwear lines,
but obviously not. Maybe underwear lines aren't a big
deal in China?

I can also see the shape of their . . . you know. It's
spandex, after all.

People cheer. Music swirls. The oldest guy takes his
turn in the middle, jumping the rope while doing a handstand. A handstand! He makes it look easy, but my brain
is flabbergasted. He's jumping rope *on his hands*.

I wonder if he's happy.

I wonder what it would be like to have biceps like that.

Penn has biceps like that. Vicks says he does a lot of
lifting at his restaurant job. I have a moment where I
imagine Penn unloading boxes of canned goods from the
back of some truck, and then I blink and look around,
embarrassed. Where did that come from?

When the performance ends, I stand up with the rest
of the people who've been watching. It's odd. Everyone
claps, and I think they mean it, and then *blam*, straight-
away they're dusting off their behinds and adjusting
their Goofy ears and checking their watches.

"I am absolutely *craving* a Ding Dong," a red-haired
lady says to her husband. "You think any of these places
sell Ding Dongs?"

I feel like there should be more, somehow. More clapping, more appreciation. Or maybe I just feel bad for zoning out when that guy was jumping rope on his hands.

I bite my lip, then straighten my spine and stride over to him. The hand-jumping guy. His hair is spiky from sweat, and I'm struck by how black it is. Jet-black. True black. Blacker than Vicks's. Way blacker than Penn's, which isn't black at all, but a nice, soft-looking brown.

"Y'all were great," I tell him.

He looks up, surprised. His eyes are so dark, I can't find the pupils.

"*Shay-shay,*" he says. At least, that's what it sounds like. "Thank you."

"You from China?" I ask.

"Hong Kong," he replies.

"Oh."

He regards me quizzically. I like the way he holds himself, as if he's capable of things.

"Have you been to Hong Kong?" he asks.

"Me? Nah." What a question! Me, in Hong Kong! I blush.

"Hong Kong very pretty," he says. "Very . . . big. You should visit."

"Um, okay."

He smiles politely, and I know that the conversation has run its course. But I'm not ready to say sayonara. Or maybe . . . I don't know.

I think about Mel and Marco. I think about Vicks and Brady. I think I don't know *what* I'm thinking.

I put my hand on the Chinese guy's shoulder, and his eyebrows shoot up. I'm fluttery inside, veering on light-headed, but what the heck? We're all gonna die anyway. I stand on my tiptoes and kiss him. He pulls back. I follow. Then there's a shift in direction, and his mouth opens against mine. His lips are soft. Warm. Salty. Out of nowhere I think of trains.

"Ninmen!" the boss lady shrieks, followed by a flurry of furious Chinese syllables. They pelt us like stones. We jerk apart.

"Ni bie! Dongshen!" Boss Lady's barreling toward us, and I don't need to speak Chinese to know she's saying to leave crazy American girl alone, or else.

My Chinese guy shoots a glance in her direction, then clasps my hand and pumps it up and down. *"Sigh jee-ahn,"* he says earnestly.

My shoulders hunch. "I don't know what that means."

"Good-bye," he says. "It means good-bye."

Boss Lady is upon us, scolding and scolding. She yanks him away and smacks his arms, back, and head. It's a slap fight, only he's not slapping back. He's cowering and looking pleased with himself while his friends crack up.

Well. People are staring, and my face is flaming. I quickly walk away, wondering what in heaven's name

I was hoping to accomplish with that little display.

When I'm a good twenty yards from the pavilion, I allow myself to peek back. The temple still stands, but the Chinese dancers have been herded into their dorm. I hope my guy doesn't get whipped or nothing.

The temple's reflection shimmers in the pond, like something from another world.

"*Sigh jee-ahn,*" I whisper.

25

VICKS

IT'S SO PRETTY here, it almost feels wrong. Even on the nicest Florida beach, like when we visit Grandma Shelly and drive up to Hollywood, you've always got some garbage left in the sand, a couple of ugly porta-potties clogging up the view, something that reminds you—yeah, this may be beautiful, but it's the real world too.

In Epcot, there's nothing like that. No telephone wires, no garbage, no radio blasting, no dead seagulls. Here, everything's so perfect that it's only when you look at the *people* that you can remember anything ugly or sad is even possible. Like there's a woman yelling at her son because he dropped his croissant on the ground right after she gave it to him. And there's a guy in a wheelchair who's missing both his legs. And a man so heavy it looks like it hurts him to walk. And a little girl crying because she's tired, and her dad telling her he won't pick her up because she's a whiner.

There are puddles on the ground from the storm, and the warm early-evening air has a wonderful, just-rained smell. But inside my ribs is a ball of crushed ice.

France, where I am, is only about two minutes away from China, where Jesse's watching some guys in spandex skip rope. Which I am not in the mood for. I'm not in the mood for much, since I will probably never have another boyfriend in my life and might just die from the cold as it spreads from my chest down my arms, into my fingers, which will turn blue and become paralyzed. Then my legs will freeze to icicles and drop off, and then finally I'll just expire, right here in Epcot, and they'll cart me away through underground tunnels so that the sight of my blue, rigor mortising body doesn't disturb the other visitors during the firework display.

I'd actually like to stay alive for the fireworks. I still remember the Magic Kingdom light show from when Grandma Shelly took me and Penn to Disney, back when I was like six.

But I may not make it, on account of the cold spreading.

This cold is a no-Brady feeling, I know that. It's been there in my chest ever since we broke up, but everything was so crazy with the party and Marco, and fighting with Jesse, and Mel, and the storm—I couldn't really pay attention to it. Now I'm somewhere where I'm supposed to be happy, where all the badness of the world is washed away or at least camouflaged by innovative placement of decorative bushes—and I've got nothing to distract me. No angry Jesse, no driving in the rain, no toll booth, no other drama. So the cold in my chest is colder than before, and I keep noticing things like that tired grandmother carrying two huge shopping bags while she follows a pair of twin twelve-year-olds, who are complaining how Epcot's not as fun as the Magic Kingdom.

In France, there's a wine shop. A fancy wine shop—not like the aisles of Publix, which are just supermarket shelves filled with wine, but a tiny, gourmet wine shop like it's off a street corner in the real Paris, maybe big enough to hold only six people. The bottles look expensive, rich dark greens with antique labels. Next door is a bistro, Les Chefs de Paris, and I look at the menu.

There's no French food in Niceville, unless you count Au Bon Pain and a bakery that sells some pretty decent cakes and calls them gateaux. My family goes out for Italian sometimes, and sometimes Mexican and P.F. Chang's, but we'd have to drive an hour to find a real French bistro like they write about in the cooking magazines. And here it is. I mean, I know it's fake, and maybe the small bit of happiness I'm feeling at reading the menu is fake too—but right now, I'll take whatever I can get. Besides, the food is real, right? It may be a fake bistro under a fake Eiffel Tower, but the steak au poivre is still steak au poivre.

I don't have the money to eat here, but I go in and ask if they'll let me use their bathroom—and they do. While I'm in there I think, *Je suis une mademoiselle* oops *jeune fille française* and *je* put on lip balm in *le mirroir de la toilette* oops *le* WC and *après le* lip balm *je* will go meet my hot *amour français* who will drive me around on *le* motorbike *et donne-moi beaucoup de fleurs* because *je suis une jeune fille très glamoreuze*. Like I have a different life. Like I'm the kind of girl who eats in bistros. Or even better, like I'm the kind of girl who cooks in bistros, then goes home through the streets of Paris.

Next door to the restaurant is a gift shop. I go in and spot the expected Eiffel statues and little Mickeys wearing berets, but there are also cookbooks. Lots of them, with beautiful photographs of France and French dishes like escargot and mussels. A small, plainer-looking one is called *Bistro Cooking*, by Patricia Wells. On the cover, it says, "Recipes inspired by the small family restaurants of France celebrate a return to generous, full-flavored cooking. Bistro is warm, bistro is family."

I want to buy it. I want to buy two, actually. One for me, and one for Penn, for when he goes to culinary school. It'd be nice to have something to give him. Like a send-off, even though the school is only two towns over. Anyway, I only have three bucks in my pocket. The book costs $10.99. So it's not happening.

I flip my phone open and hit speed dial number three. Penn answers on the second ring.

"It's me. You will never believe where I am right now."

"Where?"

"Guess."

"Just tell me it's not a police station."

"It's not a police station. Although we were at the world's smallest police station yesterday." I laugh. "From that *Fantastical Florida* book, remember?"

"You went to that?"

"And to Old Joe Alligator."

"I'm jealous. Who's *we*?"

"Jesse, me, and this girl Mel from the Waffle."

"Jesse with the long blond hair?"

"Penn, why do you always act like you don't know who Jesse is? Now guess where I'm calling from."

"I don't really have time for this," Penn complains, and then adds: "Are you on the beach?"

"No, but there's water. There's a river."

"Are you—"

"I'm in Paris! In Epcot. I called because I want to buy

you this present and I don't have enough money, so the next best thing is to call you and tell you. A Parisian present."

"You're at Disney?"

"Mel paid to get us in. Don't you want to know what the present is?"

"Where are you guys sleeping? Are you driving back tonight?" asks Penn, and suddenly it seems like he's not my coconspirator, not the other youngest Simonoff—but a guy living on his own and working a job and worrying about his stupid little sister.

"I broke up with Brady," I blurt.

"Oh, man."

"I'm never gonna see him again and I think my life might be over, but I'm shopping at this cute little store and there's a present I wanted to get for you. So I'm thinking of you, my favorite brother, in my final moments. Now, don't you want to know what the present is? Or what it would be, if I wasn't broke?"

"Listen, Vicks," says Penn. "I'm sorry about Brady, but I'm at Chang's right now and I got tons of snap peas to prep before the dinner rush starts. I'm not even supposed to be answering my phone."

"What?"

"I'm working. I'll call you later if I can," says Penn. And hangs up.

Because he's got a life. Because he knows where he's

going and he's not even that curious what the present I want to give him is. Because he doesn't need me like I need him.

We all meet in Morocco at eight, get our pictures taken on Mel's camera phone together with some second-rate characters that I think come from *Pinocchio*. (Mel says all the good characters like Pooh Bear live in the Magic Kingdom.) We ride a boat across the river. Everyone goes on a crash-test ride except me, because I had quite enough worry about crashing while driving in the hurricane, thank you, and then Mel takes us to eat in a restaurant filled with such huge tropical fish tanks, it seems like we're underwater. I have salmon with a papaya relish I've never had before, salad made with beets and grapefruit, and key lime pie.

It is nice not to be in the real world. To be somewhere sanitized, eating papaya salmon and pretending nothing can touch you. It helps you forget.

After dinner, we watch the late-night firework-laser show over the water, and Jesse and I walk away to let Marco and Mel be alone.

I can't help thinking about Fourth of July, when Brady bought fireworks and we set them off together in his family's backyard with some of our friends from school. Brady is always the one who gets the idea to do something cool, the one who buys not just fireworks

260

but chips and a big, slightly nasty-tasting creamy cake from Publix, one that looks like a flag, and has all the guys come over to his place. He even made onion dip, with dried soup and sour cream. And called Jesse himself to invite her.

And he bought me sparklers.

That hardly sounded like him on the phone the other night, talking about his English paper with red marks all over it, and being nervous about the anthropology quiz and all. Usually, it's Brady who's on top of things. Not that he's such a top student or anything, not all As, but he always keeps it together. Keeps people together. This time, it sounded like he was falling apart.

I'm actually glad Jesse's next to me while I'm watching the fireworks. If I was alone, the cold in my chest would be more than I could stand.

"I don't want to go home," I tell Jesse. "I can't go to Miami, and I really don't want to go home." I don't say this part out loud, but I don't want to go back to the empty Simonoff house, and I don't wanna see Penn, not after that call. I can't face my school friends, either, after breaking up with Brady. They'll be too sympathetic, too sorry for me, while my parents won't be sympathetic enough since they don't think I should date anyone long-distance anyway. Plus, Niceville is too empty without Brady. It's just days and days of no Brady picking me up after work, no Brady goosing me in the 7-Eleven check-out line, no Brady's sweatshirt lying on the floor of my room, no Brady, no Brady.

Whatever it is I need right now, it's not at home.

"I hear you," Jesse says. "Home is not my happy place either." She makes a face. "But then, I guess you knew that already."

"I got a clue."

"I am so *not* tired!" Jesse cries, trying to change the mood. She bounces with her hands on the railing overlooking the water. "We should go somewhere. Not home, not the hotel, but *somewhere*. I don't think I'm gonna sleep for hours and hours."

"Me neither."

"So where should we go?" Jesse muses. "I mean, we've been to China, France, and Morocco. Is there anything in Florida that can top those places? I don't think so. It's all gonna be downhill from here."

I think for a moment. "I know the place," I tell her.

"Where?"

"Coral Castle."

Jesse squints, remembering. "You mean that place the sad-sack guy built when his girlfriend dumped him? The one you were reading about in the car?"

I nod. "No one knows how he built it either. Like he didn't have any helpers or anything. Not one. He lifted thousand-pound pieces of coral in the middle of the night, all alone."

"Wow."

"It's like a heartbreak miracle palace," I say. "Don't you think we should go? I think we should go."

Jesse puts her arm around me. Like she understands.

26

MEL

"SO," I SAY to Marco, holding on to him and not wanting to let go.

It's late, it's hot, it's muggy, and the two of us are standing in the hotel parking lot. Vicks and Jesse have gone up to the room to pack our stuff so we can visit the castle of heartbreak. Or maybe it's the castle of love. Or both.

"So," Marco says. He untangles himself from me, takes my hand, and leans against the driver's side of Robbie's navy blue two-door Civic. "I had a great night."

"But was it Exceptional?"

"No, it was Fine. But Fine is better than Exceptional."

My cheeks hurt from so much smiling. We smiled while screaming on rides, we smiled while holding hands. We smiled while kissing.

After dinner, I gave Marco a special tour of Canada. I even sang the national anthem for him.

"Sure," he said. "You can sing as well as act. But can you dance?"

I contemplated busting out my old Britney moves, but decided that that could wait for another day. Instead, I found us a place to sit for the fireworks, while Marco went to get cotton candy.

When I felt an arm around my shoulder, I assumed it was him, but instead it was a seven-foot blue and orange Goofy. He tapped his heart with his giant white glove and made a swooning motion.

I burst out laughing.

"What's going on here?" Marco said, joining us, a huge pink cotton candy in hand. "Goofy, are you trying to steal my girl?"

Goofy nodded vigorously.

Marco thumped his chest. "Then it's only fair to warn you that I have an orange belt in tae kwon do."

I giggled and tore off a chunk of the cotton candy. "Um, isn't that the lowest belt you can have?"

"It most certainly is not," he scoffed. "It's the second lowest."

We laughed and watched the fireworks explode into stars and triangles.

When he took my hand, I warned him that my fingers were sticky.

"Good," he said. "Then this time you won't let go."

Now we're saying good-bye. Not good-bye forever, just good-bye for tonight.

"I'll speak to you . . . soon," I say hesitantly. I rub the back of his hand with my thumb. It's soft, the back of his hand.

"Yes, soon," he says, and nuzzles me back into him. I breathe in deeply and try to commit his minty scent to memory. "Do you guys have to drive tonight?" he asks. "Why not sleep in the pirate hotel and leave in the morning?"

"The castle is four hours south of here, and then we still have to drive nine hours home tomorrow." I shrug. "What can I say? It's a road trip. We're wired. We want to move."

"Okay. Are you driving?"

"Me? No. I hate driving. But don't worry about us. Honestly. We'll be fine. We had a nap. And Jesse's a good driver."

"I'm not worried about the driving. I'm worried about you stumbling upon another keg party."

"Ha-ha."

He wags his index finger. "And stay clear of hitch-hikers."

I giggle. "I hear they're bad news. You're sure you don't want to use the hotel?" I ask. "It's already paid for. You can crash there and drive home tomorrow."

"Thanks, but if I don't get this car back tonight, Robbie's going to kick my ass."

"I bet you and your orange belt could take him."

He poses his arms to look like a karate chop. "I'll call you when I get to Robbie's. Let me give you my number though in case you need anything."

He rattles off the numbers and I program them in. "And that's Marco . . . Exceptional?"

He laughs. "Stone."

"That's not a last name, it's a noun," I say, smiling as I type. "Want my number, Mr. Noun?"

"I already got it, Ms. Adjective. I called my phone with yours to get it in my call display."

Aw. "You did?"

"I had to. In case you pulled another Houdini on me."

I kiss him hard on the lips before it's his turn to disappear.

After an hour of driving, we realize we are about to run out of gas. Jesse follows a rest-stop sign off the highway into what looks like the middle of nowhere. Seriously, there are no houses anywhere. There are no streetlights either. There is only swampland. I'm amazed when she pulls up to an ancient Exxon with one sixty-watt bulb blinking above the sign. I swipe my credit card and Jesse pumps while Vicks cleans the windshield. I find the washroom. The smelly, lockless washroom. I somehow manage to squat, pinch my nose, and hold the door closed simultaneously.

When I get back, Jesse's in the driver's seat, Vicks takes shotgun, and I climb in the rear. We are a well-oiled machine. I reach for my iPod, scroll through "songs" until I find the one I'm looking for, then punch the "select" button. "Spirit in the Sky" rocks the Opel.

Jesse catches my eye in the rearview mirror and grins, knowing I picked it for her. I grin back.

"I hope you know how to get back to the I-95," I say as we speed down the dark road. "Because I sure don't."

"You're gonna have to stop calling it that," Jesse tells me. "No *the*. Just I-95. Better yet, just ninety-five."

I laugh. "I can't help it! Maybe it's a Canadian thing?"

"A Canadian thing, *eh*?"

I kick my shoes off, adjust my pillow, and let my mind wander back to Marco. Adorable Marco. Sweet-heart Marco. Sexy Marco.

"I think you're going the wrong way," Vicks says.

"Don't worry," Jesse says. "I know where I'm going."

Vicks looks out the window. "I think you should turn around."

"I think you should chill." She glances at Vicks. "Now who's being the tightbottom?"

"Tight*bottom*? Did you just call me a tightbottom?"

I don't really care about directions and tight bottoms. Well, except maybe Marco's tight bottom, tee hee. Who cares which way we're going when Marco likes me?

Vicks leans way over in the front seat. When she sits back up, she's got the map. She unfolds it and says, "Dude, I seriously think we're going west instead of south. We should have seen a sign to get back on the highway by now."

"Let's give it a few more minutes."

I flip open my phone to see if he's called and I missed it.

"I think you should turn around," Vicks says.

Jesse cranes back her head. "Mel, what's your vote?"

He hasn't called. Not that I expected him to call so soon. But he'll call tonight. I think. I wonder when I'll see him again? This weekend? Is that too soon? I don't want to seem like I have nothing else to do. Maybe he'll drive up to see me next weekend?

"Mel?" Vicks says.

I snap to attention. "Yes, Tight Bottom?"

"Ha-ha," Vicks says. "Don't you think we're lost?"

"Um . . . no?"

Jesse laughs. "Put that in your pipe and smoke it, baby!"

"Like she knows anything," Vicks says. "She's too busy daydreaming."

"Mel and Marco sitting in a tree," Jesse sings. "K-I-S-S-I-N-G. First comes love, then comes marriage—"

"Someone pass me the iPod," Vicks grumbles. I hand it to her and she cuts off "Spirit in the Sky," replacing it with "Bad Day."

"Aw, man!" Jesse says. "You are *such* a grouch." She sighs in a very aggrieved fashion. "Anyway, Marco and Mel are adorable together."

Yes! Yes, we are. Marco and Mel. Like M&Ms. "Really?"

"Oh, definitely," Jesse says. "So what happens now? Are you guys going out?" She does a one-handed air quote on the words *going out* while continuing to hold the steering wheel.

"Don't do air quotes," Vicks says to her. "They're cheesy."

"The word *cheesy* is cheesy," Jesse retorts. This time she takes both hands fully off the wheel for her air quotes, before putting them back. "So, Mel, are you guys going to be together?"

"I guess," I say. "I mean, we didn't discuss it, but yeah." I think.

Vicks twists to look at me. "You're going to have a long-distance relationship?"

"I guess so."

"Why would you want to go through all that with someone you just met?"

Jesse slaps her hands on the wheel. "Vicks!"

"Yeah?"

"What kind of a thing is that to say? She's in the love bubble! Why would you try to burst her love bubble?"

"I'm not trying to burst her anything," she spits out, facing the road again and waving her arms above her head. "She just has to be realistic about it, that's all. What happens when he doesn't call one Tuesday night? Is he at the library? Is he having sex with someone else? That's what's going to go through her mind. Her first instinct will be to call him. When he doesn't answer, she'll want to call him again. And again. And then she'll become stalker calling girl. Is that what she wants?" She turns to me. "Is that what you want?"

I sink in my seat. "Um . . ."

"Your issues are not Mel's issues," Jesse says.

"You have to be tough to get through it," Vicks says. "And Mel, you're a sweetheart and all, but you are *not* tough. You're going to get chewed up and spit out like a piece of gum."

271

She's right. My heart starts to beat a bit faster, and I finger the phone. I am not tough. I am not tough enough. I have already checked my phone three times since I got into the car to see if he's called. That's how I'll spend my days—checking and rechecking my phone. I'll sleep with the phone. Go to the washroom with the phone. If Vicks couldn't handle dating long distance—tough, über-confident Vicks—what chance will I have?

"Mel, ignore her," Jesse says. "You guys will do great. Bet he comes down to visit you this weekend."

"Maybe," I say, but the panic in my mouth tastes like vinegar. He could change his mind. He could meet someone else he likes more than he likes me.

Jesse whistles. "Wait till he sees your house."

See my house? I try to keep my feet planted on the floor of the car. Yes, I suppose he'll have to see my house eventually. Meet my family. Great. "Wait till he sees my sister. He'll probably take one look at her and fall in love or something," I half joke.

Jesse shakes her head. "Why would you say that?"

"See?" Vicks asks. "I told you. She's too insecure."

"I was kidding," I say.

"I don't think so," Jesse says.

True. I guess I wasn't. But I don't say anything. I flip open my phone to see if he sent me a text.

"Mel, you are way prettier than your sister," Jesse says.

272

"Whatever."

"You are. Especially if you wear a little lip gloss like I showed you."

"Look," I say, my heart now racing. "If it doesn't work out with Marco, it doesn't work out. It doesn't matter." I feel myself closing up, closing in. I pull my legs into my chest. I close my phone.

"Don't say that!" Jesse says. "If you don't give it a chance, it'll never work out. You have to have a positive attitude." Her voice is suddenly squeaky high. "You have to. You *have* to."

Vicks is shaking her head. "You can't just drive forward blind, Jesse. Be realistic. Relationships end. People go away. Even when you don't want them to. And there's nothing you or anyone can do to stop it."

Jesse tightens her fingers on the steering wheel. "That's not true. That's just not true."

"Well, yeah, it is," Vicks goes on. Doesn't she realize she's pushing Jesse's buttons? "Sometimes the end of the road is the end of the road, and a positive attitude isn't going to fix it. Nothing can. You can't. I can't. Even 'God'"—now she makes air quotes—"can't. Now, *please* turn around. We're lost."

Jesse jerks the steering wheel to the right, and I almost scream as the car swerves to the shoulder of the road. But I don't. Instead, we're all silent as she steps on the brake, grinding the car to a halt. I'm expecting her to make a U-turn, but instead, she throws the gear into park.

"What the hell?" Vicks asks.

Jesse unsnaps her seat belt, opens the door, and takes off into the dark.

I guess the truce is over.

27

JESSE

"OH MY GOD," I hear Vicks say. "You have *got* to be kidding me." Her voice carries through the open window to where I'm standing, which is ten feet from the car in a desolate patch of nothing. To my left is the road, unlit and utterly deserted, and to the right is a short dip in the dirt and then a swamp, which is swampy and full of swamp creatures. If Vicks was standing beside it, I'd push her in, I swear I would. I am done with that girl. I'm done trying and I'm done curbing my tongue and I am just plain done!

"Don't you use the Lord's name in vain!" I yell into

the nothingness. I swat at a mosquito that has landed on my leg.

"God God *God!*" Vicks yells back.

"Saying His name means you believe in Him!" I retort. And maybe that doesn't make sense, but it's what MeeMaw taught me to say when someone uses "God" or "Jesus" as a curse.

I thought me and Vicks were good. I thought we'd worked things out. But me and Vicks aren't good, and *this* is the end of the road.

"Go talk to her," Mel says. "She's upset."

"Gee, you think?" Vicks says. Her tone says she's let go of her friendly feelings toward me just as quick. "She's been upset the whole freakin' trip. She's been a pain in the *ass* the whole freakin' trip." She raises her voice. "She's been a pain in *God's* ass! And Mary's ass! And Jesus's sweet white ass!"

Ohhh, she makes me mad. I stalk farther into the night and wish I could just—*poof!* Disappear. And end up in Canada, and eat that cheese curd gravy thing that Mel talked about, and Mama would be there too, and everything would be fine. Better than fine. Clean and pure and new, like a child rising from the baptismal trough, water raining down her pretty white dress.

A sound chokes from my throat. I don't mean for it to, but it does what it wants.

"*Go,*" I hear Mel say to Vicks.

"No way," Vicks replies. "You taught her the whole stomp-out-of-the-car-and-throw-a-hissy routine. You go."

"Hissy? I didn't throw a hissy!"

"Excuse me?" Vicks makes her tone thin and reedy. *"Let me out this instant. Stop the car or I'll . . . I'll . . . throw a mango at you! I will!!"*

She is so ugly. She is so ugly to everyone. No wonder Brady let her go.

"No wonder Brady let you go," I say out loud.

Mel sucks in her breath. I hear the sound from two yards away. I also hear another sound, coming from the swamp. A splash, followed by a quack.

"Did you hear that?" Mel says.

"What do you think?" Vicks says, pissed.

"No, I meant—"

"Fuck it," Vicks says.

The car door opens and then slams. I don't turn around. From the swamp comes another quack, only it's more of a squawk. It's abruptly cut off, and not as if the squawker had any say about it.

There's something out there. I know it at the base of my spine.

"You're a pain in the ass," Vicks says when she reaches me. *"My* ass. But okay, I'm here. You want to tell me what I did *this* time?"

I burst into tears.

"Jesse . . . ," Vicks says, suddenly uncertain.

277

The noises I'm making are ugly. They rip out of me. They howl.

"Oh, Jesse, Jesse . . ." Vicks flails her arms. She doesn't know what to do, and it scares her and me, both. "Jesse?"

"My mom won first prize in a wet T-shirt contest." My body heaves. "She squeezed into her tightest T-shirt and stuck her chest out and let some stupid, drunk rednecks spray her with a hose!"

"What are you *talking* about?"

There's a swamp sound again—something snapping— and Mel calls, "You guys? I'm hearing creepy noises, and I wish you would come back to the car. I really do!"

"I called her a whore," I say. "What kind of daughter am I? What kind of daughter is so ugly? And what if God . . . what if He . . ."

"This is what you've been so freaked out about?" Vicks asks. "A wet T-shirt contest?"

"What if it's *me* He's punishing, and not her?"

Vicks pulls me into a hug. It's that same big bear hug from Epcot, and she doesn't get it, she still doesn't get it, but I let her rock me back and forth.

"Jesse, you are a piece of work," she says. "Punishing you *how*? By making me be such a bitch?"

"By giving her cancer," I say, my voice breaking. But dang, it's good to say it out loud. Good and terrible and glorious and wrong. I feel Vicks stiffen, and I press hard against her.

"Your mom has cancer?" she says.

I nod into her shoulder.

"Your mom has *cancer*?"

I nod again.

"Uh-*huh*," she says, almost like she's pissed. "And all this time, while we've been worrying about boys and hot tubs and tattletale pirate waiters . . . ?"

I sniff in a glob of mucus.

"Oh, *sweetie*," she says, and I realize that if she *is* pissed, it isn't at me. "No wonder you've been such a tightbottom."

I laugh, and then I sob, and then all kinds of slop is released from inside me, bubbling up and out, 'cause sure enough, this is what I needed: to tell my best friend, Vicks, that my mama's real sick. It's crazy how much of a relief it is, even though Mama's cancer is still there.

I'm vaguely aware that Mel has joined us, that above my head, Vicks is explaining the situation. *Mother. Cancer.*

Mel is asking, "Is it stage one? Stage two? Because there's so much that can be done. Has she started chemo?" The sound of her voice is teeny-tiny.

"Shhh," Vicks says, stroking my hair. Her voice is a river. I'm a baby in her arms. "Shhh."

The air is punctured by another squawky peep. It's coming from the swamp, only it's closer now. Much closer.

"Oh, crap," Mel says in a peed-her-pants kind of way.

Vicks goes rigid. I can feel the alarm in her body, the way her muscles change. "Jesse, don't look."

I twist from her grasp and turn around. There's a bird—no, a duck, a baby duck—fluttering up the bank, and behind it, not ten yards away, is an alligator. An enormous alligator that's alive and not stuffed and surely ten feet long, shuffling toward us in the light of the Opel's headlights.

"Oh crap, oh crap, oh crap," Mel says.

"Walk," Vicks commands. "Don't run. Just get to the car."

The baby duck flaps its tiny baby wing-nubs—I crane to see, even as Vicks pushes me forward—and I think, *Where is its mother? Where is its mother?*

"*Move*, Jesse," Vicks says.

"We have to save it!"

"Are you insane?" Her sweat stinks of fear.

The gator reaches the top of the bank, and the duckling squawks and patters in a frantic zigzag. Mel is almost to the car; she runs the last few feet and yanks open the door. The gator swivels its massive head.

"Holy fuck," Vicks whispers.

"Hurry!" Mel whimpers.

Vicks jerks my arm, but I wrench free and fast-walk toward the duck. The gator lashes its tail. His pupils are slits.

"Jesse!" Mel shrieks.

Gators can run thirty miles an hour. I am a Florida girl, and I know this. So when the gator lifts its body onto its stumpy legs and starts trotting, I know I better grab this duck now, or say good-bye to it and the world.

I don't want to watch the duck die.

I sure don't want Vicks and Mel to watch *me* die.

These thoughts flash in my head, and my heart is galloping so fast I can hardly see straight. Then I'm lunging forward, tripping and going down hard, but my fingers find feathers, and I do not let go. Rot fills my nostrils, and I make the mistake of looking behind me. Snout. Teeth. Bumps the size of peas lining the flesh of its mouth.

"Jesse, get up!" Mel screams.

My legs scrabble. My elbow drives into a rock. The duckling struggles against me, but I'm not letting it go, *Oh no, I'm not letting you go.*

A hand grips my arm. "You are an *idiot*," Vicks pants as she hauls me to my feet.

The gator hisses, and Vicks is thrusting me forward, making me run. We reach the car, and Vicks shoves me into the backseat on top of Mel. Then Vicks is on me, our limbs tangling as she yanks shut the door.

"Go!" Mel yells from the bottom of the heap.

The gator slams against the Opel.

"It's metal, you moron!" Vicks shouts. "Give it up!"

Cradling the duck to my chest, I scramble into the front seat. I twist the key, and the Opel jolts forward and dies. I try again, only this time I crank it too hard and the motor revs crazy-loud before sputtering out again. *Crap, crap, crap.*

The gator goes for the Opel a second time, launching its body up through the actual air, and I don't have to speak gator to know what's running through its cold reptile brain: *Give me back my snack, and in return I'll rip out your guts.* Its snout whams Mel's window, and there's a fearsome clicking of teeth on glass. Mel screams. The gator batters the durn door—the whole car's rocking—and Mel won't shut up.

Please-oh-please, I pray. I turn the key a third time. The engine catches, and I hear Vicks squeeze out, "Thank you, God." Vicks says this! Vicks! Mel just whimpers. Gravel pops under the tires as we gain purchase, and the duck flutters its wings for balance.

"Sweet dung on a Popsicle stick," Vicks says from the back.

"You got that right," I say. I'm light-headed and can't really feel my body.

"Is it chasing us?" Mel asks. "Please tell me it's not chasing us. Is it chasing us?"

The Opel may not be fast, but it can hit sixty miles an hour. I punch the gas pedal to the floor.

"It's not chasing us," I say. "That gator is one long-gone daddy."

Vicks is breathing hard. A glance in the mirror shows

me she's squeezing Mel tight and patting her over and over, while Mel sits frozen like a lump. Mel's face is pure white.

"Don't you *ever*," Vicks says to me. "Don't you *ever* pull a stunt like that again, do you understand?"

I'm chastened by her tone. I could have killed us all . . . and for what? A duckling that right this second is squirting green poop on my bare thigh?

But then I'm filled with euphoria, 'cause we aren't dead. We're alive, and so is the duck. *My* duck.

"Okay, maybe that wasn't exactly the smartest thing I ever did," I say. "But I sure did learn a valuable lesson." I realize I sound *exactly* like Faith Waters, and a giggle burbles up. *Me and the Gator and the Jaws of Death*, that's what I'd call this heart-stopping episode. "Don't you wanna know what the lesson is? Huh?"

"What?" Mel asks faintly. She's still shaking.

"Well . . . that life is life until you're dead."

"That's your valuable lesson?" Vicks says. "*That's* your valuable lesson?! Of *course* life is life until you're dead. What else would it be?"

"Now, Vicks—," I say.

"Nooooo," she says. "The lesson is don't get out of your car on a deserted road by a swamp, especially if it's nesting season and the mama gators are all crazy to feed their babies. And if it comes down to you or a duck?" She leans forward and thwacks my head. "Let the gator have the duck."

"Except I didn't," I say. "And now she's safe, and isn't that good?"

"She's a she?" Mel says, though this talking thing is obviously still a struggle for her. She is just paler than pale back there in the moonlight. "How do you know?"

"Well, she's not a mallard. So probably."

Vicks thwacks me even harder. "Oh, put a lid on it. You don't know crap about birds."

"Ow!" I say. My duck quacks in protest.

"And you, you pitiful feathery thing," Vicks says. "Shut. The hell. Up."

SUNDAY, AUGUST 22

28

VICKS

"LET'S CALL IT Poopy," I say, sniffing. We've been driving south for about an hour. It's one in the morning.

"It doesn't smell," says Jesse. "It's just little baby duck poo."

"That's a good name!" I cry. "Poo. Short for Little Baby Duck Poo. Alternately called LBDP. "

"Vicks!"

"Then we can shorten it to LB or DP, and then later just Pee, and then later P-Baby. It can have ever-morphing little duck names. It'll be like the rap mogul of duckland."

"No."

"Or else we could call it Turd."

"What part of no do you not understand?" Jesse asks me.

I persist. "Turdball? That's better."

"You're a sick person, you know that?" Jesse laughs.

"You're not going to keep it, are you?" Mel wants to know.

"Of course I am!" Jesse answers. "And Mama loves animals. There's no way she'll turn it out."

"Hey," I ask her, "does that guy next door to you still have that hutch outside with the guinea pigs?"

"Uh-huh," Jesse says. "Otis and Lola." When Mel looks confused, Jesse adds, "There aren't any yards where our trailer is, so you can see everyone's business."

"You think you can keep the duck in a hutch?" Mel asks, wrinkling her nose.

"Like made out of chicken wire but with a cozy place to sleep," Jesse says. "Out the back of the trailer. With hay or wood chips or something. At least until she's bigger."

"Turdball will love it," I tell her. "She'll love the hutch. I'll get Penn to help you build it, if you want."

I say this because I know Jesse thinks Penn is cute, though she fools herself that it's a secret. Besides the free Coke she always gives him, she stands in front of him too long when she brings his food, and one day I caught her in the Waffle bathroom combing her hair when he came in for breakfast and she was working the counter. She actually left her station and went in the back to fix her hair, which is not something Jesse would ever do unless she felt like her hair was really, really important just then.

Jesse pulls a strand of that very hair over her lips, and I think, *Uh-huh. Do I know my Jesse or what?*

Then she nods, which throws me.

"Are you nodding because you want me to call him?" I say.

"Um. Why don't you give me his number, and I'll call him?" she says.

"*You're* going to call *him*?"

She blushes, but she doesn't back down. "Well, yeah. Maybe."

"Okay, cool," I say. "Don't let me forget." I turn to the duck. "Turdball, don't let me forget to give Jesse Penn's number."

"Her name is not Turdball," Jesse says.

"Lucky?" suggests Mel. "Lucky Ducky?"

"Or Hope?" says Jesse.

"Hope the Duck? Please." I am indignant. "We can do better than that. Ooh, how about á l'Orange?"

Jesse squeals in horror. "You guys!"

Mel follows my lead. "What about Roast?"

"Or Peking?"

"Or Curried? Or Smoked?"

"Roast is good," I tell her. "That's funny. Hi, Roast. Hi, little Roastie."

Jesse makes a growly noise while she changes lanes. I can tell we've pushed it far enough.

"All right, what about Waffle?" I offer. "Because we all work at the Waffle."

"I like it," says Mel decisively. "That has my vote."

"It's kind of ducky, too, isn't it?" I add. "'Cause it sounds like waddle. Which is how it walks."

"Hi there, Waffle," Jesse says experimentally. "Do you like that name?"

The duckling is silent.

"If you're not answering me," says Jesse in mock irritation, "then how am I supposed to know what you think?"

We're back on the highway, headed south toward Coral Castle. I am lying down in the backseat. Mel moved up front to let me stretch out, since I didn't sleep as well as they did in the hotel. My mind was too wound up to go rapid-eye-movement or anything.

Well. We are alive, we are here.

We are badass.

We have a duckling.

We have left our families and their diseases and their worry and their expectations. We left our school friends and our work friends and our jobs and lives. We shook them all off to be here, speeding down the interstate, singing "Suddenly I See" in the dark.

Here, there's no senior year of high school, no money worries, no everyday life. Just the three of us and a small aquatic bird.

And my brain, which is still wound up. And the ball of ice that's still in my chest.

I reread *Fantastical Florida* with a flashlight Mel bought at a gas station. I figure with this short delay for a near-death experience we'll get to Homestead by about five A.M. Then we can hit a Waffle House and suck down coffee and eat some bacon hot off the grease until Coral Castle opens.

The name of the girl Ed Leedskalnin loved—Ed being the Latvian guy who built the castle—her name was Agnes Scuffs. Such a stupid name for someone so beloved.

If I were named Agnes Scuffs, I don't think anyone would ever love me.

Hell, no one loves me now and my name is Victoria Simonoff. Which is a very sexy name, actually.

Agnes Scuffs didn't love Ed back, so he moved 1,100 tons of coral by himself, using only his weird supernatural powers that he never even had until she dumped him. No one ever saw him build anything. Never saw him touch the coral. And no one ever helped him either. The guy was only five feet tall. When Agnes Scuffs broke his heart, he became magic.

I'm heartbroken.

I am.

I know I'm the one who broke it off with Brady, but I *feel* like he broke it off with me.

I used to think there was no way I'd ever build a coral castle for him, if he didn't want me anymore. I thought I'd know how to get him back. Know how to make him want me again.

And if I couldn't, I was sure I wouldn't mope around. I'd just move on.

Now, I'm wishing that my heartbreak did make me magic. So I could make something beautiful, or do something heroic, and Brady would see it and that's what would make him come back.

I would build a coral castle, if I could.

29

MEL

"**IS SHE ASLEEP?**" Jesse asks me.

I turn back to look at Vicks, careful not to wake the duck, who has tucked herself into a small fuzzball in my lap. Jesse reluctantly entrusted Waffle to my care after Waffle slipped off the driver's seat and nearly got squashed by the gas pedal.

"She's out cold," I say, and indeed, Vicks is stretched across the backseat, her head cradled between her arms like she's bracing herself for impact. I lower the volume on Macy Gray's "I Try."

"Saving me from the jaws of death must suck out the energy," says Jesse.

I've been full of fun and smiles and alligator adrenaline, but her comment stings. I sink into my seat and stare at the blackness outside. Yes, saving someone from the jaws of death would require energy. But I wouldn't know. Because I didn't save her. I didn't do anything but panic. "I'm sorry I didn't jump in to save you," I say.

"You didn't need to. Vicks did."

"I know." My voice cracks, but I take a deep breath and keep going. "I just wish I was the kind of person who could."

"Mel, you're not a bad person because you're afraid of alligators."

I turn back to her. "I hate that I'm a wimp."

"Hey. Some people are afraid of getting chewed up by alligators. Some people"—she jerks her thumb at Vicks—"are afraid of getting chewed up by other people. It's okay."

I think about my new school. My old school. My sister. The situations I was afraid to face. The people I was afraid to stand up to. The people I let slip away. "But I'm afraid of alligators *and* people," I say. I hear the whining in my voice, and I'm embarrassed, because I'm not trying to turn this into a poor-little-Mel conversation.

"You're not afraid of me, are you?" Jesse asks.

I laugh, startled out of my self-pity. Jesse. Jesse who

once terrified me. Sweet, generous Jesse. Big-hearted Jesse. "No." I pause. "Not anymore."

"I *was* pretty awful to you." She gives me a sheepish smile. "Why'd you come with us on this trip? For real?"

I run my fingers over the duck's head and down its back. "I don't know. You and Vicks seemed so close. You trusted each other. I wanted to be a part of that. And I guess . . . I guess I was *tired* of being afraid of people."

We're silent for a few minutes, while I pet Waffle and listen to the song. I wonder if you can know something about yourself and not know it at the same time. I wonder if everyone has secret fears, and not just me.

I think about Vicks, who's so scared of getting hurt down the road that she decided to hurt herself now instead. "She's making a mistake, isn't she?"

Jesse must have been thinking about Vicks too because she nods and says, "Uh-huh."

"We should stop her."

She wrinkles her forehead. "How?"

"We'll go find Brady."

"Are you kidding me?"

I stop petting to reach for the map. "No, why not? She saved you. Now we'll save her."

Jesse's forehead is still wrinkled and now she's sucking on her lower lip. "Um, okay. But Vicks and me, well, we're fixing things between us, I really do think we are, and . . . it's just . . ."

She trickles off.

"You don't want to mess things up," I fill in.

"I don't want to mess things up *again*," she says. "For the forty billionth time. I mean, I'm sure this is one of those times when the right thing to do is speak up, but—"

"It's okay," I tell her.

"I'm sorry, Mel. For real." She does look very sorry.

I realize what I have to do. "Hey, can you pull over? Just for a second."

"Excuse me?"

I may be afraid of gators, but I won't let myself be afraid of Vicks. "Your turn to hold Waffle. My turn to drive."

"Er . . . do you know how to drive?"

"Of course I know how to drive. And if I'm driving, when Vicks freaks out it will be at me."

Jesse drums her fingernails against the steering wheel, but I can tell she really does want to. "Are you sure? She's going to be *way* bent out of shape."

"I know." I can take it.

Jesse pulls over to the shoulder and puts the car into park. We both open our doors and hurry around the front of the car. I pass her Waffle like a precious baton and then slip into the driver's seat.

Well. Here I am. I notice the light creeping up over the horizon, as I adjust the mirrors. I feel my excessively pounding heart against my hand as I fasten my seat belt.

I can do this. I *can* do this. I place my foot on the brake, and shift the car into drive. Here we go. The blood rushes to my head.

Vicks might be mad, but I'm not going to lose her over this. Because it's the right thing to do; because she might hate me, but she'll get over it; and because I'm a good friend.

Bzz! Bzz!

"Your cell," Jesse says. She reaches behind her to the backseat floor, where I must have dropped it. "Bet it's your boyfriend."

My boyfriend. Marco. Marco! I forgot about Marco! I mean, not *forgot* forgot, but I haven't obsessed about him since the whole alligator debacle.

Maybe I'm tougher than I thought. I take the phone from Jesse and flip it open. "Hi there," I say.

"I almost didn't call since it's so late—well, early—but then I thought, what the hell. Anyway. How's it going?"

He's babbling! How cute. "Great. I'm driving!"

"I thought you hated to drive?"

I feel the weight of the gas peddle under my foot and weigh the truth of that statement. "No. I'm just new at it. Guess what? I almost got eaten by an alligator!"

"What?"

I laugh. "Long story. I'll tell you all about it tomorrow. Where are you now?"

"Back home."

"Good. Are you going to sleep?"

"Yup. I just wanted to check in. Call me tomorrow?"

"Sure." He wants to talk to me tomorrow. Because he likes me. Because I am likeable. Because I am going to be a great girlfriend.

"And I'll take the bus up to see you next weekend. Cool?"

I sit up straight. "Maybe I'll come see you."

"Really? You can borrow a car?"

"I have a car." My sister will have to deal. In the distance I spot a sign for Miami. "Marco, I gotta go. We're almost in Miami."

"I thought you were going to the castle."

"We were. But I'm wild and crazy and changed the plan." I laugh.

"Okay, Ms. Wild and Crazy. Have fun. Good night. I mean, good morning."

"Same to you." Adorable Marco.

I flip down the phone and hand it to Jesse.

"He's going to have sweet dreams tonight," she says. "He must be thanking his lucky stars he met you."

The words, *I doubt it,* want to slip out, but I swallow them. I laugh instead.

We follow the signs to the university. "You don't

know where Brady lives, do you?"

"No clue," Jesse says. "Let's just look for the dorms or something. And then we'll wake her up. Well . . . you'll wake her up."

I continue along the South Dixie Highway until I spot a sign to turn onto Stanford Drive, and then I see the campus. Even though it's only four in the morning, there are a few groups of students—probably drunk—milling around the lawns.

I stop the car and turn off the ignition once we've driven through the entrance gate.

It's quiet.

"You gonna do it?" Jesse asks.

"Absolutely," I say, my voice squeaky. "But you back me, okay?" I unsnap my seat belt, and climb into the backseat. I touch Vicks on the shoulder.

"Vicks," I say extra gently.

"Oh, brother," Jesse murmurs.

"Vicks," I say louder. I'm a little bit afraid she's going to punch me in the face, but I gotta do what I gotta do. An alligator she's not. "Vicks, we're here."

She unclenches her arms and lifts her head looking like a turtle stretching her neck. "At the heartbreak castle?" she mumbles.

"Close," I say. "But not exactly."

30

VICKS

"I CAN'T BELIEVE you brought me here," I moan. We are in a parking lot on the University of Miami campus. It's dark, except for a couple streetlights.

"Don't you want to see Brady?" asks Mel.

"No. He's banging some cheerleader," I protest. "He's studying anthropology without me. He's moving on."

"Vicks." Mel shakes her head. "How do you know that? You don't know that. *You* broke up with *him*." She shakes my knee.

"Why are you doing this?" I ask her. "It's like four in the morning."

"Four twenty-three," says Jesse.

"You shouldn't drink and dial, Vicks," Mel scolds. "That's a basic life lesson."

"He texted me first!"

"So you don't call him back drunk." Mel gets out of the car and stands in the doorway, looking at me. "I bet you don't even remember the details of the conversation when you broke up."

"I do too!" I say. But she's right. I don't really remember. Stupid beer. "Something about anthropology and cheerleaders that was very, very unpleasant."

"So you need to go talk to him," she says. "That's why we went on this trip, remember?"

"I'm not going to grovel at his feet after he didn't call me for two weeks," I say.

"It's not groveling," argues Mel. "You guys are in love."

"Correction," I say. "We *were* in love. It's over."

"I don't think so," says Mel.

What does she know? She's only seen Brady when he comes into the Waffle. She doesn't know whether he loves me or not. "Were you driving?" I say, to change the subject. "Why isn't Jesse in the driver's seat? Jesse, was Mel driving?"

Jesse shrugs.

"I was in the driver's seat because I was driving." Mel speaks to me like I'm delusional. "And this is where

I, as driver, thought we should go."

She wiggles her shoulders in satisfaction. Like a little I'm-in-the-driver's-seat joy dance.

Really. At a time like this.

"She went through the toll booths like a champ," says Jesse, getting out of the car and fussing over Waffle, who's still in the front seat.

"Oh, kick me when I'm down," I moan. "Throw my failures back at me."

Mel snorts.

"I can't believe you two are ganging up on me like this," I complain. "All I ever wanted was to see the Coral Castle."

Jesse reaches into the car and yanks me up and out. "Go talk to your boyfriend," she says.

"I thought you didn't condone the kind of 'talking' we do," I mutter.

"So? You love the guy, right?"

I nod.

"And any fool can see he loves you back."

"I—"

"And you're my friend, so I'm trying to help you out. Even if we disagree on like seventy-five percent of the world."

"Eighty-five," I say.

"Well, this time I'm right." She pauses. "Actually, I'm right all of the time."

"Except when you're not."

She gives a funny little half smile, and the fact that she doesn't push it registers despite my agitation. Jesse is learning to back off. *Jesse* is learning to back off.

"You have to talk to him, Vicks," Mel says.

And Mel has suddenly taken a course in assertiveness training. Great.

"I'm all bedraggled," I say. "There's papaya salsa on my T-shirt."

"There! See?" cries Jesse. "You want to see him or you wouldn't care what you look like."

"Put on a clean shirt," says Mel.

"And I stink," I add.

"So put on deodorant," Mel says. "And before you complain about your breath, I have mints in my bag."

Jesse pops the trunk and starts rooting through my duffel. She pulls out a dark green camisole top. "Here, you haven't worn this yet, and it makes your boobs look good. I'll do your makeup if you want."

"It's the middle of the night," I protest.

"You should wear the other shorts," says Jesse, looking me up and down. "The other shorts look better on you."

"Brady likes these ones," I say. "And besides, I'm not even going to go see him."

"Brush your hair," Jesse orders, handing me a brush.

"No! You guys, I just want to go back to sleep and

303

wake up at Coral Castle," I tell them. "That's what our plan was. Can't we just do that?"

"Old Joe would not be happy with you," says Jesse.

"What?"

"Old Joe."

"What do you mean? Old Joe is crazy about me."

"He is not. If he could see you now, he'd be like—"

"He'd be proud of me for kicking that other gator's ass, that's what," I say. "And saving you from the jaws of death."

"No," says Jesse. "I mean, yes. But I also think he'd be saying"—she lowers her voice to try and sound like a gator—*"Lookie here. Jesse told everyone about her mama, right? Brave. And Mel took a swing at someone twice her size—double brave—plus she scored a hot new boyfriend. But Vicks—Vicks is running away from her life like a big scaredy-cat."*

"But you haven't *called* your mama yet, have you?" I say.

She ignores me. *"And you know what I do with scaredy-cats?"* she says in her Old Joe Gator voice. *"I eat them for breakfast, with a side of* chicken."

"Ha-ha."

She goes on in a normal tone: "You act like it's—okay, I'm gonna cuss here, and don't go thinking it's a regular thing—but you act like it's *badass* to dump Brady first time anything goes wrong—"

"Because he can't treat me like that!" I cry.

"But it isn't. It's running away."

"It is not."

"It's not being honest. You don't tell Brady how you feel 'cause you're scared of how he'll react. You don't tell me you're not a virgin 'cause you're scared of how I'll react. Do we see a pattern here? I think we do. How do you expect to be in love with people and be friends with people if you're scared of what they'll do if you really let them see you?"

"You should call your mother," I say.

"We are here, Vicks," says Jesse. "This is the U, and we drove you all the way down here, and it's time for you to talk to your man."

"Where does Brady live?" asks Mel, looking at a map. "That's what I need to know."

"Hecht College, 1231 Dickenson," I say wearily.

"See? You know you want to see him, or you'd never have told me," Mel says.

I stand on the grass in front of Hecht, look up at the second floor, and wonder which room is Brady's. The Opel is in a parking lot two blocks away.

This is the hardest thing I've ever tried to do.

Because he might not want me to call.

And he really might not want me to be here. He's called my cell a few times, but he never left a single message.

It's 4:42 in the morning on a Sunday. I don't know what I'll do if he doesn't answer.

"Why didn't he call me?" I say to Jesse.

"I don't know," she says. "But if you don't go find out, you'll always wonder."

"Why are you a wise lady all of a sudden?"

Jesse laughs. "It's just a new variation."

"On what?"

"On bossy."

"Ha!" I laugh.

"Stop procrastinating," says Mel.

"Oh, now you're bossing me too?" I say.

"Just dial," she says. They stand up and she links her arm through Jesse's. "We're gonna go sleep in the car." They walk away, out of sight.

Brady picks up on the second ring. "Vicks," he says, his voice thick. "Are you okay?"

"Yeah," I say.

"Is everything all right?"

"It's fine. I mean, nothing's wrong except—"

"I was hoping you'd call. I was sleeping with the phone by my bed."

"Sorry it's so late."

"Hold on, I'm waking my roommate up. Hold on, okay? Please don't hang up."

"Okay."

"Say you're not going to hang up, all right?"

"I'm not going to hang up."

There is a scuffle and then Brady says, "Okay, I went down the hall to the bathroom. Sorry about that."

"Brady, I have to ask you something."

"Okay."

I take a deep breath. "Why didn't you call me?"

"What? I texted you Friday night and you called me back and broke up with me!" He sounds defensive.

"First of all, that was a text, not a call."

"But I've been calling you ever since then. You wouldn't pick up!"

"Yeah, but what I mean is, why didn't you call me at all, ever, since you left home? I sent you five hundred text messages and left voice mails, and you just jacked me around. You never once called me back."

"I called you at home," he said. "Didn't Tully give you the message?"

"No."

"I called and talked to him at your parents' place on like, Wednesday."

"He never told me."

"Yeah, he was over there to watch a game with your dad, I think, right? And you were at the movies."

Tully. He is the worst brother. "You didn't call again," I say to Brady. "You didn't text me back all those times I wrote you. You didn't call me after all those messages I left. You know that's true."

Brady grunts. "I know."

"Why wouldn't you just call my cell and at least leave me a voice mail? Anything. Because I was like so, so lonely for you," I say, choking. "And I would check my phone every hour to see if I'd missed your call, and I'd check it when I woke up in the morning and you wouldn't have called, and I'd put it by my bed every night to see if you'd call, and you never did!" I am angry now. "You never called me and I just felt worse and worse, until I couldn't stand it anymore. I mean, what kind of way is that to treat your girlfriend that you supposedly love?"

"I do love you."

"Well, you have a stupid, mean way of showing it," I tell him.

"But, Vicks, you always sounded so happy in those messages," Brady protests. "You were like, hey, we're at the Waffle and that guy ordered fourteen sausage patties again. Or hey, you will not believe what T-Bone just told me, call me back."

"Yeah, *call me back*," I say. "What part of that didn't you understand?"

Brady sighs. "I understood. I just—I didn't want to tell you what it's like here. I didn't want to call you back and then moan and cry on your shoulder."

"What?"

"I don't know anyone here, Vicks. My roommate

thinks I'm a jerk, like he's way too good for me. He's like a necklace-wearing surfer guy and every time I put any music on he rolls his eyeballs at me. The guys in football are huge. Really, they've all got like twenty, thirty pounds on me and there's no way I belong on the Hurricanes. I'm so out of my league."

"Oh."

"I got a C-minus on my first comp essay, I can't understand half of what they're saying in most of my lectures, and apparently I can't even do laundry properly because all my shirts are now pink."

I have to laugh.

Brady sighs. "I wanted you to think I was—I don't know. I can't describe it. Something better."

Oh.

He was unhappy.

He was ashamed.

That never even crossed my mind, but now that he's said it, I know what he means. Brady was the center of everything at school. The man on campus. The one who had the Fourth of July party. The one who brought people together. He doesn't want to weigh anyone down with bad news. Doesn't want to be the needy one.

Like Jesse. Like me.

"You have to call me back," I say. "I can't do this if you don't call me back."

"I'm sorry."

"You should be."

"I am, Vicks. I am really, really sorry."

Okay. "I'm sorry you dyed your shirts pink," I say.

"I am very, very sorry about that, as well," Brady says, and there's a laugh in his voice.

"I bet you are."

"You're not running off with a guy from that party you went to?"

"Nah."

"God, Vicks, I wish you were here."

"Do you?"

"So much. I so wish you were here."

"Look out your window."

"What?"

"Look out your window." I am standing on the lawn, looking up at Hecht. There are a few lights glowing from the second floor, and I study them, my heart thumping, anxious to see Brady's form darken the frame.

"There's no window in here, I'm in the bathroom," he says. "And a floor of freshmen guys makes that a way disgusting place, in case you were wondering." He pauses. "What window?"

So much for my big romantic gesture. "I'm downstairs."

"You are not."

"Yes, I am."

"No."

"Yes. Jesse and Mel drove me down here. They're down the street in the car."

"You're outside the dorm?"

"That's what I'm telling you."

"I'm on the stairs," he says. "I'm coming down."

"Actually, they pretty much kidnapped me and made me come. I'm kind of smelly."

"I'm going down the hall toward the lobby."

"I'm smelly because we almost got eaten by a gator, I kid you not."

"I'm sure you could give any gator what for," Brady says, probably not believing me.

"Damn straight."

"And you're never smelly."

"That's what you think," I say.

"Well, you *were* smelly that one time after touch football. Oh, and when the car broke down that time and it was like a hundred degrees out. But really, you're hardly ever smelly."

"Are you in the lobby yet?" I ask. "Where are you?"

His only answer is to hang up—and then he's in the illuminated doorway of the dorm, pushing through the double doors, and running down the path to where I am. I think he's going to sweep me up and twirl me around, but instead he just bangs into me, grabbing on, and we stumble around on the grass for a minute, and it's so good to put my arms around him again.

He's wearing warm-up pants and a stupid-looking pink T-shirt.

We get ourselves vertical and he touches my face, and then we kiss, and it's me and Brady, like we've been all year. All year, and his feelings haven't changed.

We love each other, and I know it.

We're in the love bubble.

31

JESSE

WHILE VICKS IS away, me and Mel fix up a little house for Waffle. We rip the top off the Dunkin' Donuts box and Mel hands me her super soft white T-shirt to put inside, the one she wore the day we left. When I feel it, I'm brought back to that night at the museum, how Vicks heaved Mel up and I held her steady so she could reach through the open window and unlock the door.

That was the night we met Old Joe. And Marco. And, piecing it together, I reckon it was the night Vicks broke up with Brady. Was that really only two days ago?

"Are you sure about this?" I say to Mel, fingering the

313

shirt. "It's kinda fancy for a duck."

"It's soft," Mel says. "Waffle will like it."

"But it's the shirt you wore when . . . you know."

She looks perplexed.

"When you met a certain special someone?" I prompt. "Brown eyes, nasty habit of sneaking up on folks, name rhymes with Sparko?"

Mel giggles. "'*Sparko*,'" she repeats. It's adorable how happy she gets just saying his not-even-real name.

"We can use Vicks's salsa T-shirt," I say. "She won't mind, and your shirt'll stay pure."

"*Pure?*" Mel says. "It's a *shirt*, Jesse. A soft cotton shirt that'll keep our Waffle snug and cozy, so that you can stop worrying and get some sleep. And if you go to sleep, then maybe *I* can finally go to sleep."

"But—"

Mel holds up her finger and shakes her head. "What is 'pure,' anyway?" She continues to hold up her finger, but no words spill forth.

"I'm waiting."

"Um, I have nothing more on that, actually," she says, dropping her hand to her lap. She giggles. "Except, come on. What's a little duck poop between friends?"

So I accept the shirt. I fluff it just so in the bottom of the box, place Waffle inside, and set the makeshift bed on the floor. I stretch out on the seats above and try to go to sleep. But below me, Waffle quacks and patters about, nipping at her soft white blankie like it's nice, but it sure isn't her mama's warm body.

Mel groans when I sit back up. From the rear seat, she says, "Jesse? I want you to put your hands above your head and *leave the duck alone*."

"Oh, hush," I say, scooping Waffle up and cradling her against my chest. "You sound like that itty-bitty policeman."

But Mel doesn't hush, and neither do I. Maybe 'cause we're in an unfamiliar parking lot in the middle of an unfamiliar city? Maybe 'cause we're anxious for Vicks, who by now is either sealing the love deal or saying her final good-byes. Or maybe we've gone around the bend from bone-deep exhaustion to gritty-eyed wakefulness, the sort where you can't even relax your eyelids.

Whatever the reason, sleep won't come.

So I ask Mel if she believes in heaven. I don't know how anyone couldn't believe in heaven, but then again, look at Vicks.

Mel hesitates. Then she says, "Are you thinking about your mum?"

I stroke Waffle's soft feathers. She's quiet now, and peaceful. "Yeah."

"Jesse," Mel says softly, "she's not going to die."

"How do you know?"

"Because . . . well, I don't. I guess I just said it."

"Bad things *do* happen, just like Vicks said."

315

"I know. But good things happen too."

"Huh," I say. I stare at the Opel's cracked ceiling. "Is that a Jewish thing? Focusing on the positive?"

"Maybe," Mel says, laughing a little.

"Why are you laughing?"

"I don't know. I just am. But, Jesse . . ."

"What?"

"It's great that you believe so strongly in God, but I feel like sometimes you worry about the wrong things, like what's pure and who's a virgin and what the rules are for being Christian or Jewish or whatever." The seat squeaks as she shifts. "Isn't it possible that God's bigger than all that?"

No, I think. God is God is God.

But then something in my brain shifts, opening the tiniest crack of . . . something. I don't mean for it to. It just does. And I'm not saying *yes*, but I am just possibly saying *maybe*. Maybe to the idea of one big God, expanding in all directions, reaching people however He can. Like the sun, which is officially over the horizon now.

"I think you should have a talk show," I tell her. "*Mel in the Morning*. What do you think?"

"Hah." I hear her bumping around back there. "I think you need to call your mum."

"Duh," I say. I know I need to call Mama. Why does everyone have to keep telling me to call Mama? "But it's five A.M. No way I'm calling Mama at five A.M. She'd tan my hide!"

"You need to call your mum," she says again, sounding sad.

She's silent for a long moment, so long I figure she's drifted off. Waffle breathes beside me, safe in the crook of my elbow. Her bitsy head is tucked beneath her bitsy wing, and her bitsy yellow body puffs out with each teaspoon breath.

"Jesse?" Mel says.

"Yeah?"

"You pray, right? To God?"

"'Course."

"And you, like, ask Him for help?"

"I guess. So?"

"So, you can ask us for help too, you know. Your friends. Vicks . . . and me."

"I know," I say defensively. Like, what kind of idiot doesn't know how to ask for help?

Well. My kind of idiot, obviously.

But then I realize I *do* know. I didn't used to, maybe, but now I do.

"You're not alone," Mel says sleepily. "Vicks and I, we're here."

Next thing I know, it's morning and it's bright out and I've got a stiff neck and a dented-in gut from the gearshift.

317

And as much as I don't want to disturb the peace, I can't stay in this cramped position forever. Waffle stirs when I move, pulling her head from under her wing and shaking her cotton ball of a body. She pecks at a freckle on my forearm, and I make a note to track down a Miami pet store before we drive back to Niceville. Waffle needs food, and not just potato chip crumbs. I'll get her a water bowl, too, and a duck toy. Do they sell duck toys at pet stores? What would a duck toy even be?

Mel and Vicks aren't here—the backseat is empty— and for a couple of seconds I'm confused. Then I remember: Vicks. Brady. The squat brick dorm we're down the street from.

The fact that Vicks isn't back yet is good, I think. At least, I hope it's good. I hope it means they're snuggled like puppies in his dorm-room bed, and I consider it a sign of the new-and-improved me that although the word *sin* flares into my mind, I blow it right out and let it evaporate into the air.

God is bigger than that. There is indeed a chance that He is.

I push myself up and squint out the windshield. Mel is standing with her back toward me in the half-filled parking lot, doing Pilates or some other rich-girl version of what the rest of us call stretching. Her skinny fanny pokes to one side, then the other, and I'm filled with love for that goofy girl. I'm so glad to know her—in fact

318

I can't imagine *not* knowing her—and I wonder if maybe there's room for two best friends in my heart.

On the dashboard is Mel's cell phone, and under the phone is a note scrawled on a napkin. *"Call her,"* it says, underlined three times and with a squillion exclamation points thrown in for good measure.

I exhale. Just 'cause she's grown on me doesn't keep her from being irritating as heck.

I scoop Waffle up and gently place her in her box. I get out of the car, careful to be super-quiet with the door so I don't attract Mel's attention. I extend my arms above my head, and it feels good. Oh, my spine. Oh, my knotted neck. Sleeping in the Opel isn't the same quality experience as sleeping in the Black Pearl, that's for sure.

I lean through the open window and grab Mel's phone from the dash. I flip it open. I flip it shut. I walk to the front of the Opel and perch my butt on the bumper. If I call Mama—no, *when* I call Mama—what am I going to say?

My gut clenches, but I push through it. I will say what I need to say, that's what.

I'll say that I love her, and that I'll go with her to her surgery.

That I'll be there for her, and she sure better be there for me. Forever.

That entering wet T-shirt contests is trashy, and

humiliates me, and could she please not ever do that again?

I'll tell her I'm sorry I ran away, sorry I stole her car, sorry about so many things. But I'm keeping my duck. Her name is Waffle. And—oh yeah—I almost got eaten by a gator.

I bite my lip, imagining Mama's reaction to that one.

Maybe I'll leave that part out . . . and hope that she doesn't ask about the huge gashes on the door.

Two figures appear at the far end of the parking lot, and my heart leaps when I see that it's Vicks and Brady. They're holding hands! Yay! Mel spots them and breaks out of her Pilates move. She squeals and claps, and Vicks shakes her head as if Mel is an embarrassment to the parking lot and the planet. She's grinning, though.

Vicks gives Brady a squeeze, then goes over to Mel. The two of them say some stuff I can't make out, Mel gives Vicks a happy hug, and then they turn toward the Opel. They take in the phone in my hand. Mel's eyes go wide, and Vicks nods before giving me a big thumbs-up.

I shake my head, 'cause I haven't actually dialed yet. Guess I need bravery lessons from little Mel. She and Vicks must read something into my gesture that's more than I intend, 'cause they start toward me, wearing twin expressions of concern.

"What's going on?" Vicks calls when she's close enough.

"Oh, no," Mel says. "Did something bad happen?"

"No, no, nothing bad happened," I say. I hear my words, and a skittery giggle burbles up, 'cause shoot, more bad things happened in the last two days than I can count.

But we came through them, didn't we?

And who knows? Maybe Vicks was on to something with her whole Old Joe bad-bottom appreciation ritual at the museum. 'Cause maybe, sometimes, a girl's gotta be bad in order to figure out how to be good.

I punch in the numbers before I lose my nerve. I raise the phone. I hear the first ring.

Thanks, Old Joe, I silently pray. *Long may you rock.*

thank you!

We are grateful to the superhero team of agents who assembled to represent this project: Laura Dail, Barry Goldblatt, and Elizabeth Kaplan. Also, to our editors at other publishing houses who supported our suddenly insane writing and publishing schedules. Huge thanks to Farrin Jacobs, who has edited and advocated for us, fed us Indian food, read our gazillion e-mails, and generally dealt with the fact that three authors are more neurotic than one; as well as the rest of the folks at HarperCollins: Elise Howard, Cristina Gilbert, Colleen O'Connell, Dina Sherman, Sandee Roston, Melissa Dittmar, Jackie Greenberg, Kari Sutherland, Naomi Rothwell, Melinda Weigel, Crystal Velasquez, Anne Heausler, Dave Caplan, Sasha Illingworth, and Jen Heuer. Also thanks to Tamar Ellman and all our friends in foreign places.

Novelist Kristin Harmel took us to Epcot, filmed

our hot tub adventures, and put us up in Orlando with great style and grace—plus muffins. Amber Draus was our Epcot guide extraordinaire. The helpful folks at Gatorland in Florida answered our questions and let us in free because it was research. Our gratitude to the people behind the Roadside America website and the book of the same title, which inspired and informed our story. The information on the Coral Castle and the World's Smallest Police Station is accurate to the best of our knowledge; likewise the descriptions of the other sites in Vicks's fictional *Fantastical Florida*—though Xanadu is now closed. We did relocate Old Joe Gator and added on an extra four feet to him for dramatic purposes. He actually resides in the lobby of the Wakulla Springs Hotel, where he has been known to wear a party hat on New Year's Eve. Oh, and we invented the pirate hotel.

David Levithan and Rachel Cohn inspired this project with their wonderful collaboration *Nick & Norah's Infinite Playlist*, as did Patricia Wrede and Caroline Stevermer with their book *Sorcery and Cecelia*, with its fascinating note about their working process.

John Green, Maureen Johnson, and Scott Westerfeld kept Emily company during writing, and John answered all questions on college football–related issues. Leslie Margolis, Bennett Madison, and Alison Pace hung out and wrote with Sarah. Amber Kelley and Julia Meier took care of Lauren's kids—huge! (the help, not the kids)—and the ever-friendly Starbucks morning crew kept her hopped up on caffeine and sugar.

Thanks to the FOZ (Friends of Zoe) for helping us with the title: Terry, Samantha, Maia, Lucy, Jeanmarie, Rachel, Katherine, and Roni. And of course, Zoe Jenkin for administrating.

Thanks to our friends and family, always: Elissa and Robert Ambrose, Larry Mlynowski, Louisa Weiss, Aviva Mlynowski, John and Vickie Swidler, Robin Glube, Shobie Farb, Jess Davidman, Bonnie Altro, Johanna Jenkins, Len and Ramona Jenkin, Sarah Burnett, Jackie Owens, Laura Pritchett, Don and Sarah Lee Myracle, Eden Myracle, Mary Ellen Evangelista, Tim White, Jim White, Eric Myracle, Susan White, Ruth and Tim White, and of course Ivy, Al, Jamie, and Mirabelle.

Special thanks to Elissa Ambrose and Ruth White for being such badass first readers; and to Chani Sanchez, Jess Braun, Leslie Margolis, and Lynda Curnyn for their terrific insights.

A thousand thank-yous to our super-supportive and always-loving spouses: Daniel Aukin, Jack Martin, and Todd Swidler. You guys rock.

how to be bad

How It All Began

Want to know how three people who barely knew each other came to write a novel together? Read on. . . .

Yeah, we all write fiction for teens, but the similarities pretty much end there. This is us:

Lauren: Colorado goofball. Bubbly. An adorable southern accent from her previous life. Often found in jeans and a pink T-shirt.

Emily: Brooklyn denizen. Unafraid of being ridiculous. Partial to wearing a wrap dress with her toenails painted blue.

Sarah: Canadian living in Manhattan. Ambitious. Fun. Knows how to flat-iron her hair and walk long distances in high-heeled boots.

This is how we came together:

Sarah had just started a teen lit discussion group on MySpace. (Today, the group has over 15,000 members—but in February 2006 it had, like, eight. And nearly all of them were YA authors. Check it out at http://groups.myspace.com/teenlit.) Someone posted about Rachel Cohn and David Levithan's collaborative novel, *Nick & Norah's Infinite Playlist*, and Lauren commented that she'd always wanted to write a book like that, alternating chapters with another writer.

"Anytime, baby," Emily posted. She'd only met Lauren briefly at a reading they'd done together, so she didn't really expect anything to happen. But within minutes Sarah had privately emailed something on the order of "Me too! Me too!" Which led to this exchange:

1

From: E. Lockhart
Subject: Girly Project
Date: February 28, 2006
To: Lauren Myracle
Cc: Sarah Mlynowski

Hi Lauren,
Sarah Mlynowski and I have been frantically
emailing one another since you posted on the
Teen Lit group about how fun it would be to do
a co-authored book. We'd like to do one!
We'd love you to be a part of it!
It's still very much an infant idea:
three (or possibly four) YA novelists to write
a book in three (or possibly four) voices that
intersect . . .
So: I know there's no STORY here yet, or
anything, but I think it might be a ridiculously
fun adventure . . .

From: Lauren
Subject: RE: Girly Project
To: E. Lockhart, Sarah Mlynowski

Ooooooo! Of course!!!!!! Heh heh heh. That
would be a total blast.
Have you two read the wonderful co-authored
Sorcery and Cecelia by Patricia Wrede and
Caroline Stevermer? So very fun, and ever since
reading it (and its sequel), I've thought how fun it
would be to do such a project.
Yaybies for infant ideas!

2

By the end of that day after a flurry of emails, the three of us had decided: We would write a novel.

It was like we'd all agreed to get married without even going on a date.

Fortunately, we were compatible. Though we had to toss lots of ideas into the old circular file, we eventually settled on a road trip: Three girls. Three voices. Three problems. A classic genre into which we felt we could breathe fresh life. Then we agreed on a setting:

From: E

Hello you wonder women!
I just had fifteen minutes of peace and quiet (finally) and have an idea about SETTING to share with you both.
The three girls work together at Waffle House in a landlocked Florida town . . .
If you don't know Waffle House, it's low-rent and ubiquitous. Diner food with a focus on waffles. They crop up off the interstates and make a poor showing next to the large signs of chains like Arby's and Chili's. I love them.
Anyway, I think they work there for a few reasons.
1) It allows them to be friends outside of school. Which means they might have an intense, summer-long bond, but not know all about each other's families and histories, which allows them to have more secrets from each other. It also allows them to come from more disparate backgrounds.

2) It allows me, at least, to stretch a little more out of the middle class/relatively privileged kids I've been writing about, but keeps me in a place I know and have strong affection for (Florida).

3) There are more wild tourist attractions in Florida than anywhere else.

How do y'all feel about a Florida setting? I grew up visiting my grandparents there, and have driven through it on my own quite a bit. I love it and it's insane. It's HOT, it feels wild, there's amazing foliage, it smells good; it's full of old retired people and glamorous high rollers, both. It's silly, it's all new, it's sad, in a way. Do you know it well enough to set a book there, or do you feel you can find your way in? That's it for now. Just an idea, of course! Feel free to object.

From: Lauren

Do I know the Waffle House? Do I know the Waffle House??? Oh honey chile, I grew UP at the Waffle House. I adore the Waffle House. I own the Waffle House CD. (Yes, really.) I am ALL ABOUT THE WAFFLE HOUSE.

And Florida works for me. I've been to several Florida beaches, and I bet I could fudge the sights. Florida's cool. +thumbs-up+

From: Sarah

Am happy with Waffle House. Have never eaten
there but it sounds a lot like the pancake house in
Miami that my father-in-law looooooooooooves.
Also sounds like the restaurant I was a bus girl
for when I was 17. And let me tell you—there
is nothing worse than wiping up spilled maple
syrup at 7:00 am. By 8 your shoes stick to the
floor. Slurp.

Also, occurred to me that characters don't have
to be "friends" before road trip. They could be
peripheral acquaintances who work together
who get tangled up in the adventure and
become friends. (Like us while writing this book!)

From: Lauren

Oh, yay! We have a plan!

This is how we wrote:

We all agreed to "Lauren's Entirely Negotiable Rules
of Conduct," which included elements like:

- All work must be considered pure work-
  in-progress, and all critical judgment must be
  suspended until we have a full first draft.
- No one shall consider anybody's work to be
  goofy or stupid or wrong-minded, and we shall all
  just know that in our hearts and never feel para-
  noid.
- The novel will be written by passing it from one
  writer to the next to the next, each of us adding

EXTRAS

a new chapter that moves the story along. This pattern will be repeated until the end of the novel is reached.

- We all have full liberty to write each other's characters however the muse strikes us, including dialogue. We'll do our best to stay true to the character, and we'll know that fine-tuning by the character's alter ego can be done at the end.

For the first ninety pages, we charged ahead—no plotting, no planning—just trying to surprise each other. Then the three of us had a big ROAD TRIP RENDEZVOUS in Orlando, during which we visited Gatorland, got stranded at Epcot, took silly pictures, had some major toll-booth trauma—and outlined the rest of the book. Then we all went home and wrote, wrote, wrote.

And now we have a novel! Even better, now *you* have our novel. We hope you've enjoyed the ride as much as we did.

xo
Emily, Sarah & Lauren

P.S. In case you were wondering which author wrote the chapters for which girl, we challenge you to make your own guess. Then turn to page 17 of the Extras to see if you were right!

Bad Girl Quiz

Which of the *bad* girls are you most like?
Take this quiz and find out!

1. Your heart is racing. Your skin is tingling. Your palms are sweating. That's right: crush alert! The boy who makes you stop in your tracks is . . .

   a. Drop-dead gorgeous, with eyes that you could stare into forever . . . and ever and ever and ever . . .

   b. Fun and outgoing; he'll never get overshadowed by your larger-than-life personality.

   c. Kind and thoughtful; he really gets you. Of course, that great smile of his doesn't hurt either. . . .

2. Your dream car is:

   a. A roomy BMW that will fit all your friends.

   b. Covered in so many bumper stickers that you can't even tell what color it is.

   c. One that works! As long as it gets you where you're going, you're not picky.

3. You love your BFF like a sister . . . so what exactly makes you two so simpatico?

   a. She's always there for you—even when you say or do the wrong thing. In other words, your friendship is absolutely not based on having the same sheep-skin coat. (Not that you've, uh, ever fallen into that trap or anything.)

   b. Just like you, she's up for anything. And, you've definitely managed to have some fun times together!

7

c. She respects your opinions—even if she doesn't always agree with them.

4. It's Friday night and you get a text from the boy you've been crushing on, inviting you to a spur-of-the-moment party. You:
   a. Convince your best friend to come with you; it's always easier to show up with a friend by your side.
   b. Jump in the car, what else?!
   c. Weigh the pros and cons to ensure you make the right decision.

5. How *bad* are you?
   a. Come on, admit it—you have your moments. . . .
   b. You're clearly a kick-butt, one-of-a-kind, stop-you-in-your-tracks kind of girl; in other words, bad-to-the-bone, *your* style.
   c. Bad?? You are good to the core!

6. What type of music is most likely to be blaring on your iPod?
   a. Rock, pop, classics . . . you're not picky!
   b. Indie rock all the way, baby.
   c. Country music—nothing's better to sing along to.

7. Which of the following would be most likely to come out of your mouth?
   a. "*Poutine* . . . fries and gravy and cheese curds. No, it's amazing, trust me. The most fattening thing in the world, but worth every calorie."
   b. "Whatever, I'm not going to be some whiner-baby girlfriend, all freaked because he doesn't check in every morning and every night."

c. "Fourteen dollars. Dang, what's wrong with this world?"

8. Think of your favorite jeans. You know the ones— you've worn them so many times that they're basically molded to your body. Where did you buy them?
   a. Your favorite department store . . . a great place for a little retail therapy with a friend.
   b. That funky store in town that embroiders all their jeans so each one's totally unique.
   c. The local superstore; why drop a lot of cash on jeans?

9. Your favorite possession is:
   a. You do love your pillow-top mattress. There's just something so calming about curling up in it after a long day.
   b. The *Fantastical Florida* guidebook. It's filled with all kinds of weird stuff that would be awesome to see, like a building shaped like an orange or the world's smallest police station or Old Joe Alligator, a three-hundred-year-old stuffed alligator. Who *wouldn't* want to go visit that??
   c. Definitely your TV; there's nothing quite like a night of lounging on the sofa watching Lifetime movies. . . .

10. You're on a road trip and your friends get in a fight. You:
   a. Try your best not to get in the middle of it; you'd much rather please your friends than fight with them.
   b. Tell them in your kindest loud voice to CHILL OUT!
   c. Try to explain to them exactly who is right and why.

11. Your favorite outfit is:

a. Nice jeans, a super-soft tee, and your diamond studs.
b. What you're wearing doesn't matter so much, since your hair's your *real* accessory: dyed jet black and streaked with white. Pretty rad, huh?
c. Cutoffs and a tank top—covers all the essential C's: casual, cute, and comfy!

We've all got a little *badness* buried deep inside us! Of the three bad girls, you're most like:

If you answered mostly A's

Mel! Dressed to impress and filled with good intentions, you are always trying to please others. You'll be the first to lend your BFF money or cheer her on from the sidelines—which makes you a top-notch friend. But, don't forget: Being a good friend is just one of your many great qualities. Sometimes, you need to please yourself, too! So, slip into those stylish jeans of yours and know that with or without your friends by your side you rock either way!

If you answered mostly B's

Vicks! A free spirit, you do things your way, and you know what? Your way totally works for you! You radiate a vibe all your own, and it draws people to you from all walks of life. Quirky, fun, cool, and unique are all words that could be used to describe you, but most important of all, you are strong and loyal—and that's what keeps your friends by your side through thick and thin.

If you answered mostly C's

Jesse! A good girl through and through, you have strong ideals and convictions, and sometimes get frustrated when others don't understand them. But, you're also the one with the ideas (road trip, anyone?!), and your friends love you for that. You might not take life's little setbacks lightly, but you know how to get things done—and still manage to have a little fun along the way. That's right: Underneath it all, you love a good laugh just as much as the next girl!

How to Be Bad's Oh-So-Excellent Playlist

Hello from Sarah, E., and Lauren!

No road trip is complete without TUNES, and we had a blast selecting the songs that Jesse, Vicks, and Mel listened to as they cruised through Florida. Part of the fun was introducing each other to new music; each time one of us stuck a song in, we made sure the others knew it, too. If not? iTunes, baby! We all loved getting unexpected "You have received an iTunes gift!" messages in our inboxes.

Now you can enjoy the girls' playlist, too. Rock on!

"These Boots Are Made for Walkin'," by Nancy Sinatra

This is the one song that Jesse's crappy radio could pick up—it's an oldie girl-power anthem—and Vicks was not happy. The cool thing, though, is that it ties into Vicks's life situation perfectly. She's on a mission: The reason the girls are driving across Florida in the first place is so that Vicks can tell off Brady, her boyfriend, for not treating her right.

"Drive," by Incubus

Sarah picked this one out for the list, and we were like, "Der, of *course*." It's all about taking the wheel in your own life, something we all need to do.

"Oops! . . . I Did It Again," by Britney Spears

Heh heh heh . . . this one was put in primarily to bug Jesse, who rolls her eyes at Mel for liking it. But, truth? We all really like it. It's catchy! It's addictive! It's BRITNEY!

But it also ties in with the questions Mel and Vicks are struggling with: Is he playing with my heart? Is this just a game?

"Wheat Kings," by The Tragically Hip
Gorgeous, gorgeous, gorgeous. Haunting and melancholy. A Canadian pick from Canadian Mel!

"Red River Valley," by Arlo Guthrie
Campfire song! Heartwarming! Cheesetastic. Also about a girl who's being left by the boy she loves, so more Vicks and Brady connections here. The girls have a moment with a taxidermied alligator, and they sing this song together.

"Drops of Jupiter," by Train
This is one of the songs Lauren had never heard of until Sarah introduced it to her. (E. had heard of hardly anything, so it goes without saying this was new to her as well. She likes show tunes. She's not embarrassed, either.) Now Lauren has it on her iPod and listens to it all the time, because it speaks of hope and love and sadness, all swirled up together. Jesse, Vicks, and Mel understand that mix completely.

"London Bridge," by Fergie
Ha. What's not to love about this song with its nonsensical, sexy lyrics? (And what does it mean exactly, anyway?) Yet Jesse is *totally* offended by it cuz of her Christian ways, and Vicks rolls her eyes at Jesse's reaction.

"Where Is the Love," by Elvis Costello
No, not the Black Eyed Peas song. No, no, no. This

one is a gorgeous sad ballad, and when Jesse hears it, she thinks about Vicks's brother, Penn, whom she has a crush on. All three girls long for love, so they can all relate to the drama Vicks is going through.

"Let's Get It On," by Marvin Gaye

More sexiness to make Jesse squirm. Mel accidentally selects this song after Jesse orders her to stop playing "nasty" songs like "London Bridge." Jesse gets pissed, Mel is horrified, and Vicks thinks it's hilarious.

"So Sorry," by Feist

Do y'all know Feist? If you don't, you need to. She's Canadian, too . . . just like Mel! And Sarah! And she has one of the funkiest, raspiest voices ever. In a good way.

"Miami," by Will Smith

The girls' destination is Miami!!!! Gotta play "Miami"!!!! Plus, Will Smith has such a beautiful, full-of-life smile. Sigh . . .

"Girls Just Want to Have Fun," by Cyndi Lauper

A goofy one that just makes you dance in your seat. A classic from when Lauren and E. were teenagers.

"Walking on Sunshine," by Katrina and the Waves

Mel puts this on in an attempt to nudge Vicks and Jesse out of their funk, during a point in the road trip where they're mad at each other. She figures, "How can they not cheer up when listening to this?" Annoyingly, they prove amazingly resilient even to this superhappy tune.

"Who Did Swallow Jojo?" by The Veggie Tales

Okay, listen (says Lauren). The singing veggies in

"The Veggie Tales" rock, and E. and Sarah are just going to have to accept it. Case closed, the end, finis. ~~Eat your veggies~~ Listen to your veggies, ladies!!! ☺

"Spirit in the Sky," by Norman Greenbaum

You know how Vicks rolled her eyes at Jesse for not digging "London Bridge"? Well, Jesse rolls her eyes at Vicks for not digging the gospel-inspired "Spirit in the Sky," which Mel plays especially for Jesse. Note to readers: *Both* songs rock, and there is nothing wrong with liking them both.

"Bad Day," by Daniel Powter

You know it, and you love it. We all love it!

"Suddenly I See," by KT Tunstall

If Lauren had to pick one song to be the theme song for her life, she'd pick this one. (At least, she would today.) Upbeat, optimistic, and with a touch of "here's the answer to life's big question" thrown in, it's tailor-made for all three girls as well.

"I Try," by Macy Gray

To listen to this song is to become addicted to it. Check out the chorus and see if you don't agree. We dare you! As for why we picked this one for the book, it's about trying to leave someone you love—just like Vicks is trying to leave Brady, and Jesse is trying to leave her mom. But it's not that easy. . . .

Bonus songs which almost made it into the novel (all of which are quite excellent). The themes in these songs connect to the themes in *How to Be Bad*, so you should listen to them all as soon as possible:

"Soak up the Sun," by Countdown Singers
"Small Town," by John Mellencamp
"When I Come Around," by Green Day
"I Fought the Law," by Hank Williams, Jr.
"Shut Up and Drive," by Rihanna
"Umbrella," also by Rihanna
"Is She Really Going Out with Him?" by Joe Jackson
"Big Girls Don't Cry," by Fergie

Spread the love, spread the tunes!
Friends + music = very VERY good.

☺ S, E & L

Who wrote what?

Lauren wrote Jesse's chapters, Emily wrote Vicks's, and Sarah wrote Mel's.
But really, we all wrote them all. ☺